"Beth Pennington has no use for a houseboat."

Charlie's sister, Lucy, made a sound of disgust before continuing, "I don't know why Abraham Steele left it to you and Beth in the first place. He knew you were divorced. And Beth's afraid of water—or have you forgotten?"

Charlie didn't want to admit there were few things about his ex-wife he had forgotten. "As soon as Beth comes home, she'll sign her half over to me."

"Beth's coming back to Riverbend? I wonder why."

Talk of Beth made Charlie's breakfast stall on its journey to his stomach. He took a sip of coffee in an attempt to wash it down. "You sound like Mom— always trying to remind me Beth's never going to be a part of my life again." He pointed at her with a strip of bacon. "In case you haven't noticed, I'm not exactly losing sleep over Beth."

"We're just worried. She already hurt you once."

Charlie was spared further discussion when a customer signaled for Lucy. He decided to make good his escape, but as he left the café, he glanced back to see his sister chatting with Evie Mazerik. Much as he wanted to think Lucy was talking to the cashier about work, Charlie had a pretty good idea they were discussing the one subject he didn't want to share with the town. Beth.

Dear Reader,

Ask my dad about his youth and you'll hear all about the guys from Thirty-third and Third Street in Minneapolis, just two blocks from the Mississippi River. They were the kids he played ball with, the ones he worked on cars with and with whom he sneaked down to the river for a swim. They were also the friends who introduced him to the girl he would marry.

Growing up on the Mississippi and hearing my dad's tales, I felt an immediate affinity for the River Rats of Riverbend. There's a mystique about life in a river town that has been part of American culture since Mark Twain plunked Huck Finn, Tom Sawyer and Becky Thatcher down in Hannibal, Missouri, over a century ago.

I was delighted to be asked to participate in this series so that my very own River Rats, Charlie and Beth, could come to life and tell their story. Like my mom and dad, they fell in love as teenagers, but unlike my parents, they couldn't make it last. Now, as adults, they have a second chance. I hope you enjoy their adventure on the river.

Sincerely,

Pamela Bauer

P.S. I enjoy hearing from readers. You can write to me c/o MFW, P.O. Box 24107, Minneapolis, MN 55424.

THAT SUMMER THING
Pamela Bauer

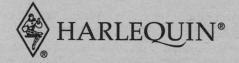

HARLEQUIN®

TORONTO • NEW YORK • LONDON
AMSTERDAM • PARIS • SYDNEY • HAMBURG
STOCKHOLM • ATHENS • TOKYO • MILAN • MADRID
PRAGUE • WARSAW • BUDAPEST • AUCKLAND

ISBN 0-373-70930-7

THAT SUMMER THING

Copyright © 2000 by Pamela Muelhbauer.

Visit us at www.eHarlequin.com

Printed in U.S.A.

For my wonderful sister and brother-in-law,
Sharon and David Lingren

With a special thank-you to Courtney Burken

CAST OF CHARACTERS

Charlie Callahan: Contractor, temporary guardian and River Rat

Beth Pennington: Physician's assistant, athletic trainer and Charlie's ex-wife

Nathan Turner: Charlie's fourteen-year-old ward

Abraham Steele: Town patriarch and bank president, recently deceased

Lucy Garvey: Charlie's sister, Beth's former best friend and waitress at the Sunnyside Café

Ed Pennington: Beth's brother, lawyer and River Rat

Grace Pennington: Ed's wife

Aaron Mazerik: Former bad boy, current basketball coach and counselor at Riverbend High

Lily Bennett Holden: Golden Girl, widow, artist and River Rat

Evie Mazerik: Cashier at the Sunnyside Café, Aaron's mother

Dr. Julian Bennett: Town doctor, Lily's father

Wally Drummer: Former basketball coach at Riverbend High, now retired

CHAPTER ONE

"YOU'RE UP BRIGHT and early this morning," Lucy Garvey said to her brother, Charlie, as he sat on one of the counter stools at the Sunnyside Café. She reached for the coffee carafe and poured him a cup.

"You know what they say. The early bird catches the worm." He took a sip of the coffee, needing the jolt of caffeine.

"You want the usual?"

He shook his head. "Just coffee this morning."

She clicked her tongue. "Now what would your mother say if she heard that?" She turned to face the window separating the kitchen from the dining area. "Two eggs over easy, bacon and a side of hash browns." She turned back to Charlie with a smug grin, then made her way down the counter to refill the cups of the other customers.

Charlie could only shake his head. Lucy was a lot like their mother. She had the same blue eyes, the same dimpled smile and a light dusting of freckles that his mother managed to hide with make-up, but Lucy didn't bother to camouflage. Both thought he needed to be fed every time he walked into the diner. Anyone watching would have thought Lucy was the older sibling, the way she fussed over him.

"So what worm you trying to catch this morning?" Lucy asked when she finally made her way back to his section of the counter. "And how come you look like you're going to either a wedding or a funeral?"

"I'm going over to West Lafayette."

"To see your little brother?"

Nathan Turner wasn't Charlie's brother in the literal sense of the word. Four years ago Charlie had met the boy through the Big Brothers program. They'd been friends ever since and were more like father and son than brothers.

"He's got himself in trouble. Threw some rocks and busted a few windows in what he thought was an abandoned building."

"Doesn't sound like a felony offense."

"It's not, but it's enough to land him in juvenile court this morning."

"Ah. Now I get the reason for the shirt and tie."

He grimaced as he tugged on the silk knot, attempting to loosen its grip on his neck. "I hate these things."

She leaned over the counter and pushed his hands away. "Here. Let me fix it for you." As she straightened his tie, she asked, "So, are you going to go put in a good word for the kid?"

"I have to. I promised Amy that I'd always be there for Nathan, and I intend to keep that promise."

"He hasn't exactly made it easy for you, has he?" Satisfied with her work, she stepped back. "There. Isn't that better?"

"Much, thanks." Charlie took another sip of his coffee. "Nathan's not a bad kid. He's just had a lot to deal with for someone so young. Tomorrow it'll be exactly one year since his mother died."

"Then it's a good thing you're going to see him. This past year can't have been easy for him."

"No, and I haven't spent very much time with him since he moved to West Lafayette with his grandparents. I hope to change that."

"You said he was coming to spend a couple of weeks with you this summer."

He nodded. "Next month. I think his grandparents could use a break. He's a handful."

"Isn't every teenage boy?"

Charlie smiled. "I know I was."

"Yes, and look at you now." A bell rang and she scurried over to the window to retrieve a plate of bacon and eggs. "So what kind of punishment will Nathan get?" she asked when she returned, setting the plate in front of him.

"That's what I'm going to find out. I want to make sure the judge understands I'll do whatever it takes to keep him out of trouble."

She pulled a bottle of ketchup from her apron pocket and placed it on the counter. "It'd be a shame if he couldn't visit you this summer."

"If we're lucky, that won't happen." He poured a liberal amount of ketchup onto his potatoes.

"You should enroll him in one of Aaron Mazerik's sports programs while he's here. Two weeks shooting hoops and hanging out with other boys his age would do him good. Speaking of basketball, I heard there's going to be a pickup game Wednesday at the gym."

"Yeah. A few of us got together after Abraham's funeral and decided to shoot some hoops on a regular basis."

She sighed. "I envy you. It's been years since I was on a court."

If it hadn't been for an injury, Lucy would have gone on to play basketball in college. Unfortunately a torn ligament in her knee had ruined her chances for an athletic scholarship. Instead of going away to university, she'd stayed in Riverbend, married and started a family.

"Why don't you stop by and play with us?" he suggested.

"As if the guys would want a woman crashing their night out," she drawled.

"Hey, anyone would be nuts not to want you on their team. You were always better than I was."

She punched his arm playfully. "I do believe brotherly love has caused your memory to fade. It was nice seeing so many of the River Rats at Abraham's funeral, though. Weren't you surprised by how many came?" The River Rats was the name given to the bunch of kids who used to hang out down by the Sycamore River.

He *was* surprised. Abraham Steele might have been the bank president and town patriarch, but he hadn't exactly been the most popular man around. "Most of us showed up out of respect for Jacob."

"I still can't believe he wasn't there. No matter what happened between him and his father, he should have been here for his father's funeral and the reading of the will." Charlie knew she was only saying what many folks in town were thinking. "Is it possible he doesn't know his father died?"

He wrinkled his brow. "Could be."

"People are wondering if maybe Jacob's dead."

Charlie raised an eyebrow. "People being you?"

"I'm not the only one." The bell sounded again and she disappeared briefly to deliver breakfast to the waiting customers. When she returned she said, "It's funny how things work out. Twenty years ago, who would have thought the richest man in town would die estranged from his son?"

"Or that he'd leave me a houseboat—or I should say, half of one." Charlie shook his head. "When Nathan comes for his visit next month, we're going to spend some time on the river, but first I have to work out a few details."

"You mean Beth being part owner, don't you?"

He took a sip of coffee. "I'm sure that'll change. Ed says she wants to sell her half."

"Didn't I tell you she wouldn't want it? She has no use for a houseboat." Lucy made a sound of disgust. "I don't know why Abraham left it to the two of you in the first place. He knew you two were divorced. And Beth never liked the river. She's afraid of the water—or have you forgotten?"

Charlie didn't want to admit that there were very few things about Beth Pennington he had forgotten. Only time and distance had allowed him not to think about them.

"Well, he did leave it to her, and now we have to figure out a way for me to become the sole owner. Ed's working on it."

Her sister frowned. "You did hire your own attorney, didn't you?"

"Of course."

"Good. As much as I respect Ed, he *is* her brother."

"Yes, and for that very reason he'll do what he can to get this legal stuff taken care of as smoothly as possible. He knows our situation. As soon as Beth comes home, she'll sign the necessary papers and that will be that.''

His words stilled Lucy's hands, which had been busy rearranging the condiment tray. ''Beth is coming back to Riverbend?'' she demanded. ''When?''

''I'm not sure.''

''How long is she staying this time?''

''I don't know,'' he said, which was the truth. Despite the divorce, he and his ex-wife's brother had managed to remain friends by *not* talking much about Beth. As much as Charlie had been tempted to ask Ed the details concerning her visit, he had kept his questions to himself.

Lucy wouldn't let the subject rest.

''I wonder why she's even coming. She doesn't want to be here. Not that I blame her. She's made a new life for herself. She doesn't fit in here anymore.''

Talk of Beth made Charlie's breakfast stall on its journey to his stomach. The food seemed to stick in the middle of his chest. He took a sip of his coffee in an attempt to wash it down. ''You're sounding like Mom again.''

Lucy threatened to smack him with her order pad. ''Oh, hush!''

''It's true. Every time Mom hears that Beth is coming back to Riverbend, she starts saying things like, 'Beth doesn't belong here, she doesn't like it here'—as if she needs to remind me that Beth's never going to be a part of my life again.'' He pointed at her with a strip of bacon. ''In case you and Mom haven't noticed, I haven't exactly been losing sleep all these years over my ex-wife. I have a life.''

''Of course you do, and the reason Mom and I say those things is that we don't want your life getting messed up by her again.''

''That's not going to happen,'' he stated firmly.

''I hope not. She was all wrong for you, Charlie.''

''I agree. Now can we drop the subject? I'm trying to enjoy my breakfast.''

She looked as if she wanted to continue the discussion, but the bell rang again, indicating more food hot off the grill.

When she had gone, Charlie took a bite of the whole-wheat toast. It tasted like cardboard. What little appetite he'd had when he'd come into the diner had disappeared, thanks to Lucy.

It wasn't really fair to blame his sister, he knew. She hadn't said anything he himself hadn't been thinking the past week. Ever since he had learned that Abraham Steele had left the houseboat to him and his ex-wife, he'd been bothered by memories of Beth. He knew what his mother and sister said were true. Even Beth's brother had voiced pretty much the same thing. Beth had made a life for herself that didn't include Riverbend. Or him.

And that was fine. He didn't want to share the houseboat with her, anyway. According to his attorney, there was no need for them to see each other. Papers could be signed without any contact between them.

''Are you thinking about her?'' his sister's voice interrupted his musings.

''Who?'' he asked, feigning ignorance.

She gave him a disbelieving look as she refilled

his coffee cup. "If you're lucky, this visit will be no different from the others. It'll be short, and neither one of us will be on her calling card."

"Hearing you talk, no one would ever guess that you and Beth used to be best friends," he said dryly.

"That was a long time ago. People change." A spoon fell to the floor and she bent to retrieve it. "I don't plan to see her and neither should you, especially not now."

"Why not now?"

"You're vulnerable."

He looked at her over the rim of his cup, trying to hide his amusement. "I am?"

"I'm not stupid, Charlie. I know that men have certain…needs."

He chuckled. "You think I'm going to fall for Beth because I'm lonely?"

"She's always been able to do a number on you."

This time he laughed out loud.

Lucy planted her hands on her hips. "I'm serious. I'm worried about you. Owning this boat with her…well, it could present all sorts of problems."

"None I can't handle," he assured her.

Her sister harrumphed. "She hurt you once. What makes you think it won't happen again?"

"I learned a long time ago that even if I could ride a white horse, they don't make shining armor in my size."

Charlie was spared Lucy's reply when a customer signaled for her attention. He ate as much as he could of the breakfast and finished his coffee.

With luck he figured he could exit the diner with a simple wave in Lucy's direction. But luck wasn't with him. As he paid the cashier, his sister caught up with him.

"Here. Let me give you a hug for good luck at the hearing today." She wrapped her arms around him and squeezed.

"Thanks. By the way, I'm going to be gone for the weekend. After I get this stuff straightened out with Nathan, I'm going to Indianapolis."

"Who's in Indianapolis?" she asked, her eyes widening with interest.

"Not who. What. A trade show. Mitch Sterling and I are going."

As he left the café he glanced back through the plate-glass windows and saw his sister chatting with Evie Mazerik, the cashier. As much as he wanted to think Lucy was talking to the older woman about work, Charlie had a pretty good idea the two were discussing the one subject he didn't want to share with the town. Beth.

BETH PENNINGTON breathed a sigh of relief as she crossed the Illinois border into Indiana. At least twice during her trip from Iowa the engine light had come on, giving her cause to believe her car had mechanical problems. At least now she was close enough to Riverbend that she wouldn't feel guilty about calling her brother, Ed, if she needed help.

As she left the gently rolling farmland behind and the brick buildings and treed streets of Riverbend came into view, she was surprised by the nostalgia that washed over her. Seeing her hometown sent a shiver through her—and not an unpleasant one.

Just the opposite, in fact, which was why it caught her off guard. She didn't expect to feel good about coming home—although she really couldn't call it home anymore. Once she'd crossed the Sycamore River she took a right, instead of proceeding straight through town, inexplicably wanting to drive through her old neighborhood.

She felt a catch in her chest at the sight of her childhood home. It was a two-story frame house, nothing fancy, but full of memories. Most of them good, but a few painful. Along the walkway day lilies bloomed in a profusion of orange, a legacy of her mother, who'd planted them only a few weeks before she'd died.

"You're still here, Mom," Beth murmured quietly. As a nine year old, she'd taken her grief out on any weed that dared to pop up in that garden, tugging at it with a vengeance and tossing it aside. Every spring and summer that followed, she'd nurtured those lilies with the same tenderness her mother had nurtured her, knowing that when the flowers bloomed, she'd feel her mother's presence again.

As Beth glanced at the wooden porch, she imagined her father lying in his hammock, the newspaper propped on his belly. How many times had she and Lucy Callahan run past him in a hurry, slamming the screen door on their way inside, only to have her father holler, "Where's the fire?"

Up the stairs to the second floor they'd race, eager to plop down on her double bed and dissect everything that had happened at school that day. Although Lucy was the same age as Beth, she'd been a year behind her in school because Beth was in the accelerated program. That hadn't stopped them from being the best of friends, sharing their fears and disappointments, along with their hopes and dreams.

Automatically Beth's eyes sought the Callahan house next door. Although her father had moved away, Beth knew that Lucy's parents still lived there. Time was, she would have never dreamed of passing their house without stopping to say hello. They would have scolded her if she had.

A honking horn startled her out of her musings. She wasn't twelve, she was thirty-one, and Mr. and Mrs. Callahan no longer regarded her as a daughter. There was no point in stopping, so she turned her attention to the street and drove away.

As she reached the heart of town, she saw that, although time had brought some changes to Riverbend, most of the commercial district looked the same. There was Steele's bookstore and the Sunnyside Café, two of her favorite places. The Strand Theater still showed movies nightly, according to the marquis, and Beck's was selling shoes right next door.

Beth continued down Hickory Street, suddenly impatient to see her brother and his family. When she reached his home, the excitement bubbling inside her had her hurrying out of the car and up the front steps.

"Omigosh! You're here!" Grace Pennington's mouth dropped open when she saw Beth standing on the front step. "Ed didn't think you'd come."

"Should I leave?" she joked.

"No, this is wonderful. Come on in." After a warm welcoming hug, Grace ushered her sister-in-law inside.

As she stepped into the living room, Beth saw Grace's parents seated on the sofa.

"Mom and Dad are here for the weekend," her sister-in-law told her. The two seniors smiled and greeted Beth warmly.

"I should have called before I came," Beth apologized. "I didn't even think that you might have company." For once in her life she'd made an impulsive decision and it looked as if it was the wrong one.

"We're not company," Grace's father bellowed. "We're family."

"That's right, and there's always room for family," Grace assured her, pulling Beth into the living room with a loving hand.

In their hearts maybe, Beth said to herself, but in her brother's house there was only one guest bedroom, which was now occupied. Maybe she could bunk in with one of her nieces. She was about to make that suggestion when her niece Kayla came bouncing into the room followed by a set of twins.

"Hi, Auntie Beth," said Kayla. "Look who Grandma and Grandpa brought with them. My cousins Erin and Jenny. They're sleeping overnight, too."

Beth's eyes met those of her sister-in-law. "The more the merrier, right?" Grace said in her usual calm manner. "I bet you could use a cold drink. Why don't you come into the kitchen with me. While I put the finishing touches on dinner, you can bring me up-to-date on everything that's happened."

"I feel really stupid," Beth told her as she took a seat at the wooden table. "I should have called before I came."

"Nonsense. We love surprises—especially ones that bring us our favorite people. Now, don't even worry about the sleeping arrangements. We'll figure something out after dinner." She gave Beth's arm a squeeze. "I'm so glad you're here—Ed's going to be delighted."

"Where is my brother?"

"Working, but he'll be home for dinner." Grace opened the fridge and took out a pitcher of lemonade. She poured a large glass for Beth. "He's going to be surprised. Now that July's half gone, he thought you'd keep postponing your visit until the summer was over."

"It was tempting," Beth confessed, accepting the cold drink gratefully. "I can't remember the last time I didn't work over a summer break."

"You work too hard, Beth. You and your brother have that in common."

"Guess it's in the genes," she said lightly. "If I didn't work I'd get bored." She watched her sister-in-law tend to the pots on the stove. Despite having a houseful of kids and extra guests for dinner, she looked her usual calm self, not a hair out of place on her blond head, her makeup as fresh as if she'd just put it on.

"You won't have to worry about being bored here. We'll find plenty of things for you to do. The girls were counting on you coming and they've made plans to take you on picnics and a dozen other things."

The girls were Beth's nieces—Kayla, who was eight, Allison, five, and little Cierra, who was three. "They're the real reason I'm here. It'll be good to spend some time with them."

Grace grinned. "They love being with you, but I have to warn you. They'll run you ragged if you let them. No reason you can't lie around and do nothing if that's what you want."

Beth had never been very good at doing nothing, which was why she said, "Ed mentioned that Dr. Julian Bennett might be looking for someone to help out at his clinic."

"Are you thinking about working while you're here?" Grace asked.

Beth shrugged. "It would only be part-time."

Just then her brother walked in through the back door. "Hey! I thought I recognized that car out front." He spread his arms to welcome his sister, who jumped up to give him a hug. "It's good to see you, sis. You look great." He pushed her back at arm's length and let his eyes take her in.

"You don't look so bad yourself," she told him, returning his gaze with the same affection. "I see you cut your hair." Ever since she could remember, his dark, wavy hair had reached the edge of his collar.

He rubbed a hand over his closely cropped brown hair. "Thought I should start looking like a thirty-five-year-old attorney instead of an aging rebel," he said. "Besides, it's easier this way."

"I like it," she stated sincerely.

"Has Grace been bringing you up-to-date with what's been going on around here?" he asked, giving his wife an affectionate nuzzle on the neck as she stood next to the stove stirring a pot.

Grace replaced the lid on the pan and said, "I'll let you do that, Ed. I'm going to set the dining-room table and get the kids washed up for dinner."

"Let me help." Beth started to rise to her feet, but Grace put a hand on her shoulder.

"You sit and visit with your brother," she ordered, then grabbed a stack of plates and disappeared into the other room.

"So what's wrong?" Ed asked as soon as they were alone.

"Nothing's wrong," Beth denied indignantly as he sat down across from her. "Have you forgotten that you invited me to come spend the summer with you?" She spread her arms. "So here I am."

"It's mid-July."

"All right, so I missed the first part of summer."

He smiled slyly. "You cost me a hundred bucks."

"How's that?"

"I bet Grace you wouldn't come at all."

Beth chuckled. "No wonder she was so happy to see me."

"I'm happy to see you, too. You haven't exactly been a regular visitor to Riverbend," he reminded her.

"I have a very demanding job," she said, then immediately added, "Or I should say I *had* a very demanding job."

"Does that mean you're still unemployed?"

She could see concern in her brother's eyes and it touched her. Even though they were separated by distance, they had remained close over the years, and she had confided in him often about the difficulties she'd had getting along with the athletic director at the college for the past year. Ed had been a rock of support when she'd made the decision to quit her job, and he understood her anxiety about her uncertain future.

"Yes. I told them in the spring I wasn't going to renew my contract," she said, not wanting to rehash the betrayal she'd felt on not only a professional but a personal level. As an athletic trainer she had always put the well-being and safety of her students first. To have someone question her judgment, then overrule her decision to keep a player out of a game was a breach of professional conduct she couldn't tolerate.

"I'm glad to hear that. I was worried they might have coerced you into returning to your position."

She shook her head. "That won't happen. I think it's probably a good time for me to take a break from working in college athletics, anyway. I plan to do some clinical work."

"I bet Julian Bennett would find a permanent spot for you if you asked him."

"My home is in Iowa," she reminded him gently.

He smiled. "I know, but you can't blame a brother for trying."

Their conversation was halted as Grace announced it was time to eat. Dinner turned out to be a bit chaotic as the five little girls chattered and giggled their way through spaghetti and meatballs. By the time it was over, Beth was convinced that her sister-in-law had her hands full and didn't need to worry about another houseguest, even if that guest was family.

She brought up the subject as she and Grace finished cleaning the kitchen. "I think I should check into a motel—just for the weekend."

"You will not," Grace stated emphatically.

"She will not what?" Ed asked, coming into the kitchen.

"Beth wants to go to a motel for the weekend."

"You already have a full house," Beth told her brother. "You don't need me."

"Yeah, we do. To help clean up," Ed teased.

"I can do that without putting someone out of a bed," Beth said.

"This is really bothering you, isn't it?" Ed returned.

"Yes." She set her dish towel aside. "You're not going to be offended if I go to a motel, are you?"

"No," her brother replied slowly, "but it doesn't make any sense to pay for a room when you have a place of your own at your disposal."

She gave him a puzzled look. "What do you mean?"

"The *Queen Mary*. Thanks to Abraham Steele, it's half yours."

Beth shook her head. "Oh, no. I couldn't sleep there."

"Why not?"

"You need to ask?"

He gave her a look of disbelief. "Because of Charlie?"

She hated the way her stomach muscles tensed at the mention of her ex-husband. For fifteen years she'd been able to pretend that Charlie Callahan didn't exist. But now, thanks to one legal document, the window to that corner of her memory was reopened. A beneficiary of Abraham Steele's last will and testament, Beth was now in the uncomfortable position of being in a partnership with a man she hadn't expected to ever see again.

"I told you I wanted to sell my half to him," she said as calmly as possible.

"Yes, but right now that half belongs to you and you have a right to use it. Besides, Charlie's not even going to be in Riverbend this weekend. I talked to him yesterday and he told me he was going out of town. Some builders trade show in Indianapolis."

She chewed on her lower lip. Using the houseboat would solve the problem of where she was going to sleep tonight. And it would be nice to have a quiet room all to herself where she wouldn't feel she was inconveniencing anyone.

"Why are you hesitating? You have every legal right to use the boat, Beth," Ed assured her.

This wasn't about her rights. It was about memories. Ever since she'd learned she'd inherited the houseboat, unwelcome images had begun creeping into her consciousness. Too much had happened on that houseboat, things best forgotten.

"I'm just not sure it's a good idea, that's all," she told him. "I can go to a motel."

"Trust me, Beth. The *Queen Mary* is nicer than any motel around here. Abraham completely remodeled it before he died."

Which meant she might not even recognize the place. Maybe she could stay on the boat and not be plagued with memories of the past. "Don't I need a key or something?"

"I have one." Ed disappeared, only to return a few minutes later carrying a small key ring and a black leather-bound folder. "You'll need this, too."

"What is it?" she asked as he handed her the folder.

"All the information you'll need to use the boat. I've already looked at it and it's pretty self-explanatory. Basic stuff about the water and electricity. There are diagrams in there, as well.''

Seeing the amount of information in the folder added to Beth's trepidation. ''Maybe this isn't such a good idea. I don't know the first thing about houseboats.''

''Don't worry about it. I'll go with you to Steele's marina and answer any questions you have. Do you remember the way, or do you want me to drive and you can follow in your car?''

''I remember where it is, but I'm not sure I should drive my car.'' She went on to tell him about the engine light coming on.

''Why don't you leave it here and I'll take a look at it in the morning?'' he suggested. ''I can drive you to the marina tonight and pick you up in the morning.''

''I'd appreciate that.''

''Are you sure you won't stay with us?'' Grace asked as they prepared to leave.

Beth was tempted to take her up on her offer, but she knew she couldn't. Like it or not, the houseboat was the best place for her to sleep this weekend. She would just have to do what she'd done for the past fifteen years. Forget about that other long-ago night she'd spent on the *Queen Mary*.

Forget about Charlie Callahan.

CHAPTER TWO

JUST AS IT HAD BEEN all those years ago, the *Queen Mary* was docked at the small private marina just south of town. As Ed's Jeep traveled across the gravel road with nothing but blackness on either side of it, Beth tried unsuccessfully to suppress a shiver. She couldn't help but remember the last time she'd been down this road. She'd been with Charlie, on her way to what he'd promised would be a night she'd never forget. Little had either of them known how true those words would be.

"Here we are," Ed announced, turning into a small parking lot. "If you wait a second, I'll get a flashlight and light the way."

She did as he suggested, remaining in the Jeep until he'd retrieved a portable lantern from the back. As she climbed out of the vehicle, he aimed the beam of light toward the ground. "Watch your step."

Beth stayed close to him as he led her onto the pier and over to the houseboat. "So this is it?" she said, thinking that it didn't look as big as it had when she'd been a teenager.

"Like I said, it's changed since you were last here. Abraham spent a pile of dough remodeling it. Wait until you see all of the conveniences he added."

Beth saw what her brother was talking about when they stepped inside. The salon had a white leather sectional sofa that allowed occupants a good view of the water, as well as the big-screen TV built into a cabinet against one wall. Next to it was a stereo system and a VCR. All the windows had custom-made deep blue drapes that matched the carpet beneath her feet.

"This is nicer than my apartment," she said, admiring the oak cabinetry in the galley. She fingered the shiny black front of a microwave suspended beneath one of the cabinets.

"The guy had the bucks to spend and he liked nice stuff."

Beth sat down on one of the high-backed stools next to the bar and twirled around. "It's hard to believe all this was someone's toy, isn't it?"

"It's your toy now," he reminded her.

She shook her head. "It doesn't make any sense. Why would he leave something like this to two people who haven't seen each other in fifteen years?" The question had been nagging her ever since she'd received the letter from the attorney stating she was one of Abraham Steele's beneficiaries.

He sighed. "Who knows what motivated him to leave any of the River Rats anything? Whatever the reasons for his bequests, the fact remains you own half this place."

"Yeah, me, who never liked the river," she stated dryly.

"Well, lucky for you, Charlie does."

Beth knew all too well how much her ex-husband enjoyed the river. The memory of a fifteen-year-old boy splashing in the water surfaced in her mind. She had gone down to the river to look for Ed, who was supposed to be fishing with a couple of the other River Rats. To her surprise, the boys weren't dangling their lines in the water. They were skinny-dipping.

There had been four naked bodies frolicking in the river that day, but Beth's eyes had only noticed one. Charlie's.

At thirteen, she'd had a limited knowledge of male anatomy, gained mainly from science textbooks and baby-sitting ten-month-old Billy Benson. The shock of seeing a nude teenage boy had frozen her to the spot.

She wasn't sure how long she had stood there staring at him, but as she raced back to her house on wobbly legs, she knew that from that moment on, she could no longer regard Charlie as the boy next door, the boy who was good friends with her older brother, Ed, the boy who walked her and Lucy to the school bus stop. Things had changed.

To the rest of Riverbend he might still look like her second big brother, but to Beth he had become something more. Every time he smiled at her, she'd felt warm inside, and when he casually touched her, she'd gotten all tingly. It had been the beginning of an infatuation that would last through high school.

She shook her head, hoping she could toss the memories aside as easily as she flipped back her hair. "He must be remarried by now."

"Do you really want to know the answer to that question?" Ed asked with a lift of one eyebrow.

Beth didn't. For fifteen years she'd avoided asking any questions about Charlie Callahan. Ignorance had been bliss while living in another state. But now she was in Riverbend and she needed a few answers. Only a few.

"I think I should know his marital status, since we've inherited a boat together, don't you?"

Ed sighed. "All right. He hasn't remarried."

So he was single. The rumor she'd heard a couple of years ago hadn't been true. She took a deep breath, trying to calm her jangled nerves. "Maybe I should just give him my share of the boat. It's not like I will have any use for this place after this weekend."

"Now, *that* would be foolish." He spread his hands. "Look around you. Abraham Steele wanted you to have a share in all of this. As your brother and your lawyer, I can't let you give it away. Especially if the only reason you're doing it is to avoid a confrontation with your ex-husband."

"I'm not," she fibbed. "I just don't want the hassle of dealing with this right now."

"You get bequeathed a boat we used to call the floating palace and you don't want it." He shook his head in disbelief.

She looked about the place in bewilderment. "What would I do with something like this?"

Ed shrugged. "Take off on a river adventure?"

"No, thank you. I'd probably get seasick. Remember that time Dad took us out on Lake Michigan when we were kids?"

"Everyone was a little queasy on that trip because the waters were rough. You won't have to worry about any motion sickness tonight. You're docked. This boat isn't going anywhere." He pulled open the door to the built-in refrigerator. "This is on, but it looks like there's nothing inside but a few cans of mineral water. Should I take you to a convenience store so you can pick up a few things?''

She shook her head. ''It's all right. As long as there's mineral water, I'll be fine. Besides, if I have food here, you might forget to come get me.''

''I won't forget,'' he assured her. ''Do you need a tour of the boat, or do you remember where everything is from all those parties the River Rats had here?''

''I didn't party with the River Rats, or have you forgotten?''

''Ah, yes. You were always afraid we were going to get caught sneaking onto the boat, weren't you?''

''I wasn't officially a River Rat.''

''No one was *officially* a River Rat, Beth. You lived in the neighborhood and you hung out with the rest of us.'' A faraway look came into his eyes. ''Gosh, we had some great parties on this boat. Do you suppose Abraham knew what went on when he was out of town?''

''Probably.''

''Jacob never got into any trouble—at least none he told us about.''

The image of a fair-haired boy popped into Beth's head. Jacob Steele had been the unofficial leader of the River Rats, the golden boy of Riverbend. Even though he was Abraham's son, he wasn't allowed to bring any friends onto the boat that Abraham considered his private retreat. That hadn't stopped the River Rats from using it when he was out of town.

''That's another thing that bothers me about this bequest,'' she told him. ''Besides the fact that we've been divorced for fifteen years and shouldn't be sharing anything, Charlie and I shouldn't get the boat. It should go to Jacob. He was Abraham's son.''

''A son who didn't even come home for his father's funeral,'' Ed reminded her.

''Whatever happened between him and his father must have hurt him deeply. Jacob's not the kind of guy to turn his back on his family without good cause.''

''None of the River Rats are, Beth. Sure, we got into a few scrapes when we were growing up, but we were all pretty good kids.''

''Abraham must have thought we were special. He included all of us in his will,'' she said, running a finger along the shiny countertop.

He chuckled. ''Yes, I now have a vintage 1957 Chev and you have half a houseboat.''

''At least your gift will fit in your garage. I don't have a lake or a river for mine.''

''Then it's a good thing you're spending the rest of the summer here.'' He waved a hand at her. ''Come. I'll show you a few things.''

She followed him around the cabin and listened as he explained the water system and electrical circuits. ''If you get too warm and don't want to open the windows, you can turn on the air-conditioning. The control's next to the instrument panel,'' he said, slipping into the captain's seat to point out the various gauges.

''For someone with no experience of houseboating, you sure seem to know an awful lot.'' She eyed him suspiciously.

He gave her a sheepish look. ''I have a little experience,'' he admitted. ''I was here with Charlie one day recently and we took a ride on the river.''

She crossed her arms over her chest. "Without asking me?"

"I only went because I wanted to protect your interest. It was my duty as your legal representative."

Beth thought it was more likely that he went along because he wanted to spend time with Charlie. She didn't tell him that, however. She might not be able to stop her brother from remaining friends with her ex-husband, but she certainly didn't have to hear the details of their friendship.

"The master bedroom's in here," Ed told her, opening a door on the other side of the bathroom.

"It's all right. You don't have to show me." The last thing she wanted was to look inside the room where she and Charlie had made love—even if it had been remodeled since.

"Where are you going to sleep?"

"Aren't there beds below?"

He led her down a small flight of steps to the lower cabin, which had two bunks, both covered by brightly patterned quilts in a kaleidoscope of colors. There was also a small cedar chest and a built-in wardrobe.

"This isn't quite as fancy as the master bedroom," Ed commented as she opened a narrow closet.

"No, but it's cozier." She sat down on one of the beds to test its firmness. "I think I'll feel less like an intruder down here."

"You have every right to be here, Beth," Ed stated firmly.

"So you keep telling me, but for whatever reason, I still feel like I'm sneaking onto a houseboat that's off-limits.'' She stretched her arms over her head, then sighed. ''I don't know. Maybe I'm just tired. What time should I expect you in the morning?''

''How about if you give me a call when you wake up? That way if you want to sleep in a bit later than usual, it won't matter. You have your cell phone, right?''

She nodded. ''It's in my purse.''

''Good. Now lock the door behind me and get a good night's sleep.'' He gave her a kiss on the cheek, said good-night, then headed back to his Jeep.

After twelve hours in the car and with a headache throbbing in her temples, Beth wanted to follow her brother's orders, but ever since she'd stepped on the boat, she hadn't been able to shake the uneasiness that lingered from her past. Even though remodeling had made the *Queen Mary* barely recognizable, it was still the place where she'd made what had turned out to be the biggest mistake of her life.

She squeezed her eyes shut, refusing to give in to the temptation to remember that night fifteen years ago. She was tired, she needed sleep, and she would not let the past haunt her. Not now. Not here.

Taking a deep breath, she opened her eyes and put an Enya CD in the stereo system, allowing the soothing sounds to flow around her. And just in case Enya failed to lull her to sleep, she pulled a bottle of pain-relief tablets from her purse. When she opened the refrigerator to get a can of mineral water, she saw one lone beer on the bottom shelf. Michelob. Charlie's favorite.

Seeing that can was a reminder that he had been on the houseboat only a few days earlier. He'd walked barefoot on the carpet that was beneath her feet, stood on this very spot with the door open, contemplating the contents of the refrigerator.

"We're not trespassing, Beth," he'd told her when she'd expressed reservations about being on the boat the night of the spring formal. "Abraham said I could use the place if I wanted. That's why I have a key."

She remembered the smile on his face, the gleam of desire in his eyes as he'd pulled her along the wooden pier. It hadn't taken much convincing to get her to spend the night with him on the boat. Little had she known that that one night would bring so many changes to her life.

Her dress had cost a small fortune—a sapphire-blue satin off-the-shoulder gown that had swished when she walked. And after two hours at Clip Curl and Dye, she had never felt more confident. One of the stylists had managed to make her short boyish curls look glamorous and chic, her makeup as professional as a cover girl's. But it was the glitter that Beth had loved. It had dusted her bare skin in a most enchanting way.

She remembered the look on Charlie's face when he'd picked her up for the dance. She'd fantasized a guy looking that way at her—as if she were the only girl in the world for him.

Then her dad had barked, "Don't forget she's only sixteen, Charlie."

She could have died of embarrassment. Because she'd been accelerated, she was the youngest in her class. All the other girls were seventeen and eighteen. Academically it had been easy fitting in with the older girls, but socially she'd had problems.

Having eighteen-year-old Charlie Callahan as her date for the dance was her chance to be accepted, and she didn't need her father to throw a bucket of cold water on the evening.

Not that he really could have. Charlie made sure she had a night she'd never forget. Any worries she'd had about what people would think were cast aside when they were voted the cutest couple at the dance. At midnight, when the chaperons had chased everyone home, Charlie hadn't taken her to the pizza party at Josh Parker's house. Instead, the two of them had gone down by the river for a moonlight picnic.

Beth knew now they should have gone to the party with the rest of their classmates. As her father used to say, hindsight is twenty-twenty. If they hadn't been alone in the moonlight, they would never have kissed, and if they hadn't kissed, they wouldn't have touched, and if they hadn't touched, they wouldn't have... She shook her head, not wanting to think about that night.

She wouldn't think about it. She closed the door quickly, leaving those memories in the cold. She opened the can of mineral water and poured its contents into one of the crystal goblets she'd found in the cupboard. Then she shook two of the pain-relief tablets from the bottle. They were extra strength, with an additional ingredient to induce sleep.

It was time for her to stop worrying about what she would encounter in Riverbend. She knew that if she took the pills, she'd be a bit groggy in the morning, but she didn't care. At least her headache would be gone and she wouldn't toss and turn in an unfamiliar bed. With a long gulp of the sparkling water, she swallowed the tablets.

Then she turned up the volume so the Enya music could be heard in the cuddy. As she lay flat on her back staring up at the dark ceiling, she closed her eyes and waited for the music to calm her active mind.

But no matter how hard she tried, she couldn't stop thinking about Charlie. When she closed her eyes, she saw him. Shirtless. Drinking a beer. Staring at her with that look that used to make her feel as if she was standing on the edge of a steep cliff. The last thought she had before she fell asleep was to wonder why he had never remarried.

"JEEZ, CHARLIE! The sun's not even up yet!" fourteen-year-old Nathan Turner grumbled as he carried his duffel bag out to the pickup.

"Best time of the day. Wait until you see what sunrise looks like on the water."

"I only got five hours of sleep last night. Isn't there a law against dragging kids out of their beds without the proper amount of sleep?" the boy muttered belligerently.

"Not when it's the kid's fault because he stayed up half the night playing video games," Charlie tossed back at him.

Nathan was uncharacteristically uncooperative as they loaded the pickup with fishing gear and supplies. He was not happy to be up so early. Actually he hadn't been happy since Charlie had seen him sitting in the courtroom yesterday morning.

"Hey! Be careful with the bag. There are eggs inside," Charlie said as the teen tossed a paper sack of groceries into the truck as if it was a bag of garbage.

By the time they were ready to leave, Nathan's squinty-eyed frown had become a stubborn scowl. Charlie was losing patience. "Look, I realize this is earlier than you're used to getting up—"

"No kidding."

Charlie ignored the sarcasm. "But we only have two days to spend on the houseboat. If we wait until noon to go out, we'll miss the best part of Saturday. You do want to take the houseboat on the river, don't you?"

The only response Nathan gave was a grunt, but to Charlie it sounded like a positive grunt, which he took as a good sign.

"It should be a perfect weekend to be on the river," Charlie said cheerfully. "If it gets as hot as they're predicting, you'll be able to swim right off the back of the boat."

Mention of the houseboat had Nathan's scowl softening, although he was reluctant to let Charlie see. He turned away, bunching his sweatshirt into a ball and propping it between his head and the window to use as a pillow.

Charlie didn't say anything, but continued driving. It was hard to believe that this disgruntled teen with the streak of blue in his hair and the gold ring through his nose was the same clean-cut kid he had been a surrogate parent to for the past four years. What had happened to the even-tempered, happy-go-lucky Nathan?

His grandfather blamed it on the group of boys Nathan called his friends, but his grandmother insisted the moodiness had more to do with puberty.

Charlie could see the obvious signs of adolescence. Nathan's voice had changed, he'd grown four inches in four months, and it wouldn't be long before a razor would be needed to take off the light coating of peach fuzz on his chin. Charlie was inclined to think they were probably both right, but suspected the boy's rebellious behavior also had a lot to do with losing his mother.

After several minutes of jostling and fidgeting, Nathan said, "I don't see why I couldn't have taken a shower before we left."

A shower? This from the kid who had barely raised a wet cloth to his face, let alone taken a shower, the last time he'd stayed with Charlie.

"We're going down the river, not to the video arcade," Charlie answered. "It'll be like that camping trip we took last summer. Remember? Guys are allowed to be slobs on camping and fishing trips, as long as there aren't any women around."

His reasoning brought another sound of disgust from his temporary ward. "I hate that stupid judge. If it weren't for him, I'd be home in my own bed."

It bothered Charlie that Nathan didn't want to be with him in Riverbend. In the past he'd complained about there never being enough time for the two of them to be together. Now that the judge had ordered him to spend six weeks in Riverbend, Nathan acted as if it was a punishment, not a reprieve.

Maybe that was why Charlie's voice was a bit harsh as he said, "You're wrong, Nathan. The reason you're not home is that you chose to use someone else's property for target practice."

"I said I didn't try to break those windows, but nobody believed me. Just because I hang out with the BDs, everyone wants to think I'm a juvenile delinquent,'' he muttered sullenly.

"Who are the BDs?''

"What do you care?''

"Because I'm your buddy. Or have you forgotten?''

That took a bit of the sting out of his attitude. "They're the bad dudes.''

Charlie frowned. "And you're one of them?''

"I want to be. And I was just getting to where they would accept me when you had to drag me here.''

"I didn't drag you here,'' Charlie refuted. "You were ordered here by the judge because of something you did, not because of what I did. And I really don't think being in a gang is a good idea.''

"They're not a gang, just some guys who hang around together. They're my friends and they'd do anything for me. I can count on them.'' The defensiveness in his tone made Charlie uneasy.

"You can count on *me*,'' he said firmly.

Nathan gave a snort of disbelief. "That's why you're making me get up with the cows.''

"You mean chickens,'' Charlie said, trying to inject a little humor into their discussion.

Again Nathan turned toward the door and tried to position his head against his makeshift pillow. Charlie gave him his space and kept quiet.

That didn't stop him from thinking about the teenager. Had he made a mistake sticking his neck out to help the kid? When he'd left for West Lafayette yesterday morning, he hadn't expected to be returning with the fourteen year old in tow. It was one thing to have Nathan spend two weeks with him; quite another to have him spend half the summer.

Ever since Nathan had gone to live with his grandparents, distance had prohibited them from spending much time together. Until yesterday Charlie had thought that they had a pretty good relationship. Now he could see that the two of them had grown apart, and it saddened him, because at one time they had been like father and son.

As the truck ate up the miles, Charlie thought back to those days. He had just turned thirty, and at his surprise birthday party he'd been warned by his friends that the big three-O could cause a man to change his entire way of thinking.

Charlie had laughed and told them how wrong they all were. The reason he was still single and doing all right was that he worked hard Monday through Friday and made the most of his weekend playtime. The latter had been accomplished mainly with women who weren't looking for the house with the picket fence, two kids and a dog.

But shortly after his birthday he'd found himself reflecting on his life and came to the conclusion that something was missing. Although he wasn't about to change his life-style, he did want to do something different. When one of his friends mentioned that the local Big Brothers program was having trouble finding volunteers, Charlie decided to answer the call.

He could still remember that first day he'd met Nathan. He'd expected that things would be awkward, that Nathan would be a bit reserved, maybe defensive about not having a father. He wasn't. He was just like any other kid and reminded Charlie of himself at that age. So full of energy. So eager to learn everything he could about the world around him. Unlike Charlie, who'd had a great relationship with his father, Nathan had never known his dad.

They soon became best buddies, and before long, Nathan's mother, Amy, joined them on their outings. They were the closest thing to a family that Nathan had ever known, and it wasn't long before he was asking Charlie if he could call him Dad. Charlie saw no reason he couldn't, for he truly did feel like a father to Nathan.

Charlie knew that Nathan harbored the hope that one day he would marry his mother and become his real father. For Charlie, who'd never expected to entertain such a thought, it had come as a shock when he'd realized Nathan's idea wasn't so outrageous. He had no reason not to believe that, in time, he and Amy might find happiness together.

But then one night Nathan called to tell him his mother was sick—real sick. Charlie went over to see what was wrong. It didn't take a doctor to see that she was seriously ill. He rushed her to the hospital, where she died two days later from bacterial meningitis.

In the blink of an eye, everything changed. Nathan's grandparents became his legal guardians and took him home with them to West Lafayette. Charlie knew that Amy's folks were good people and would give Nathan the kind of family he needed—something he couldn't do without Amy.

Charlie vowed to remain a part of Nathan's life, acting as a father figure whenever he could. Which wasn't often. Construction was booming in Riverbend, forcing everyone at Callahan Construction to work long hours.

No matter how hard Charlie tried to make his visits with Nathan special, he could feel the bond between them weakening. Nathan no longer had that childlike eagerness in his voice when they talked, and gone was his enthusiasm for "hanging out" in Riverbend.

Charlie glanced at the boy beside him and felt a wave of guilt. He hadn't kept his promise to Amy. He'd let work and the fact they lived in different towns keep him from being the father figure he should have been. Maybe the judge's ruling was exactly what they both needed to put their relationship back on track, to help them reestablish the bond that had allowed Nathan to call him Dad.

"We're here," Charlie announced as the truck came to a stop next to the pier where the *Queen Mary* was docked. Dawn was brightening the sky, changing it from darkness to deep purple, which was the precursor to a beautiful sunrise. Charlie hoped nature's beauty would lighten Nathan's mood.

It didn't.

As the boy awoke from his nap, he said, "Why couldn't we just stay home?"

Charlie had to bite his tongue. "What do you think of that sky?" He nodded toward the horizon. "Isn't that a beaut?"

"'Red sky in morning, sailors take warning,'" Nathan recited ominously.

Charlie said, "We're not sailors. We'll have a roof over our heads should it rain, and an engine to get us to shore."

Nathan mumbled something under his breath as he fumbled with his seat belt.

"There she is. The *Queen Mary*," Charlie boasted as they climbed out of the pickup. "How's that for a floating palace?"

Nathan shrugged. "It's all right, I guess."

Charlie knew the boat was more than all right, no matter what the surly teenager thought. "Come on. The sooner we get this stuff onboard, the sooner we'll be cruising on the river," he said, lifting a duffel bag from the back of the truck.

Emptying the truck caused less grumbling than loading it had, giving Charlie hope that even a teenager wasn't immune to the lure of the river. They left the fishing rods and tackle box on the deck, then carried their duffel bags and groceries into the main cabin. Nathan said nothing other than to heave a sigh when Charlie told him where to set the food.

Although the teenager tried to pretend he wasn't impressed by the comforts on board the boat, Charlie didn't miss the way Nathan eyed the entertainment center. "Not bad for a prison, eh?"

The teenager shrugged. "If you'd told me there was a TV, I would have brought my video games along."

"We're going to be too busy having fun. We won't have time for TV." Charlie didn't mention that he'd already decided to rent a Nintendo and some other games after the weekend.

"Who listens to this crap?" Nathan asked, lifting a CD case from the entertainment center.

Charlie glanced at the Enya CD. "It's not mine. Must have been Abraham Steele's or one of his guests'. Now make yourself useful and put away those groceries, while I get the boat ready."

Nathan wandered over to the captain's console. He plunked himself down on the chair and examined the controls. "Am I going to be able to drive?"

"I may let you take the wheel once we're away from the dock," Charlie answered, pulling the cord that opened the blue draperies across the front of the boat.

"How far up the river are we going?"

"Here. I'll show you." Charlie reached into his pocket and pulled out a folded piece of paper. "This is a marine map. Shows all the hazards on this section of the river. It's important that we keep it handy at all times."

He spread the map out on the console, noting the way Nathan studied it curiously. It was the first time the kid had actually shown any interest in their adventure. Maybe it would turn out to be a good weekend, after all, Charlie thought.

"We're going to stop right about here," he told Nathan, pointing to a hook in the river. "As soon as you've put away the groceries, I'll give you a lesson in navigation, all right?"

Again the shoulders shifted, but the hostility was gone from the teenager's face. "Can I use the bathroom, or do I have to wait until the engine's running?"

"No, go ahead. Flush away," Charlie told him, indicating the door to the head. While Nathan was inside, Charlie checked the fuel gauge and water supply.

He was on his knees connecting a wire that had come loose on the control panel when he heard Nathan say, "Your girlfriend left something in the bathroom."

Charlie straightened. "I don't have a girlfriend." From the silly smile on Nathan's face, he knew that it was something the teen found amusing.

He went to see for himself. A bright red bra hung on the doorknob. The first thought that crossed Charlie's mind was that Mitch Sterling had had a woman onboard when he'd used the boat last week.

"Well, that sly old…" he began, then noticed Nathan's rapt attention. "Must be from a previous guest," Charlie said, snatching the bra from the doorknob and shoving it into the vanity drawer. "Follow me."

He opened the door to the master bedroom and tossed his duffel bag onto the bed. "I'll sleep here."

"Where do I sleep?" Nathan asked.

"You have two options. One is the cuddy below. There are two beds down there. It's private, though a little cramped. The other is to use the sofa bed."

Nathan looked at the white leather sofa. "You mean it's one of those you pull out and have to make every night?"

Charlie nodded. "You'd probably be more comfortable below." Nathan glanced down the stairway. "It is rather dark down there. The windows are more like portholes."

He could see the boy considering the possibilities—downstairs in the cuddy with little natural light, or on a sofa in the salon with a big-screen TV. He had no doubt that the teenager would opt for the sofa. That way he could watch television as he lay in bed.

"I'll sleep up here," he said sullenly, as if it was a sacrifice to sleep on a sofa bed.

"All right. That's fine with me. Now get that food in the refrigerator and I'll prepare us for departure. We need to disconnect the shore cable and switch over to the generator before we leave."

Nathan shoved cans into the cupboard, acting as if putting away the groceries was some sort of penance. Charlie left him alone and went off to tend to the tasks that needed to be done before launching the boat.

A short while later he announced, "We're ready. We can either navigate from in here or go up to the flybridge. What do you think?"

Nathan shrugged. "I don't care."

"Then we'll go up to the flybridge." Charlie headed for the steps leading to the upper portion of the houseboat. Nathan followed.

Once on top, Charlie stood behind the control panel. "We'll crank this baby's engine and get moving." He turned the key in the ignition, producing a low hum.

"It's pretty quiet, isn't it?" Nathan said as the engine sprang to life.

"She purrs like a kitten," Charlie agreed. "You ready?" Nathan nodded and Charlie slowly maneuvered the boat away from the dock.

The sky had become a vivid pink, thanks to the dawn's paintbrush. "See what I mean about the sunrise?" Charlie commented as the sky's resplendent colors reflected on the river's surface.

"It's kinda spooky. It's almost like the air is painted pink," Nathan said, losing his insolence long enough to be a bit awed by nature.

Charlie understood his sentiment. "When I'm in a boat this time of morning, I feel a little bit like I'm on a mystical journey. Better enjoy the show before it disappears. It's already starting to fade."

"I'm hungry. What's there to eat?"

Charlie smiled. Beneath the streaked blue hair and nose ring lurked a regular kid. "As soon as we get to our fishing spot, we'll anchor and I'll cook us some breakfast. Until then, why don't you go down and get yourself a doughnut and a glass of milk?"

"I'd rather have a soda and some chips."

"Whatever," Charlie mumbled, and watched the boy disappear into the cabin. His last thought as the blue head bobbed out of sight was that it was going to be a long six weeks. A very long six weeks.

BETH WASN'T SURE what woke her. Maybe it was the sound of a motor humming in the background. One of the neighbors mowing the lawn perhaps. As she opened her eyes, however, she realized that she wasn't in her own bed or even in one of her brother's. She was on the houseboat. *Her* houseboat.

And it was swaying ever so slightly, something her brother had told her wouldn't happen. She swung her legs over the side of the bed, standing ever so carefully, worried that she might experience a bit of motion sickness. To her relief she didn't.

Thinking the wind must be responsible for the slight sway of the boat, she reached for the curtain behind the bed and pulled it aside to look out the rectangular porthole. To her surprise, there was a rather large expanse of river between her and the shore. She padded across the room to the opposite side of the boat and lifted the curtain on the other narrow window.

A gasp escaped her as she realized that the boat was no longer at the pier. Had the wind become so strong that it had broken loose from its moorings? Suddenly her brain put two and two together. The hum of an engine, no pier in sight. The boat was moving!

Her heart beating rapidly, she scrambled up the steps to the salon. Seated on the white leather sofa with the TV remote in his hand was a teenage boy. He wore baggy carpenter jeans and his shirt was open, revealing an expanse of flesh. He was at the gawky stage—caught somewhere between man and child—with long, lanky limbs and an awkwardness only time would eliminate.

"Who are you and why is this boat moving?" Beth demanded.

He looked as surprised by her appearance as she was by his. "I'm Nathan. What are you doing on my dad's boat?"

His *dad's* boat? "This is not your father's boat. It's my boat and I don't know what makes you think you can just take off with it."

"We didn't know you were on it," he said weakly, then, gaining his courage, added, "You shouldn't be on it. It belongs to my dad."

Fear caused Beth's skin to prickle. "I'm going to get my cell phone and call the police. You just can't get on someone else's houseboat and take it for a ride." She was about to head back down to the cuddy when she heard a man's voice.

"Nathan, I could use your help. Come on out here."

The voice was vaguely familiar. Beth's stomach plunged. "What's your father's name?"

Before the boy could answer, the man called out, "Nathan! Did you hear me? Get out here. Now!"

When the boy would have moved, Beth raised a hand and used her schoolteacher voice to say, "You stay right here and answer my question. What is your father's name?"

"You're going to be in big trouble, lady, when my dad finds out you stowed away on his boat," the teenager said, getting bolder by the minute. "This is private property and..." He stopped, his eyes on the sliding door behind her.

By now Beth's heart was in her throat. She swallowed with difficulty, then turned to see a man step into the cabin. He was big, brawny and bare-chested. Dark sunglasses hid his eyes and his jaw was unshaven.

Beth didn't need the boy to tell her his father's name. It was Charlie Callahan, her ex-husband, looking lean, tanned and even more attractive than he had fifteen years ago.

She had often thought about what they would say to each other when they did finally meet again. Now she knew. There was no, "Hello, Beth, how are you?" No, "It's good to see you."

The first words out of Charlie's mouth were angrily uttered. "What the hell are *you* doing here?"

CHAPTER THREE

CHARLIE HAD EXPECTED the day would come when he'd meet Beth again. What he hadn't foreseen was the turmoil of emotion it would create in him. Seeing her standing in front of him, looking as if she'd just crawled out of bed, made him feel as if someone had given him a stiff punch to the gut.

She looked as shocked to see him as he was to see her. Folding her arms across her chest, she demanded, "What do you mean, what am I doing here? What are *you* doing here?"

Before Charlie could answer her question, Nathan stepped forward. "I tried to tell her it's your boat, Dad, but she wouldn't listen. She must have stowed away in the cuddy."

Charlie didn't miss the fact that he had once more become "Dad" to the teenager. Or that Nathan showed signs of a vivid imagination. He was looking at Beth as if she could be someone on the run.

"I'm not a stowaway. This happens to be my boat," Beth stated in a tone that left no doubt that she didn't appreciate Nathan's implication that she'd done something illegal.

Nathan looked at Charlie. "*Her* boat? I thought you said this was your boat."

"It is—at least, half of it is. The other half is Beth's. Nathan, this is Beth. Beth, Nathan." He made the introduction as brief as possible, hoping to avoid the questions that would result if Nathan learned Beth was his ex-wife.

He'd never told the teenager he'd been married. There'd never been any reason to, and until just a few moments ago, it had been a nonissue in his life. Four weeks of marriage hardly qualified as a treasured memory. His summer thing with Beth—which was how his buddies had referred to it—felt as if it had happened in another lifetime.

Only now he was reminded that it had happened. He watched Nathan extend his hand to her, revealing the manners Amy had instilled in him as a child. "How do you do."

Beth took his hand cautiously, eyeing Charlie suspiciously as she returned Nathan's greeting.

"You haven't told me what you're doing here," Charlie said to her, trying not to notice that, instead of short curls, her dark hair now hung in long kinky waves that fell to her shoulders in a rather tantalizing way.

"Obviously the same thing you're doing—using my property."

He didn't care for the tone of her voice. Or the fact that he was responding to her scantily clad body. She wore skimpy pajamas made to resemble a T-shirt and shorts—very *short* shorts. Although she was still slender, there were curves that hadn't been there fifteen years ago. She'd filled out in all the right places, and Charlie had to force his eyes away from her figure to her face.

She moved over to the windows and asked, "Where's the pier?"

"In Riverbend."

"We're moving?" She pressed a hand to her stomach.

"No, we're anchored."

"This boat is supposed to be docked at River-bend. You had no right to take it—or me—any-where," she said haughtily.

"Do you honestly think I would have taken it anywhere if I'd known you were onboard?" he countered. "What are you doing here? Why aren't you at Ed's place?"

"Because his guest room is occupied. Grace's parents are here for the weekend."

"So you came here to sleep?" he asked in dis-belief.

"And why is that so hard for you to believe?"

"You're not exactly crazy about the water."

"It didn't feel as if I was on the water when the boat was moored at the marina. Are you sure we're anchored?" she asked, her hand flying to her mid-section once more.

"We are." She looked unusually pale, prompting Charlie to ask, "You're not going to be sick, are you?"

"No, but I need to use the bathroom. Excuse me." She left in a hurry, slamming the door as she disappeared into the head.

"What's she doing on a houseboat if she gets seasick?" Nathan asked.

"She said she wasn't sick," Charlie answered.

"She looked like she was gonna hurl."

"I'm sure she's fine," Charlie said, although he really wasn't sure of anything concerning Beth at this point in his life. When several minutes had passed and she still hadn't emerged from the head, he went over to the door and knocked. "Beth, are you okay in there?"

"Yes." The response was muffled. "I'm fine."

"Are you sure?"

"For Pete's sake, Charlie, I said yes, didn't I?" she snapped.

Maybe she'd changed physically, but emotionally she was still the same old Beth, hating it whenever anyone showed concern for her. She still didn't want to admit that she needed anybody.

When he returned to the salon, Nathan had flopped down onto the leather sofa, sprawling in the way only a teenager could. "Does this mean we're going back to Riverbend?" His expression brightened.

"There are places between here and there where she could get off the boat," Charlie answered, which caused the sullen look to return to Nathan's face.

"Wait a minute. You're not dumping me off like some unwanted cargo," Beth said from behind him.

He turned and saw that she had come out of the bathroom. Her face was still pale, but she looked ready to do battle with him, hands on her hips, eyes flashing.

"I'm not going to dump you anywhere," Charlie told her.

"No, you're going to take me back to Riverbend." It was more of a command than a statement of fact. "Ed's expecting me to be at the marina, not in the middle of a cornfield."

"I wouldn't leave you in a cornfield. I just thought that if the motion of the boat makes you feel sick, you might want to get off upstream. I'm sure Ed wouldn't mind if he had to drive a little farther to get you.''

''I told you I'm fine,'' she insisted. ''And you haven't told me what you're doing here. Ed said you were at some trade show this weekend.''

''My plans changed,'' he said, avoiding Nathan's eyes.

''So you decided to use the boat without asking me?''

''I don't recall *you* asking *me* if you could spend the night onboard,'' he retorted. Again the look on Nathan's face reminded Charlie that he needed to be careful what he said. He didn't want the fourteen year old to see him in a shouting match with his ex-wife.

''It's obvious there's been some miscommunication,'' he said in a calmer voice, raking a hand across the back of his neck. ''You thought I was out of town and I thought you were still in Iowa.''

That piqued Nathan's curiosity. He got up from the sofa and went to stand beside Beth. ''I've never met anybody from Iowa before. What do you do there?''

''She works,'' Charlie answered for her, trying to preempt Nathan's interest, then addressed Beth. ''So we both had plans for the boat for the weekend. Now what?''

''Obviously one of us will have to find another place to sleep tonight.''

''Since Nathan and I want to go fishing, I'm willing to buy out your interest for tonight,'' he proposed.

''Meaning what?''

''I'll give you the money for a motel.''

He could see she wasn't happy with his suggestion. Nor was Nathan, who said, "I don't care if we don't go fishing."

"But I do," Charlie told him, annoyed that the teen was willing to let Beth have the boat. Nathan was gazing at her as if she was an ally, not an intruder. Charlie looked Beth squarely in the eyes and said, "Since you're only looking for a place to sleep and we want to use the boat for recreation, wouldn't it make more sense for you to go to a motel?"

One thing Charlie knew about Beth was that she wasn't obstinate. Some women might have refused to find another place to sleep out of sheer stubbornness. Not Beth. Decisions were made after careful consideration—a trait he'd admired in her.

That was why he wasn't surprised when she said, "You can have the boat for the rest of the weekend, but I don't want your money. I'll find another place to stay without your help. Now, if you'll take me back to Riverbend, I'll get off this boat and you two can have it all to yourselves."

Charlie had won, but there was no thrill in the victory. "I appreciate that," he said. "We'll leave right away."

"Thank you."

Unfortunately her gratitude was premature. When Charlie sat behind the controls and turned the key in the ignition, the engine wouldn't start.

"What's wrong?" Beth asked, hearing his unsuccessful attempts to get the boat running.

"I'm not sure, but I'm going to find out." With that he got up out of his chair and headed outside. Beth and Nathan followed him, watching as he lifted a hatch in the deck.

"Well?" she asked when he didn't volunteer any information.

"I need my tools." He retrieved a gray metal box from the storage closet and again bent over the hatch. It only took him a few minutes to find the problem.

"Do you know what's wrong?" she asked when he straightened.

"We're out of gas," he announced.

She didn't believe him. "You're joking, right?"

"Nope."

"How could we run out of gas?" she demanded.

Charlie said nothing, just let the hatch door slam shut.

"You didn't answer my question. How could we run out of gas? Didn't you check the gauge before you left Riverbend?" She was drilling him as if he was her employee, not the co-owner of the boat.

"The fuel gauge says we have a full tank," he informed her.

She frowned. "So what are you saying? That the gauge isn't registering?"

"Bingo," he retorted, wiping his hands on a cloth rag. "There's probably a short in the wiring."

"Does that mean we're stuck here?" Nathan wanted to know.

Beth answered before Charlie could. "We're not stuck anywhere. I have my cell phone in my purse. I'll call for help."

"And who are you going to call?" Charlie wanted to know. "Ed?"

"He must know someone who could bring us gas."

"I'm sure he does, but it's not necessary," Charlie told her. "This is a public waterway and it's Saturday morning. I'm sure a boat will come by sooner or later."

"That may be, but I'd rather not wait to find out," she said, then disappeared inside.

As she walked away, there was only one thought going through Charlie's mind. Time had been damn good to Beth's body.

BETH FELT WEAK and her hands were shaking by the time she reached the narrow confines of the lower cabin. She collapsed on the bed and took several deep breaths, hoping her stomach would quit acting as if it were moving independently of the rest of her body.

Yet how could it when Charlie was here on her boat? Correction. On *their* boat. She was stranded in the middle of the Sycamore River with her ex-husband.

No wonder her stomach felt so unsettled. It had been a shock to see him again—a shock that was intensified by the discovery that he had a son.

When Ed had told her Charlie had never remarried, she'd assumed that meant he had no children. Why should she think any differently? Charlie had always been a man of principle. After all, when he'd found out their one night together had resulted in an unplanned pregnancy, he had married her, saying he would always do the right thing when it came to kids.

But they hadn't had a child. The thought sent a sharp pain through her chest. She bit down on her lower lip, forcing the memory from her mind.

"No. I will not think about what happened between us, Charlie Callahan,'' she said aloud. ''I won't go there.''

She couldn't go there because she knew if she did, it would be like opening the lid of a jack-in-the-box and the pain she'd managed to bury for so long would pop right up in her face. She pulled off her pajamas and tossed them aside, hoping she could discard the memories with them.

Living in Iowa had made it easy to forget that she'd been married and divorced. No one there knew Charlie, and she had little contact with anyone in Riverbend. Leaving for college had given her the opportunity for a fresh start, a chance to forget the painful past and begin a new life.

Now she was back and her new life felt threatened. Would she be able to pretend Charlie Callahan didn't exist? That they hadn't been married?

Thanks to Abraham Steele, it wasn't going to be easy, but she'd figure out a way to do just that. It would help if she felt nothing for him. She'd hoped that when the day finally came that she did see him again, she would be indifferent toward him. Now that day was here, and it was as if all those years spent learning to live with her mistakes had been stripped away. Instead of a responsible mature adult, she was once more a vulnerable teenager.

It didn't help that he'd stood before her shirtless, his tanned flesh bulging with muscles strengthened by years of construction work.

As a kid he'd been lean. Even when the other guys who were River Rats had begun spending a lot of time after school in the weight room, Charlie hadn't cared about building muscles.

And it hadn't mattered to the girls of Riverbend,

either. Charlie was cool. And fun to be with. His popularity had little to do with the size of his biceps. Every kid at Riverbend High knew that Charlie's appeal was in his personality.

As Beth dressed, she tried not to think about the good times. She needed to remember that they had come with a price. But suddenly all the years she'd spent pretending she'd never been married evaporated as quickly as puddles in the sun.

Her marriage was no longer conveniently buried deep in the cellar of her mind. Its memories were right up front, pushing their way into her thoughts, begging her to remember that Charlie was her first love.

She took a deep breath and willed her body to be calm. She couldn't think about the past. Not now. She needed to call Ed so she could get off this boat as soon as possible.

It was a good thing she'd brought her cell phone along, she thought, turning it on. In the right-hand corner, a light glowed, indicating the battery was low. She punched in Ed's number, hoping there was enough of a charge left for her to complete the call, but she was out of luck.

With a frustrated sigh, she tossed the phone aside. She was stuck here with Charlie.

"Damn."

If only she didn't have to go back up on deck and see him. Time was supposed to heal all wounds, so why did seeing him again affect her this way? It had to be the shock, she told herself.

Theirs was an awkward situation, but she'd get through it. And as soon as she was back in Riverbend, she'd make sure their paths didn't cross the remainder of her stay. No matter what Ed advised her, she would get rid of her share of the houseboat in the fastest way possible.

And as for those painful memories...she'd locked them away once before. She could do it again. She just needed to get away from Charlie Callahan.

BETH WASN'T GONE LONG, and judging by the frown on her face when she returned, she hadn't gotten the answer she'd expected from her brother.

"Did you talk to Ed?" Charlie asked as she stepped outside into the sunshine. She'd changed into a pair of jean shorts and a yellow top that clung as closely to her curves as the pajamas had.

"My phone isn't working," she said, averting her eyes. "Battery's low. So now what do we do?"

"I told you. We wait for a boat to come by." With effort, Charlie tried not to notice how the fabric stretched across her breasts.

"Can't you use the radio?"

"I'm not calling for someone to come give us gas when we're in the middle of the river on a beautiful sunny day. This isn't an emergency situation," he told her.

"So how long do you plan to wait before you consider it an emergency?" she asked tartly.

"We have plenty of food to last until tomorrow if necessary," he answered.

"Tomorrow?" Her brow wrinkled in a fierce frown. "You told me you'd take me back to Riverbend today."

"And I will. You're getting all worked up over nothing."

"I'm not worked up," she denied. "It's just that

I'm worried Ed's going to wonder where I am. He's expecting me to be at the marina, not in the middle of the river.''

''If that's what's worrying you, I'll call him as soon as I get to shore,'' he told her.

She shaded her eyes with her hand, then peered up and down the river. ''There's not a boat in sight.''

''Not yet, but there will be,'' he stated confidently.

''And until then?''

''Until then I might as well make us some breakfast,'' he said, getting up out of the chair. ''Are you hungry?''

He could see the thought of eating wasn't a tantalizing one. ''No, actually I'm not.''

''Then you don't want to join us?''

''No, I'll pass.''

Charlie wasn't sure she'd refused because her stomach was unsettled, or if she just didn't like the idea of eating breakfast with her ex-husband.

''You go on inside. I'll sit out here and keep an eye out for a boat,'' she told him.

Charlie watched her lower her long slender legs into a lounge chair and thought it best that he did go inside. She was a distraction he didn't need at the moment. Lucy was right about Beth having an effect on him. There was no point denying that he'd always been physically attracted to her.

But he was no longer a teenager. He only wished his hormones would listen to the message his brain was sending them. Beth was beautiful and smart, but she was *not* the woman for him. He knew it. She knew it. Everyone in town knew it.

So why did he still want her?

"THE PAN'S SMOKING."

Charlie turned and saw that Nathan was right. He had set the skillet over the flame and forgotten about it. He switched off the gas.

"You're not supposed to leave oil in a pan un-attended," Nathan told him.

"Who are you? Smokey the Bear?"

The teenager shrugged. "They taught us safety in the kitchen in 'living skills' at school."

"Did they teach you how to cook?"

"Some stuff. Not bacon and eggs, though."

Judging by the mess Charlie had made, it looked as if he didn't know much about cooking breakfast, either. He'd already burned the bacon and over-heated the skillet.

"What about toast? Can you manage that?" he asked.

Nathan shrugged. "I guess."

"The bread's over there." Charlie motioned to the loaf at the end of the counter.

With about as much speed as a turtle, Nathan am-bled over to the counter and plugged in the toaster. He popped two slices of bread into the slots, then watched as Charlie cracked eggs into a bowl. All but one broke.

"I like my eggs runny," Nathan informed him.

"Well, you're getting them scrambled," Charlie said, taking a fork to the eggs and whisking them.

"Maybe we should ask Beth to cook for us."

"Maybe we shouldn't," Charlie replied.

"Why not?"

"Because I said no." He poured the eggs into the pan.

"She might as well earn her keep," Nathan said.

"She doesn't need to. As I told you, she owns half this boat." He sprinkled shredded cheese and onions over the eggs.

"So this Steele guy left both of you the boat?"

"Yes."

"Weird."

"Yes, it is."

"He must not have known she gets seasick."

"Possibly." Charlie pushed the eggs around with a wooden spoon.

"How come you don't like her?"

Charlie paused to look over at Nathan. "What makes you think I don't like her?"

"Duh. You were pretty rough on her."

"Me? You're the one who accused her of being a stowaway."

"She didn't tell me it was her boat. Is that why you're pissed off at her? Because you didn't get the whole boat?"

"I hope you don't talk that way around your grandparents," Charlie said, tempted to give Nathan the treatment his own father would have given him had he used profanity in his presence. "You could get grounded for such language. And just to set the record straight, I'm not *angry* at Beth."

It was the truth. Anger was definitely not what he'd felt when he'd seen her standing there in her skimpy pajamas with her hair falling about her face in disarray. *Bothered* would have been a better word to use, but he didn't want Nathan to know that she caused such a reaction in him.

"Who is she, anyway?"

"I told you. Her name is Beth Pennington. She was a close friend of my sister Lucy when we were kids. She lived next door to us."

"Was she a River Rat?"

"Sort of. Your toast is up. Butter's in the fridge."

Charlie was relieved that Nathan had a one-track mind, and the task of getting the toast buttered appeared to be the track it was taking. However, the subject of Beth apparently held enough fascination for him, because he quickly came back to it.

"That must have been her titty-holder in the bathroom," he said as he put two more slices of bread in the toaster.

Charlie could hardly believe that Nathan had used such a word. "It's called a bra," he said in his sternest voice.

At the memory of the lacy scrap of material, Charlie's body warmed. Then he remembered what it had been like as a teenager when he'd seen Beth naked. Heat rushed through every limb in his body, and he forced himself to push such thoughts aside.

He needed to deal with the issue of Nathan's vocabulary, not daydream about an old lover. "I don't think your mother would have appreciated you calling one of her undergarments by that name."

"I wouldn't have used it around her."

"Do the BDs talk that way?"

"I didn't swear. I just called it a titty-holder. I suppose you're going to ground me for that, too." He stalked away and threw himself down on the sofa.

"Come back over here and finish making the toast," Charlie demanded.

"What's the point?" Nathan said sullenly.

Charlie counted to ten, then walked over to the sofa. He stooped in front of the teenager so they were face-to-face. "Look, Nathan, it's been a long time since I was fourteen, and until I met you and your mother, I had no idea how to be a dad, either."

Nathan didn't meet Charlie's gaze. He sat with his eyes downcast, arms folded across his chest, mouth tight.

"I want this six weeks to be a good time—like we used to have. You want that, too, don't you?" Charlie pleaded.

Nathan nodded, but continued to look down.

"Great. Now, we can do one of two things. Continue on as we have been, or forget about everything that's gone wrong this morning and start over. Clean slate. What do you say?"

He waited while Nathan contemplated his options. Charlie wondered what the big decision was, but knew better than to voice that thought. Nathan's grandmother had warned him that trying to be a parent to a fourteen year old was tricky. He now knew what she was talking about.

When Nathan finally raised his head, his eyes didn't meet Charlie's, but looked beyond him to the galley. As they widened, Charlie turned around to see why.

Beth was at the stove. "Good grief, Charlie. Only you would leave eggs frying unattended. What are you trying to do? Burn up our inheritance?"

CHAPTER FOUR

BETH GRIMACED at the mess in the pan. "I thought you would have learned to cook by now," she said to Charlie as he came up behind her.

"I know how to cook," he told her.

"No, he doesn't," Nathan piped up. "That's why he eats breakfast at the Sunnyside every morning."

"I don't eat there *every* morning," Charlie said.

"Lucy says you do," Nathan shot back, then made a face as he gazed over Beth's shoulder into the contents of the frying pan. "That stuff looks disgusting. It smells bad, too."

"Nathan, that's enough." Charlie's voice held a hint of censure.

Beth reached for the pot holder on the hook behind the stove. "This isn't going to be easy to clean," she said, eyeing the scorched mass of eggs, onion and cheese that coated the bottom of the pan.

"Let me do it." Charlie tried to reach for the frying pan, but she pushed his arm away.

"No. I want it done properly."

"Properly?" Charlie echoed. "You think I don't know how to scour a pan?"

"I know you don't," she told him, relieved to see he'd slipped a T-shirt on over his bare chest. It was less intimidating staring at white cotton than sunbronzed pecs. He was still standing much too close for her comfort, though.

"He hates doing cleanup. That's why he never cooks," Nathan added.

"That doesn't mean I don't know how," Charlie insisted.

"Throwing a pan in the garbage is not cleaning it," Beth told him, remembering when they were newlyweds and he'd burned spaghetti sauce in an old pot. Instead of trying to clean it, he'd chucked it into their garbage container.

The look he gave her told her he was remembering the same incident. "That was then."

"What was when?" Nathan asked.

Beth expected Charlie to avoid answering the question, but he didn't.

"When we were kids, I once burned some spaghetti sauce in this big old black kettle that was well dented and looked like it should have been in the trash heap. So instead of wasting time trying to clean it, I threw it out."

"It could have been scrubbed clean," Beth said.

"Didn't your mom get mad?" Nathan asked.

"It wasn't my mom's pan," Charlie answered.

No, it had been Beth's, and it had happened a long time ago, although standing here in the close quarters of the galley, it felt like yesterday that they'd stood side by side in the kitchen of their efficiency apartment. She'd cooked him dinner on the tiny two-burner stove with pots she'd found at a garage sale. They'd eaten by the light of candles stuck in empty bottles and made love late into the night on their pull-out sofa.

To Beth it had been like playing house, which

was probably why it had been so easy to end their relationship. It hadn't had the ingredients that made real marriages work—love and commitment. They'd been young, impatient and looking for easy answers during a difficult time. If only they'd waited, instead of rushing into marriage; so much heartache could have been avoided.

She didn't want the memories that seemed to be worming their way into her consciousness. Nor did she want to be standing next to the man who provoked them.

"Excuse me," she said, ducking between Charlie and Nathan. She emptied the contents of the skillet into the garbage, then put it in the sink, where she watched the water sizzle into a cloud of steam as it hit the pan. "This is going to need to soak for a while."

"Does that mean we don't get breakfast?" Nathan asked.

"You'll get to eat," Charlie assured him.

"When?"

"Nathan." Charlie's voice carried a warning.

"What's wrong with asking if I get to eat?" the teen questioned. "I'm hungry."

Aware of the tension between the two of them, Beth said, "There must be another pan we could use."

"*We?*" Charlie cocked an eyebrow.

"Since it looks like I'm the only one who knows how to cook on this boat, I should be the one doing the eggs," Beth stated pragmatically.

"You're offering to make breakfast for us?" he asked in disbelief.

She really didn't want to do anything for Charlie,

but found herself saying, "Only because I need to protect my investment."

"Not funny." Charlie stepped around her and opened a cabinet. Out came a second skillet, which he set down on the stove with a clang. "Your offer is appreciated, but not necessary. I can make breakfast."

Nathan groaned. "Oh, great. More burned eggs."

Charlie gave the boy another glare. "Maybe you want to try cooking for us."

"No, but if she's willing to do it, why not let her?" Nathan answered, nodding toward Beth.

"Because it's not her job to cook for us," Charlie replied a bit impatiently. "And I would appreciate it if you would remember your manners."

"What did I say now?" Nathan rolled his eyes in exasperation. "Forget I even asked. I don't want any breakfast." Then he stomped away, slamming the sliding screen door as he left.

When he was gone, Charlie apologized for him. "I'm sorry about that."

She shrugged. "There's no need to apologize."

"He's usually not like that."

"Like what?"

He chuckled. "Come on. You know what I'm talking about."

"He's just being a kid. And an honest one at that. He said the pan smelled bad, which it did, and that he was hungry, which should come as no surprise. Teenagers are always hungry."

"You're defending him?"

"Is there a reason I shouldn't?"

"You mean, besides the fact that he was rude?"

''He was just being a typical teenager. Besides, he's right, you know. You *are* an awful cook.''

''You think so?''

She glanced at the skillet in the sink. ''There's the evidence.''

''No, it isn't. That could have happened to anyone.''

''Fine, it could have. Since you're such a great cook, I guess I should let you get back to it,'' she said, trying to sound bored with the whole affair.

''What does that mean? That you're taking back your offer to help?''

''You just said you don't need it,'' she reminded him.

''All right, I lied.'' He sighed in resignation. ''You know I've never been any good at this kitchen stuff.''

She did indeed. Their marriage may have been brief, but it had lasted long enough for Beth to discover that Lucy and her mother had spoiled Charlie. He could barely put together a sandwich, let alone cook something on the stove.

''Maybe it's time you learned,'' she suggested with a lift of one eyebrow.

''You're not going to leave me to feed a starving teenager by myself, are you?'' There was a hint of a familiar smile, the one that had helped him cajole others into doing what he wanted.

She would be stupid to let it affect her. ''Sorry.'' She gave him an apologetic look. ''I'm going to retire to my half of the boat. The air's less aromatic down there.'' When she started to walk away, his hand grasped her arm to stop her.

"Beth, wait." Dark eyes met hers with an interest that made her breath catch in her throat.

"It's been fifteen years. Don't you think we should talk about something other than burned eggs?" he asked.

The feel of his fingers on her skin sent a tiny tremor through her. She slid her arm out from underneath his hand. "What do you want me to say, Charlie? That it's good to see you again?"

"Is it?" She felt as if he studied every pore on her face, so intense was that gaze.

"No." He winced and she immediately added, "I'm sorry. I shouldn't have said that."

"You don't have to apologize for being honest. It was a dumb question and one I shouldn't have asked."

Beth hated the coldness that hardened his features. She longed to see a glimpse of the old Charlie again, the old smile.

"I didn't mean the way it sounded," she apologized lamely, but he would have none of it.

"Yes, you did. If there's one thing you've always been, Beth, it's to the point."

"Yes, but the point you're missing is that you startled me, Charlie. I thought I was alone on the boat, and then I discovered that not only am I not alone, I'm floating in the middle of the river with..."

"Your ex-husband." He finished the sentence when she didn't.

Denial may have worked while she was in Iowa, but here on the boat there was no way she was going to be able to forget he had been her husband. The look in his eyes reminded her that even though their marriage had been brief, it had been real.

"Even you have to admit this is a little awkward," she said, averting her eyes from his penetrating gaze.

"Well, maybe it wouldn't be if you hadn't worked so hard at avoiding me every time you came back to Riverbend in the past fifteen years," he said coolly.

Of course she'd avoided him. What did he think? That they could marry, divorce and then go back to the way things had been when they were kids? His next words told her that was exactly what he thought.

"Considering the amount of time we spent together when we were growing up, I thought we could at least remain friends," he said, his voice warming a bit.

Friends? She repeated the word over and over in her head. Didn't he realize what an insult that word could be? "I guess you thought wrong, didn't you?" she said pointedly.

His eyes darkened. "Guess I did. Maybe Lucy was right, after all."

She didn't want to be curious but couldn't help herself. "Right about what?"

He shrugged. "It doesn't matter."

It did matter to Beth, but she didn't want to admit that. At one time she and Lucy had been the best of friends. Beth had thought nothing would ever come between them, but then, it would have been tough for any friendship to survive what they'd gone through the summer she'd married Charlie.

"How is Lucy?" she asked. "I was sorry to hear about her husband's death."

"She's doing fine."

"The girls must be getting big."

"Yes, they are. They look a lot like Lucy. Same blond hair and blue eyes."

"How old are they?"

He didn't answer but said, "Instead of asking me these questions, you could stop in at the Sunnyside and ask Lucy. She still works the counter."

"I don't think that would be a good idea. Lucy made it perfectly clear to me the last time we met that she didn't want me taking an interest in any aspect of her life." Beth didn't want to remember her best friend's parting words, but they echoed through her mind with a startling clarity now.

It had been her freshman year of college and she hadn't wanted to come home for Christmas, but the thought of being away from her family during the holidays wasn't appealing, either. She also knew that her friendship with Lucy had been strained ever since her divorce from Charlie, and when she'd heard the news that Lucy had sustained a season-ending injury in basketball, Beth knew she needed to talk to her childhood friend.

But Lucy had wanted nothing to do with Beth or her words of encouragement. "Is that what you think I should do, Beth? Just forget about playing basketball and move on to something new? The same way you forgot about your marriage to my brother and went off to Kansas?"

"You know why we got married, Lucy."

"And why you got divorced. Isn't it convenient the way things worked out for you?"

"Convenient? You think losing my baby was convenient?" Beth had choked back the tears, stunned that her best friend could think such a thought, let alone voice it.

"You're not going to try to tell me you weren't happy with the way things turned out, are you? I'm the one who listened to you cry over the thought of losing your opportunity to take that scholarship at Kansas. You didn't want that baby, Beth. You wanted to go have a fabulous time at college. Well, you got what you wished for, didn't you?"

Beth had started to cry. "You're supposed to understand. Best friends don't judge one another. They understand." With tears streaming down her cheeks, she'd run from the Callahan house, confused and disappointed.

Just thinking about that conversation made her hands tremble, but Charlie didn't appear to notice.

He rubbed a hand down the side of his face. "Just because you and I didn't work out doesn't mean you and Lucy shouldn't be friends. Ed and I have managed to get beyond what happened back then."

"Well, good for you." She couldn't keep the bitterness from her tone. "Look, do you want me to cook breakfast or not?"

"Yes, I do."

"Fine." She nudged him aside and began scrubbing the pan soaking in the sink.

Just then Nathan's voice called out, "Charlie, come here!"

Charlie paid no attention to the boy. "I may not be the world's greatest chef, but I can make toast."

Again Nathan hollered at them, and Beth said, "Maybe you should go find out what he wants."

"He can come in here if he wants to talk to me. The kid needs to learn to have patience." Ironically he sounded a bit impatient himself.

"And you're going to teach him? Is that it?"

"You don't think I'm familiar with the subject?"

"I didn't say that," she answered. Beth knew that when it came to working with his hands, Charlie had an abundance of patience. He would spend hours crafting a piece of wood, never hurrying a project but taking the time necessary to be precise and detailed.

He'd been that way since he was small. Whether he was sculpting in the sandbox or constructing buildings out of plastic blocks, he made sure that every corner was square, every line straight. Patience was definitely one of Charlie's virtues—at least when it came to his work.

His personal life was quite a different story. At least it was in terms of his relationship with her. There had been no waiting when it had come to his physical attraction to her. No methodical courting. All it had taken was one night for them to go from childhood friends to lovers.

The memory of that long night filled with passionate lovemaking flooded her mind and warmed her body. A longing she'd thought was buried for good made its presence known, tempting her to remember the way her body had responded to his touch.

She didn't want to think about it. Nor did she want to acknowledge that not all of her memories of her marriage were painful ones.

Again Nathan's voice drifted into the cabin. "Charlie, did you hear me?"

"Yeah, I heard you," he shouted back, then continued putting things away.

Beth noticed that for the second time Nathan had called Charlie by his name, instead of Dad.

"Doesn't it bother you that he's calling you by your name?" she asked.

"No, why should it?" Before she could answer he added, "He's not my son, Beth. You'd know that if you hadn't given Ed strict orders to make sure he didn't pass on any news about my personal life."

"Don't flatter yourself," she drawled, knowing perfectly well it was true. "I don't live here anymore, and when I do come to visit, I'm catching up on news about my family, not you." She scrubbed the skillet more vigorously.

"If you say so."

His smugness annoyed her. "I do say so," she repeated, then felt a bit churlish. They were two adults, yet they were behaving childishly. "I'm sure there have been a lot of changes in your life, just as there've been in mine."

"But you don't want to talk about any of them, right?" Before she could deny that, he held up his hands. "It's all right with me. No questions, no answers—that works for me, too."

So he wasn't curious about her. Nor did he want to tell her about his relationship with Nathan. Ed had told her Charlie was single, yet that didn't necessarily mean he wasn't dating someone. Maybe he was involved with Nathan's mother right now.

Suddenly Beth wished that all those times Ed or Grace had tried to bring up the subject of Charlie, she'd listened, instead of shutting them up. There had been an occasion when she had asked Grace if

Charlie was involved with anyone, but before her sister-in-law could answer, Beth had begged her to forget she'd asked the question.

Getting over Charlie hadn't been easy, and she would never have been able to do it had she not totally blocked him from her mind. Beth had learned that what she didn't know wouldn't hurt her. It was something she needed to remind herself right now. Whether or not Charlie was involved with Nathan's mother was of no concern to her, and she would be wise to stifle any curiosity about his personal life.

Just then Nathan appeared at the screen door. "Why didn't you come when I called you, Charlie? There's a guy in a canoe out here. He says he'll take you to get some gas."

Charlie turned to Beth. "You're off the hook for breakfast." Then without another word, he slipped through the sliding door.

WHILE CHARLIE WAS GONE, Beth offered to make Nathan breakfast.

"Do I have to have eggs or can I have a pizza? We have some in the freezer."

She shrugged. "Pizza's okay by me," she said reaching into the freezer compartment of the refrigerator. While the pizza baked in the oven, Nathan took a shower, then sat down in front of the TV, flipping through the channels with the remote control.

When the pizza was ready, Beth suggested Nathan sit at the bar.

"Aren't you going to have some?" he asked as he took one of the high-backed stools.

She shook her head. "I'm not hungry."

With an "okay," he dug into the pizza, gobbling down the slices with a speed that fascinated Beth. Between gulps he said, "It's really hot in here. Charlie said there's air-conditioning. Can we turn it on?"

"I don't see why not." She walked over to the control panel and found the switch. "There. That ought to help." She checked to make sure all the windows were closed, then grabbed a can of mineral water and took another of the stools at the bar. "How's the pizza?"

"Great," he said.

"So what do you think of the *Queen Mary*?"

He gave a casual glance around the salon. "It's nice. They must have a really powerful satellite dish, 'cause you can get all sorts of stations on the TV. Want to see?"

Beth really didn't, but neither did she want to discourage him from talking to her. "Sure," she agreed.

"Come sit down and I'll show you." He walked back into the living area and picked up the remote. Beth sat down at the opposite end of the sofa, listening as he gave a brief explanation to identify each station that appeared on the TV.

"Isn't it cool?" he asked, then went on, not waiting for her response, "I'm going to watch the Cubs play the Braves." He pressed the remote once more, tuning in a baseball game.

Sensing that the teenager was more comfortable with her presence, Beth said, "I'm sorry I spoiled your plans to go fishing with Charlie this weekend."

He shrugged. "It doesn't matter to me. I think

Charlie's a little ticked off about it, though. He's usually not so grouchy."

His bad mood was probably because of her, Beth thought. The last thing he'd expected when he'd planned a fishing trip was having his ex-wife tag along uninvited. Aloud she said, "Running out of gas can try anyone's nerves."

He eyed her suspiciously. "Were you really one of the River Rats?"

"You know about the River Rats?"

He nodded. "Charlie told me. He likes to tell me stories about when he was my age. He's never mentioned you, though."

She was hardly surprised. "I wasn't exactly a River Rat. I was younger than most of them, but I still got to hang out with the group because of my brother. He graduated the year ahead of Charlie."

"Who's your brother?"

"Ed Pennington."

"I know him. He's cool. You must know Lucy, too."

She nodded. "I haven't seen her in a long time. I haven't lived in Riverbend for fifteen years."

"Why did you move?"

"Because I went away to school and then I took a job at a college in Iowa."

"You're a teacher?" She could see by the expression on his face that his opinion of her just dropped several notches.

"I'm an athletic trainer, but I also teach classes at the college. Do you know what an athletic trainer does?"

"You take care of the injured players?"

"That's only part of my job. My first priority is

to prevent injuries. I tape wrists and ankles before players go into a game, and do whatever I can to make sure they're in top condition before they start. But if someone does get hurt, I have to see that proper treatment is given.''

"So you know all about sports.''

"I know about injuries that happen when people play sports. It's actually a pretty cool job.''

"Do you get summers off like the other teachers?''

"Yup. Only, athletic trainers usually go back the first week in August. That's when football practice starts. I'm also a physician's assistant.''

"Is that like a nurse?''

"Actually it's more like a doctor, because I can do a lot of the things a doctor does, including prescribe some medication.''

"But you're not a doctor?''

"Uh-uh. If you had to come to the clinic for a physical exam, though, I could give you one.''

"Do you give shots?''

"I can.''

He shivered. "That's one thing Charlie and I both hate. Shots.''

At the mention of her ex-husband's name, Beth decided to take advantage of Nathan's willingness to talk. "So tell me. Where did you meet Charlie?''

"Through Big Brothers.''

Charlie had volunteered to mentor a young boy? It wasn't something she had expected he'd do. It also meant that Nathan's father probably wasn't in the picture. "I notice you sometimes call him Dad.''

"Yeah, sometimes,'' he said noncommittally.

"Sometimes, but not all the time,'' she prodded.

He shrugged. "It'd be different if he'd married my mom." Before she could probe further, he said, "Oh, look! It's a grand slam." It was obvious he was more interested in the baseball game than in talking about Charlie.

"Do you play baseball?" she asked.

"Are you kidding? I'm not a jock." There was derision in his tone, and Beth wondered what had made this young man feel he needed to be so tough.

"What do you like to do during summer break?" Beth asked.

"Hang out with my friends."

"I bet you hang out at the same places we did when we were kids—down by the river where the big sycamore tree hangs over the water."

"I used to when I lived here, but now my friends are in West Lafayette, so I hang out there."

"Then you're just visiting Charlie for the weekend?"

"Don't I wish," he said sarcastically. "I'm stuck here until school starts."

Stuck? So she hadn't imagined the tension between Charlie and Nathan. "If I remember correctly, Charlie was a pretty fun guy when we were kids. There are probably worse places to be stuck."

Nathan simply rolled his eyes. A commercial break on the TV had him flipping the channels again. Soon a rock-music video blared.

She didn't want to see their conversation come to an end, so she said, "I bet Charlie has all sorts of fun things lined up for the two of you."

"I'd rather be home," he said sullenly. "It's going to get boring if I have to sit around his house all day and do nothing."

"Where does he live?" she asked, ignoring the twinge of guilt that surfaced as she shamelessly pumped the kid for information.

"Over on Morgan. It's this old house he's been remodeling, and it's a pretty big mess right now. Half the walls are missing. And there's no cable TV. I never heard of anyone not having cable or satellite in their house, have you?"

Actually she had, but didn't say so.

"I've never had a TV with so many channels as this one," Nathan said. He took a long drink of his soda. "I didn't think I was going to like it on a houseboat, but this is turning out to be kinda cool."

"Yeah?"

"Yeah. I wish Charlie would let us stay here the rest of the summer. It'd be a lot better for me here than at the house. I mean, I could get hurt in that place. It's under construction. Nails everywhere. There's even a hole in the floor."

Beth had the feeling that he was making a plea for her sympathy so that she'd ask Charlie on his behalf. Little did Nathan know that she'd be the last person to have any influence on Charlie.

The longer Beth talked to Nathan, the more curious she became about her ex-husband. He lived in a house that was under construction, was responsible for a fourteen-year-old boy who was not his son, and had almost married the boy's mom. It was the last part that piqued her interest.

When Nathan punched the channel selector on the remote and a fishing program appeared on the screen, she asked, "So do you and Charlie plan to catch some fish this weekend?"

"My grandpa says there's not much in the river

except catfish and bullheads," he stated with a defeatist attitude.

"Catfish are good when they're cooked right," Beth told him. Suddenly she remembered Charlie saying those exact words to her. They'd only been married a couple of weeks, and he'd come home with the biggest catfish Beth had ever seen.

The weather had been hot and humid, and without air-conditioning the apartment was downright stifling. He'd stood in the tiny kitchen wearing only his boxers, dipping the fish in his specially prepared beer batter before frying it in the pan.

Beth had never seen her father or her brother in the kitchen in their underwear. She'd told Charlie he needed to put on more clothing, but he'd laughed. It was too darn hot, he'd said. Besides, they were husband and wife.

She warmed at the memory of how that evening had ended. Unable to stand the heat, she'd finally allowed him to convince her to take off everything but her bra and underpants. They'd sat there in their underwear eating dinner. And then, after dinner...

"Do you care if I play the stereo?" Nathan broke into her musings.

"No, go ahead. I think I'll step outside and see if there's any sign of Charlie returning," she answered, getting to her feet.

Stepping outside was like walking into a sauna. Sweat beaded on her brow as she grabbed a chair and sat beneath the canopy. Despite the heat, it was quite pleasant to be on the river, the silence soothing her frazzled nerves.

When a motor sounded in the distance, she walked to the forward deck and saw a small boat heading in her direction. Seated in front was Charlie, a pair of sunglasses shading his eyes. At the sight of him her heartbeat increased.

The boat drew up alongside the *Queen Mary,* and Charlie set a gasoline container at Beth's feet.

"Here's your ticket home," he said to her as he climbed onboard. "As soon as I pour this in the tank, we'll be able to start the engine."

"What happened to the guy in the canoe?" she asked, following him as he carried the red container to the rear of the houseboat.

"Another guy in a motorboat offered to give me a ride from the marina to save time, so I took it," he explained. "You should be happy. It means we'll be able to get out of here sooner."

"Is that enough fuel to take us back?"

"No, but it'll get us to the marina not far from here. We can refuel and you can call your brother on the pay phone there and tell him what's up. Before you know it, we'll be back in Riverbend."

Watching him work, seeing the way his muscles bulged as he emptied the fuel into the tank, reminded Beth again of how much he had changed. Gone was the teenager with the boyish good looks. In his place was a handsome, virile man whose muscles had been honed by hard work.

Annoyed with the direction her thoughts had taken, she wished there was some way she could get off the houseboat right now. "I've been thinking," she said to him. "You don't have to take me back to Riverbend."

He looked up at her, but she couldn't see his eyes through the dark lenses of the sunglasses. "You want to stay on the boat with me and Nathan?"

"No," she answered quickly. "But if I'm going to call Ed from the marina, I might as well have him come get me there."

"Why inconvenience him? We can take you back."

"No. I'd rather get off at the marina."

He looked as if he wanted to argue, but finally said, "That's fine by me." He finished pouring the gasoline into the fuel tank, then rose to his feet. "We should be on our way in a few minutes."

Beth nodded, then went back inside to the air-conditioning. She needed to cool down. But even more important, she needed to get away from Charlie. Fifteen years might have passed, but he still had the power to make her heart beat a little faster than it should. And that was something she didn't want to happen. Something she couldn't *let* happen.

CHAPTER FIVE

As soon as the fuel had been poured into the gas tank, Charlie chased Nathan out of the air-conditioned salon and up onto the flybridge. Beth chose to stay inside, which Charlie figured was for the best. At least he didn't have to worry about being distracted by those shapely limbs. Or that dark curling hair. Even though she'd tied her hair back from her face, he couldn't look at her without imagining what it would be like to run his fingers through her shiny tresses.

He had thought that after all this time he wouldn't have had any physical reaction to her, yet in only a few hours she'd been able to turn him inside out. It was probably a good thing he wasn't taking her all the way back to Riverbend. The less time he was around her, the less likely he'd start thinking about her as something other than his ex-wife.

It was a short distance to the landing known as Al's Place. More of a small convenience store than a marina, it sold bait, fuel and groceries to river travelers.

While he guided the houseboat to the pier, Beth stood on the deck with her suitcase at her side. She looked fragile standing there—which Charlie knew wasn't the case at all. Beth had always been able to take care of herself. For a long time he'd thought it was because she'd lost her mother at an early age, but once they were married and he'd lived with her, he realized it was simply the kind of person she was. Strong. Independent. Determined.

The very reasons he found her so damn attractive. Maybe if she'd been some whimpering female who'd clung to him as their marriage had come to an end, he wouldn't now be wishing things could have been different between them.

He forced his attention to docking the boat, instructing Nathan on what needed to be done. Beth wasted no time getting off. She didn't wait for Charlie to carry her suitcase, but dragged it behind her up the pier.

It looked as if she wasn't even going to say goodbye. When he'd secured the houseboat to the pier, he told Nathan to stay put while he made arrangements to refuel. Once he was inside the shop, he saw that Beth was at the pay phone. Charlie walked over to her side, noticing that the look on her face was one of concern, not the relief he'd expected.

"Are you taking her to the hospital?" he overheard her say.

"Who?" he mouthed as she looked at him.

She didn't answer but held up a finger, a plea for him to be patient. "I'll get home as soon as I can," she said. There was a brief silence, "Are you sure?" Another silence. "I should be there to help."

Charlie saw Beth's eyes narrowing at whatever was being said to her. She turned her back to him again and spoke in softer tones, which made it difficult for Charlie to understand what was being said. Not wanting to intrude on her conversation, he stepped away and waited near the magazine rack.

Within a few seconds, she turned around and motioned for him to take the phone. "Ed wants to talk to you."

Judging by the look on her face, she didn't like what her brother had had to say. Charlie grasped the receiver and said hello.

"Listen, Charlie, there's no way I can come get Beth. Grace's mother fell and they think she may have broken her leg. They took her by ambulance to the hospital only a few minutes ago, and now I need to get Grace and her father there. Can you see that Beth gets home?"

"Sure, no problem," Charlie told him, surprised that his friend felt the need to ask.

"I told Beth not to worry about getting back here to help. Between Grace's sisters and her aunts, we have more people than we can handle at the moment."

"I understand. Look, Ed, if it'll help, Beth can stay on the houseboat tonight." He shot a glance at Beth and saw her shaking her head vigorously.

"It would probably make things easier on this end," Ed replied. "I'm sorry about the mix-up in plans. I had no idea you were taking Nathan fishing this weekend. Otherwise I never would have suggested Beth sleep there."

"Don't worry about it."

"Thanks. I know this is going to be awkward for the two of you. Neither of you expected to be together, and now this... Beth isn't going to be happy."

"You're right, but there are more important things to consider just now."

"Yes, there really are."

"Everything'll be fine. I'm sure Beth and I can come to an arrangement that will work for both of us," he said with more optimism than he felt. "Don't worry about your sister, Ed. I'll take care of her."

"Thanks, Charlie. I appreciate it."

As soon as he'd hung up the phone, he knew he was in trouble. Beth looked as if she was ready to blow smoke through her ears.

"I don't need a man to take care of me," she said, folding her arms defiantly across her chest.

"Well, you need this one to get you back to Riverbend," he reasoned, leaning closer so that his face was only inches from hers. "Now, do you want to accept my help or not?"

She inched backward. "Why did you suggest I spend the night on the boat?"

"Because Ed and Grace have company crawling out of the woodwork. With everything that's going on, they don't need another person in the way tonight."

"I'm not going to be in the way. I'll help with the kids," she insisted. "Grace is going to want to go to the hospital."

"He said Grace's sisters are already on their way. They don't need you."

He could see she knew that what he said was true. "Maybe not, but I don't need to stay on the boat. I can get a motel room in Riverbend."

He rolled his eyes. "Are we back to that again? Beth, you own half of the boat. Why don't you just sleep on it tonight?"

"No, thank you."

"If you're worried about having to share your

space with me and Nathan, we can stay somewhere else.''

She couldn't hide her surprise. ''But you want to go fishing.''

''That was the plan.''

''You'd give up your weekend on the river for me?'' she repeated, her expression as dubious as her voice.

''Not for you—for Ed,'' he told her, then immediately regretted his words. Of course he was doing it for Beth. He just didn't want to admit that, not even to himself. ''Nathan and I can get off the boat, but it would be better if we didn't go back to Riverbend.''

The touch of wonder that had lit her face only moments ago was replaced by a shadow. ''What do you mean?''

''Would it be so difficult for all of us to spend the night here?''

''You want me to stay on the boat with you and Nathan?''

''You don't have to look at me as if I'm asking you to donate a kidney. It's only for...what?'' He glanced at his watch. ''Another twenty-four hours?''

She shifted from one foot to the other. ''I don't think I'm the only one who doesn't think it's a good idea. Judging by Nathan's behavior, he doesn't want to spend the night on the boat, either.''

Charlie sighed and looked away. ''I know he doesn't, but it's better if he does.''

''Better for whom? You?''

''No, there's a reason I don't want to go back to Riverbend, and it isn't because I have a great desire to stay on the houseboat with a kid who's sullen and contests every suggestion I make,'' he said irritably.

''So tell me this reason.'' She was staring at him as if nothing he could say would make her change her mind.

Maybe that was why he didn't preface his next words. ''It was one year ago today that his mother died.''

Her expression softened to one of sympathy. ''Oh. I'm sorry. That's awful. No wonder he's so unhappy.''

Charlie went on to briefly explain the trouble Nathan had gotten into in the past year, including the reason he was now in Charlie's temporary custody. ''According to his grandparents, he's been having problems for quite some time, but I'm sure it doesn't help that it's the anniversary of his mother's death.''

''Of course it doesn't.'' Her eyes were compassionate, her voice understanding. ''I know what he's going through, Charlie. I've been there.''

He could see by the play of emotions across her face that she truly could empathize with Nathan. ''That's why I'm asking you to reconsider staying out here on the river with us. You know better than I do how to handle a kid in this situation. You've walked in his shoes.''

He saw her shoulders sag slightly, as if in resignation. ''This isn't going to be easy.''

''This isn't about us, Beth.''

She chewed on her lower lip as she contemplated his request.

''I need to get the boat refueled. You can let me know what you decide.''

It didn't take her long to arrive at a decision. He

hadn't taken but a few steps out of the store when she called out to him.

"I'm not sure I can help him, Charlie, but if you don't want to go back to Riverbend tonight, I guess it doesn't really matter whether I sleep on the river or back at Steele's private marina," she finally said.

"Thank you, Beth. I know how awkward this is for you."

"I don't think you do, Charlie," she muttered to herself, then picked up her suitcase and headed for the pier.

"I THOUGHT I'D MAKE something to eat. Anyone else hungry?" Beth asked when Charlie announced he was dropping anchor to try fishing.

"I'm not hungry yet," Nathan said without hesitation.

"That's because you already ate a whole pizza," Charlie remarked.

"What about you?" Beth directed her question to him.

"I'll have whatever you're having."

She quirked an eyebrow. "You don't know what I'm having."

"You don't have to worry he won't like it—he'll eat anything as long as he doesn't have to cook it," Nathan informed her.

"He's right." Charlie admitted with a half grin. "Would you like some help?"

"No." The word came out so quickly there was no mistaking her reluctance to have him anywhere near her. "I can manage."

Charlie didn't doubt that she could. Since Beth didn't want his help, he went out to the deck to set up his fishing rod. From his chair he could see her moving about inside. With her hair pulled back by a clip, her facial features looked delicate. He liked watching her work; she had an air of concentration that reminded him of how determined she could be when she set her mind to something.

It was that very single-mindedness that had contributed to the demise of their marriage. Not that he didn't appreciate ambition. He did. But Beth hadn't wanted their marriage to work because her heart had been set on going away to college. Ever since he could remember that had been her goal. She was going to be somebody. A doctor or a veterinarian or some other professional. What she wasn't going to be was stuck in Riverbend.

Although she was neither a doctor nor a lawyer, Charlie knew she'd achieved more than most women her age, earning not one, but several college degrees. Over the years he'd heard about her accomplishments—it was hard for a brother not to boast about his younger sister to his friends in town. According to Ed, Beth was good at whatever she did.

That came as no surprise to Charlie. Even as a teenager Beth had been an overachiever. Goals were set and attained. It was just too bad that staying married hadn't been one of her goals.

He squeezed his eyes shut, not wanting to think about the past. It was over and done with. Lucy was right. Beth had made a new life for herself outside Riverbend, one that would never include him again.

Not that he wanted to be a part of her life. He didn't. Just because he became a little nostalgic watching her work in the kitchen didn't mean he was interested in starting something up again. He was just a normal healthy American male admiring an attractive woman.

And she was attractive. Once more his eyes were drawn to her. He'd forgotten how delicate her lips were, how flawless her skin. But it was her eyes that were her best feature. Long-lashed and luminous, they were the color of dark chocolate and just as tempting. As his body responded to her physically, he was forced to look away. He didn't need to be aroused by his ex-wife.

When Beth announced that the food was ready, he told himself that he'd pay no attention to her. He'd simply pick up his plate and carry it outside. But then he saw that her cheeks were flushed and several curly tendrils had come loose from her clip.

"You look warm," he told her.

She swiped her forehead with the back of her arm. As she did, the hem of her top rose, exposing the bare skin of her midriff. "In case you haven't noticed, it's hot."

"Yeah, I've noticed. The temperature's climbing fast." And so was his, which was why he disappeared into the bathroom and splashed cold water on his face while washing his hands.

When he returned to the salon, he said, "Nathan, just holler if you want to go in the water. There's a sandbar not far from here that's perfect for swimming."

"Maybe," the boy answered, his attention on the TV.

"What about you?" he asked Beth. "Did you bring your swimsuit?"

"No," she answered shortly.

He wondered if she even owned one. When the

rest of the River Rats had gone swimming, she would sit on the riverbank. Ed had said his sister had an inner-ear problem that kept her from going in the water, but Charlie knew better.

One summer Lucy had made him promise that he would never tell any of the other River Rats that it wasn't her ears keeping Beth out of the river but a fear of the water. Charlie had never understood how someone who was set to take on the world could be afraid of getting her feet wet.

But then he'd discovered for himself that what Lucy had said was true. Shortly after they were married, he was working on the *Queen Mary* when Beth had stopped by with his lunch. She'd tripped over his tool chest, which had been sitting on the deck, and fallen into the river. Even though the water was only waist-deep, she'd flailed about, crying and choking until Charlie jumped in and pulled her out. He had held her shaking body in his arms, trying to calm her.

She'd clung to him as he rubbed her shivering limbs and tried to console her. It wasn't long before kisses had replaced words of comfort, and the shivering was no longer from the cold water but from the passion that had ignited between them.

Suddenly it didn't matter that they'd only married because she was pregnant. The promise he'd made to himself that he would not rush her into an intimate relationship fell by the wayside.

They'd made love as they had that night of the spring formal. She was as hungry for him as he was for her. From that day forward, they had made passionate love without any awkwardness between them. And although Charlie knew that Beth wasn't happy at having to give up her dream of going away to college, he thought that with time she'd adjust to married life. He hoped that once the baby came, she'd be happy being Mrs. Charlie Callahan, happy being a mother.

Only she never had the chance to become a mother.

"Is there something wrong?" Beth asked, interrupting his memories. "You said you'd eat whatever I was having."

He could see by the way she was looking at him that she had mistaken his frown for a criticism of the food she'd set in front of him.

He glanced down at the fried eggs and ham. "No, this looks good."

"I think I'll take mine outside," she said, carrying her plate toward the patio door.

Charlie thought that if he was smart, he'd let her go outside by herself. But he wasn't feeling smart at the moment. "We can eat out on the deck at the picnic table," he suggested, following her.

A silence stretched between them as they sat down across from each other. Beth acted as if she was alone, ignoring him as she ate, her eyes on the river, instead of him. Charlie could feel the tension, as thick and as heavy as the humid summer air.

Nevertheless, he wasn't going to force her to talk to him. He wished he could ignore her the same way she was ignoring him, but as hard as he tried, he couldn't keep his eyes off her.

She was so damn beautiful. He'd thought she was cute as a kid. She'd been a bit of a tomboy and nothing at all like the other girls he'd dated. Girls who made sure they didn't step through the school doors without having their nails polished, their eye-lashes curled.

Beth still didn't polish her nails and she didn't need to curl her lashes. They fanned out across her cheeks with a naturalness most women would envy.

The night he had taken her to the spring formal he had thought he'd caught a glimpse of the woman she would become. Her hair had been done up in fancy loops and swirls, and the beautiful floor-length dress she'd worn had shimmered when she walked. But today she looked nothing like the girl he'd escorted to the formal. And he discovered that he liked the Beth sitting across from him much better than the one who'd worn glittering rhinestones.

She continued to eat in silence, as if there wasn't a single thing she could possibly think of to say to him. The longer they ignored each other, the thicker the tension became. Finally, he could take her indifference no longer.

"So how long are you planning to stay in Riverbend?" he asked.

She looked up at him and said, "Till the end of next month."

"Then I suppose it's back to school."

"No."

"No? You're not going back to work at the university?"

She took a sip of coffee. "No."

"So what are you going to do?" he asked when she wasn't forthcoming with more.

She stared out at the landscape. "I'm not sure. Maybe work in a clinic."

"Maybe? Are you saying you don't have a job lined up?"

"I've interviewed at a couple of different clinics, but nothing's certain at this point," she answered flatly.

"The hesitation must be on your part. Ed said you have three degrees." When she raised an eyebrow, he added, "I know you told Ed you didn't want to hear any news about me, but I did want to know about you."

She squirmed and continued to stare out at the river.

"We go back a long way, Beth. My mom has pictures of you when you were barely big enough to sit at the kitchen table with Lucy."

She smiled then, a rather fragile smile that appeared more sad than joyful. "I spent a lot of time at your house. Both Ed and I did."

"My parents still live on Third Street."

"I know. I drove through the old neighborhood on my way into town and saw your dad's truck in the drive," she confessed, finally looking at him.

"Did you stop in and say hello?" As soon as he'd spoken, he knew it was a dumb question.

She shook her head. "Is your dad retired now?"

He chuckled. "He says he is, that I'm in charge of Callahan Construction, but he still shows up for work and bosses everyone around. Claims he's just helping out."

This time she grinned. "Your dad's a nice man."

"He always thought you were pretty special, too. You should visit him. I know he'd like to see you."

"I don't think that's a good idea. Your mom..." She trailed off, as if thinking twice about what she was going to say. "Our parents were such good friends. It's too bad that what happened between us had to change that.''

"They still talk, Beth. Your dad visited my folks last time he was here."

"He did?'' She looked surprised. "Did he bring Marsha?''

"His new wife? Yes. She seems nice, and from what I hear, she and your dad are happy together.''

She nodded. "They are. It seems a little odd—all those years we were growing up and he never dated another woman, then he retires to Arizona and ends up getting married again. Did you know Ed and I have a couple of stepsisters?''

"He did tell me that.''

She took a sip of her coffee, then looked at him over the rim. "They seem nice. Both of them live in Arizona.''

"Not a bad place to have family when you live in the Midwest. You can escape to warm weather in the winter if you like.''

He thought it was odd that they were talking about their parents when he really wanted to talk about her. Were there any men in her life, or more specifically, one special man?

That was a line he hadn't crossed when it came to Beth. Over the years he'd made small talk at the café with friends they had in common, and he hadn't hesitated to ask about her, but never had he asked about the men in her life.

The sound of rock music cut in on the quiet summer air. "Nathan must be watching music videos,'' he said.

Beth grimaced. "Heavy metal, if I'm not mistaken.''

"Hey! Turn it down a bit in there," Charlie hollered to the boy.

There was an ever-so-slight decrease in the volume, which had Charlie shaking his head. "I probably should have disconnected the TV before we came onboard." He went over to the patio door. "Come on, Nathan, give us a break."

The music stopped abruptly. "Thank you," he said, then walked back to the picnic table. He hadn't been sitting but a couple of seconds when the music blared again.

"It's not disturbing me," Beth told Charlie.

"Well, it's bugging the hell out of me," Charlie admitted. "I don't understand kids nowadays. I mean, when we were his age, we didn't sit in front of the TV for hours, watching rock stars with painted faces scream their way across the stage."

"Are you forgetting Boy George?"

He winced. "You're right. I had forgotten him. Another generation, same criticisms, right? But our generation was taught to treat adults with respect."

"Maybe, but that didn't stop you from giving the teachers at school grief, did it?" she reminded him. "Correct me if I'm wrong, but weren't you the one who had 'no respect for authority' checked on his eighth-grade report card?"

He grinned sheepishly. "All right. Maybe I did, but I didn't dye my hair blue and I would never have stuck a ring through my nose."

"He's just expressing himself. There are worse things for a kid to do."

"This is the second time you're defending him. Why?"

She shrugged. "He seems like a good kid." She

got to her feet, picking up her empty plate and cup. "Do you want me to take yours in?" she offered.

"I can carry my own," he said, also rising to his feet.

And once more they were like two strangers, politely tolerating each other's company. He followed her inside, set his dishes in the sink, then called out to Nathan, "Come on. I'll let you take the wheel while we look for a place to swim."

AS THEY APPROACHED a sandbar dotted with swimmers, Charlie said, "There's the best beach on the river. Who's going in the water with me?"

When he looked in her direction, Beth said, "I don't have a suit, remember?"

"Don't need one. It's so shallow here you can take your shoes off and wade in your shorts." Despite her lack of enthusiasm, Charlie steered the boat toward the sandbar and dropped anchor. "Nathan, put on your suit and we'll go for a swim."

Beth noticed that Nathan didn't move from his spot on the deck, but sat with a sullen look on his face.

Charlie pulled off his T-shirt and tossed it aside. Once again Beth found herself staring at his sunbronzed chest. She had to turn her head or risk getting caught ogling. She walked the length of the boat, pretending to survey the swimming area. When she returned, Charlie had shed the rest of his clothes and wore only his blue swim trunks. A mixed bag of thoughts entered her head—all of them inappropriate for a woman to have about her ex-husband.

"Nathan, what are you waiting for?" Charlie

asked when the teenager still didn't move from his spot in the chair.

"I just took a shower. I don't want to get all dirty in the river," he responded.

"The water's muddy, but it's not that bad," Charlie told him. "Come on, it'll cool you off."

"I'll get some towels," Beth said, hoping that if she left the two of them alone, they would talk.

When she returned to the deck, she heard Charlie say to him, "I'll wait for you in the water." During her absence he must have convinced Nathan to go swimming.

Beth watched Charlie climb down the ladder into the river. Once again her body reacted physically to seeing him in nothing but a pair of swim trunks.

"I'll leave the towels on the railing," she told him, draping the thick, white terry-cloth towels over the side of the boat.

"Aren't you coming in?" he called up to her.

"I'd rather not."

"Look at how shallow it is." Charlie demonstrated by wading toward the riverbank. "The current's barely moving. You'll be perfectly safe."

Beth was awfully hot and the water did look inviting, yet the thought of going in the river caused her skin to prickle. She knew there was no danger in wading in shallow water, yet it wasn't only her fear of water that was stopping her. It was Charlie. The less interaction she had with him, the better.

"No, thanks," she said. "I'd rather watch you and Nathan."

"If it'll make you feel better, there are life vests down below," Charlie told her.

"No, it wouldn't make me feel better," she shot

back. What was wrong with him? Didn't he realize how silly she'd look wearing a life vest to wade in water only inches deep? Especially when there were tiny tots splashing about.

He didn't force the issue, but plunged beneath the water. Beth took a chair on the deck and leaned back, closing her eyes. She tried to think about anything other than Charlie's near-naked body cutting through the water, but was unsuccessful.

"Aren't you going in?"

Nathan's voice made her open her eyes. "No, I didn't bring a swimsuit."

He shrugged, then joined Charlie in the river. Again Beth leaned back and closed her eyes. It was hot. Too hot to be sitting on the deck, yet did she really want to go into the air-conditioned salon?

The sounds of laughter coming from the water tempted her. Charlie thought she was afraid of the water. She'd show him.

She kicked off her sandals and rolled up the hems of her jean shorts, then carefully climbed down the ladder attached to the side of the boat. As she reached the bottom rung, she felt a pair of hands around her waist.

She flinched. "I don't need any help."

"You're trembling," Charlie said close to her ear. "There's no reason to be afraid."

She stepped onto the sandy bottom, wobbling a bit as she secured her footing. He steadied her and held on to her protectively.

"I'm not afraid. I've just never been comfortable in water where there's a current," she answered, clinging to his side like a leech.

"Here. Just hold on to me and I'll take you to

those rocks over there.'' He nodded toward a small mound of boulders piled along the riverbank. ''You can sit there and dip your toes without having to worry about the current.''

She did as she was told, her fingers tightening around his arm as he pulled her through the water. When it became shallower, she shook off his assistance.

''I'm fine. You can let go now.'' She perched on a boulder, allowing her feet to dangle in the river.

Charlie shrugged and waded back into deeper water, submerging his entire body and floating on his back in the bright sunshine. She watched him and Nathan dive under, then resurface, cutting through the water like a pair of dolphins.

Feeling a little surer of herself, Beth stood and walked along the sandbar, letting the water lap against her calves. Nathan was right. The water was muddy. In the heat of the day, though, it felt refreshing to splash about like a child.

Before long, Charlie was at her side. ''You're in the water and you're smiling and I don't see any panic in your eyes.''

''I told you I'm not afraid of the water,'' she said, stepping backward.

''I know. You just don't like currents.''

''Exactly.'' She took another step back and nearly stumbled over a rock.

''Careful,'' he said, his hands reaching out to grab her.

Beth looked up at him, and his eyes pinned hers with an intensity that had every nerve in her body tingling. His touch was hot, his gaze fiery and she felt as if she was burning up, despite the cold water.

"Hey, do we really have to catch fish for supper?" Nathan's voice broke the spell that held both of them motionless.

Charlie released Beth and turned to the boy. "It's called working for your supper."

Nathan groaned.

"If I remember correctly," Beth said, "I saw hamburger patties in the freezer."

She began wading toward the *Queen Mary.* Charlie came alongside her and took her by the arm. The teasing flirtatious look that had been in his eyes earlier was gone, replaced by something far deadlier. Tenderness.

She didn't need or want her ex-husband's concern, and if she hadn't been in the middle of the Sycamore River, she'd have shaken off his hold. But she was in the river, and his strong arm gave her peace of mind as she made her way back to the boat. Besides, she liked his touch.

And that caused her more anxiety than her fear of the river.

CHAPTER SIX

BETH DISCOVERED Charlie wasn't kidding when he said they'd catch their dinner. Despite a protesting teenager who insisted there was no way he was going to eat any fish even if he did catch them, the three of them sat down on the deck later that evening to a meal of fried catfish.

And while Nathan grumbled at least three times throughout dinner that he'd rather have a hamburger and fries, Beth didn't miss the fact that the teenager ate several helpings. After dinner was over, Charlie insisted Nathan do the dishes, since Charlie had cleaned the fish and Beth had prepared it.

Beth was a bit surprised that the boy didn't complain more about the assignment. Risking Charlie's disapproval, she offered to help Nathan. To her surprise, Charlie didn't comment nor did he give her any stern looks. He simply went out on the deck and put away his fishing tackle. When the last of the dishes had been put away, Charlie came back inside and challenged the two of them to a game of darts.

Beth passed on the opportunity, preferring to watch them battle each other. Nathan agreed to play on one condition. If he won, Charlie would let him watch TV the rest of the evening. Nathan won the first game, Charlie the second. Then came the tiebreaker. A shout of victory resonated through the cabin as Nathan's final dart scored the winning point.

As the blare of a music video came from the entertainment center, Charlie said to Beth, "I don't know about you, but I'm getting as far away as possible from that." He went to the refrigerator. "I'm going to grab a beer and go outside. Want to join me?"

"No, thanks. I'll go to my room," she told him.

Keeping his voice low, he said, "We can sit on opposite ends of the boat. A summer night like this shouldn't be spent in the cuddy."

She knew he was right, but still said, "I have things to do."

He shrugged and went outside.

It was stuffy in Beth's room. Through the small porthole she could see the sun had already set, but dusk lingered, making everything look as if it was caught in a snapshot that had been underprocessed. After only a few minutes of eyeing the outdoors with longing, she decided to risk Charlie's smug look of "I told you so" and go up to the deck.

On an impulse she grabbed a beer from the refrigerator before stepping outside. Charlie had lit the cane torches that rimmed the deck, creating a mood reminiscent of the tropics. Although the air had cooled slightly, it was still warm and humid.

The setting was about as romantic as anyone could ask for—except Beth hadn't asked for it. Nor did she want it. She dragged her chair to the opposite corner of the deck and sat with her back to Charlie. Propping her feet up on the railing, she gazed out at the disappearing sunset.

"I was kidding," she heard Charlie say.

She turned around to look at him. "About what?"

"Sitting on opposite sides of the boat." When she didn't move her chair, he pushed his closer to hers. "If you're going to drink my beer, you can at least put up with my company."

She felt her face redden. "I thought you wanted to be alone."

"I'd like for us to be able to be civil to each other," he said, his eyes directly on hers.

"I'd like that, too," she admitted, then took a sip of beer. "I wish there was a way I could call Ed and check on Grace's mother."

"There is," he said. "I have a cell phone."

She gasped. "Why didn't you tell me that when I told you the battery was low on mine?"

"What good would it have done for you to call Ed when we were stranded in the middle of the river?"

She was too annoyed at him to say anything.

"So do you want to use it or don't you?"

"Of course I want to use it," she snapped. "Where is it?"

He disappeared inside briefly, then returned with the phone. Beth took it and dialed Ed's number. After a brief conversation with her brother, in which she learned that the preliminary diagnosis had been correct and Grace's mother had broken her leg, she gave it back to Charlie, relaying what Ed had told her.

"See? There was nothing you could have done, was there?" Charlie said.

She shook her head. "I still wish I could be there. And the only reason I'm not is that I don't want to be in the way," she added, just in case he had any doubts as to why she was still on the houseboat.

"I understand."

They sat in silence, neither one saying a word. Beth thought she could feel his eyes on her, but she couldn't be sure and she wasn't about to look. After the initial awkwardness passed, she was able to lean back and relax once more, enjoying the sights, sounds and smells of the river.

"What are you thinking?" he finally asked.

"That there must be hundreds of different sounds out here at this time of day. I'd forgotten what it's like to be on the river on a hot summer night."

"Yeah. It reminds me of when we were kids and we'd sneak out to party down by the shore. Those were some fun times," he said with a nostalgic sigh. "It was great being a River Rat, wasn't it?"

Beth didn't comment, reluctant to admit that she'd never really felt like a River Rat, just Ed's little sister tagging along.

"Don't you ever miss it, Beth?" he asked.

She shrugged. "I don't share the same River Rat memories as you and Ed do."

"What's that supposed to mean?"

"You and the rest of the group were well liked at school, but I wasn't exactly popular," she reminded him.

"Beth, everyone liked you."

She chuckled. "You could have fooled me."

"They did," he insisted.

"Is that why the guys all fought over who was going to get to take me out?" she asked with heavy sarcasm.

"Did you ever think that maybe you intimidated them?"

"*I* intimidated *them?*"

"Of course you did. You were so smart."

"Are you saying I seldom had a date my senior year because the boys were worried they'd look dumb next to me?"

"No teenage guy wants to be shown up by his date. It takes more courage than most boys possess to ask out a smart girl."

"You did." Before he could comment she added, "But that was because of Ed, so I guess it didn't count."

"What do you mean it was because of Ed?"

"Come on, Charlie. I know that my big brother talked you into taking me to the county fair *and* to the spring formal."

He shook his head. "For a smart girl, you didn't have much insight into guys back then, did you?"

"Are you saying you didn't take me out as a favor to Ed?"

"It's true Ed and I discussed my taking you to the county fair on your sixteenth birthday, but it was my suggestion, not his."

That sent a tiny thrill of pleasure through her, although she didn't want him to see it. "Oh, I forgot. Shauna Lovett's claws were digging in, weren't they?"

"You think I took you out to get rid of Shauna?"

"Didn't you?"

He gave her an unabashedly wicked grin. "Well, maybe the thought crossed my mind that Shauna might get the message if I went out with another girl, but the truth is, I wanted to go out with you, Beth, because you were cute and fun to be with.''

The tone of his voice was like soft velvet. *She was cute and fun to be with?* After fifteen years he could still lay on the charm, and what was worse, her body responded to it.

''I had fun that night,'' he said with unmistakable sincerity. ''I must have told you that at least a dozen times.''

He had, which was why she'd been positively glowing by the time he'd brought her home. ''The Sycamore County Fair is a lot of fun.''

''Remember the dunk tank? I don't know how they managed to coerce Mr. Biden to sit on that shelf and let the kids throw balls to try to dunk him.''

''He was a good sport, wasn't he? Of all the teachers at school, I thought he was one of the nicest,'' she recalled.

''Maybe when you're a straight-A student, he was, but he wasn't particularly nice to me at report-card time.'' He raised his beer to his lips and took a long swallow.

''Is he still teaching?'' she asked.

He nodded. ''I ran into him just a couple of weeks ago at the hardware store.''

''Ed told me Mitch runs Sterling's now.''

''Yeah, although he'll be lucky to hang on to it. One of those big chains is looking to expand here. If they do, that'll pretty much be the end of the mom-and-pop hardware store.''

''How is Mitch?''

''Good. He has a ten-year-old son.''

She smiled. ''Just one? I remember when you and

Mitch used to come over to the house and tell Ed that when you grew up, you were both going to have five boys so that you could each have your own basketball team.''

Charlie chuckled. ''Well, he only has one so far and I have none.'' He nodded toward the cabin. ''After listening to that kind of music, I'm not sure I could put up with four more of them.''

''How long have you been Nathan's Big Brother?''

''You know about that?''

She nodded. ''Nathan and I talked while you went to the marina for gas.''

''I met him four years ago, when he was ten.''

''Then you knew his mother before she died?'' She asked the question even though she already knew the answer.

''Yes. Amy was a very special lady. Never said a bad word about anybody. Always had a smile on her face.''

Beth thought she detected more than affection in his tone, and she wondered what exactly his relationship with Nathan's mother had been. Nathan had made it sound as if they'd almost gotten married.

''She and Nathan moved here from West Lafayette when the insurance company she worked for opened a branch in Riverbend. She hadn't wanted to transfer because she was worried the move would be difficult for Nathan.''

''Was it?''

''At first, but once he settled into school here, everything worked out.''

Beth wondered what ''worked out'' meant. Nathan had made it sound as if he didn't have any friends in Riverbend—not something one would expect of a kid who'd lived here for three years.

Charlie finished the beer, then crushed the can between his palms. "That's why I can't understand why he doesn't want to be here now. Unless it's the timing."

"He told me he's made new friends in West Lafayette."

"Some friends," Charlie sneered. "More like kids to get him into trouble. He'd be better off looking up the old friends he made here in Riverbend. They were good kids, but he doesn't want to have anything to do with them."

"So what's he going to do while he's here?"

Charlie shrugged. "The same things other fourteen-year-old kids do in the summer. Hang out."

"Maybe you should take him to work with you," Beth suggested.

He frowned. "He's only fourteen."

"You don't have to make him an employee. Just let him help you the way you helped your dad when you were his age."

Charlie appeared to consider her suggestion. "It might work out. After all, I was swinging a hammer with my dad when I was his age. And he does have to pay back the money it cost his grandparents to replace the windows he broke."

It made sense to Beth, yet something tugged on her heartstrings. She'd only met Nathan this morning, yet he'd managed to carve a place for himself in her heart with no effort at all.

As much as she didn't want to admit it, she knew the reason. Nathan was fourteen. The same age her child would have been had she not miscarried early on in her pregnancy. Had she delivered a healthy baby, it could very easily have been someone like Nathan. And Charlie wouldn't have been a surrogate father, but a real dad.

It suddenly struck her that if she hadn't had the miscarriage fifteen years ago, she and Charlie could have been in this very spot doing the same thing they were doing now. Talking and waiting for their teenage son to get tired of listening to his rock music.

It was a disturbing thought. She stood, needing to get away from Charlie and such memories.

"How late do you suppose we're going to have to stay out here before that noise stops?" he asked, unaware of the thoughts going through her head.

"I'm not sure, but music or no music, I'm going to bed."

Charlie jumped up. "I'll tell him he has to turn it down."

She held up her hand. "No, it's all right. I can sleep through anything." She chuckled. "This morning was proof. I didn't even know the boat had left the marina."

"You always did sleep soundly, didn't you?"

She was grateful it was dark, for she was certain she blushed. He knew exactly how she slept. When they were married, he'd teased her often, saying that fire sirens could blare outside her window and she wouldn't wake up. That was why, instead of using an alarm clock, Charlie liked to wake her with a caress. She'd always responded to the slightest of his touches.

"I'm sure I won't have a problem sleeping tonight,'' she told him with more confidence than she felt.

But she did. Not because of the noise coming from the television above, but because she couldn't stop thinking about Charlie.

He'd said the reason he'd asked her to the county fair on her sixteenth birthday was because she was cute and fun to be with. Beth wished she could believe that, but like everyone else in Riverbend, she knew that, had Shauna Lovett not been on vacation in Colorado, Shauna would have been Charlie's date at the fair. She went out with Charlie more than any other girl in Riverbend, and it was understood by everyone that she was Charlie's steady girl.

Only Beth knew better. Having lived next door to Charlie all of her life, she knew that he didn't go steady. There were plenty of girls who wanted to believe he would, but the truth was, Charlie liked having a good time. He also liked hanging out with Ed, and no matter how much he denied it, Beth believed it was her brother who was responsible for Charlie's taking her to the fair.

He'd been helping Ed work on his car when she'd gone out to the garage to tell her brother he had a phone call. While Ed was in the house, Charlie had flirted with Beth, something she'd grown accustomed to over the years. What she hadn't expected was that he'd say, ''Now that you're going to be sixteen on Saturday and you can have a real date, how about coming with me to the fair?''

For Beth, who normally spent most of her time at the county fair working in the animal barns, the chance to be seen with one of the coolest guys in town was an opportunity she wasn't going to miss.

Even without her brother's encouragement, she'd have accepted the invitation. So what if Charlie had only asked her because she was Ed's little sister. So what if Shauna's friends had warned her not to take Charlie seriously. She was determined to make the most of her date with him and use it to her advantage. And even if she was simply a substitute for Shauna, she'd still have fun and learn how to be a bit more like him.

Only she should have known she could never be like Charlie. As her father used to say, he could fall into a pile of manure and come out smelling like a rose. No matter what he did, he managed to come out on top. And with little effort. That was what was so infuriating about him. He never planned anything in his life. Good things just happened.

Good things definitely happened that night at the fair. Beth had a wonderful time. Charlie made her feel special, treating her like a real date. He'd even kissed her at the top of the Ferris wheel, telling her she could no longer say she was sweet sixteen and never been kissed.

She'd fallen a little in love with him that night. It hadn't mattered that the following day he went back to treating her with the same brotherly affection he'd shown her before. Or that Shauna Lovett had called her every dirty name in the book when she'd come back to Riverbend and found out Beth had been Charlie's date for the fair.

She punched her pillow and buried her face in its softness, but she was too restless to sleep. It was still warm and she decided to look for something to drink. The cabin was in darkness, she discovered as she padded up the steps, except for the light over the stove, which glowed like a beacon in the night.

Without turning on any additional lights, she made her way to the galley. The windows were wide open, which meant Charlie must have turned off the air-conditioning before going to bed. That would explain why it was so stuffy in the cuddy.

She pulled a can of mineral water from the refrigerator and was about to make her way back to her room below when she heard voices. Curious, she glanced into the living area and saw that the white leather sofa had been pulled out into a bed, but there was no one in it. Covers lay in disarray across the mattress.

Tiptoeing over to the window, she slid her hand beneath the curtain. As she pushed the brocaded fabric aside, the voices became more distinctive. They belonged to Charlie and Nathan. The two of them sat outside on the deck, each wearing nothing but a pair of cutoffs.

"I miss her, too. Why else do you think I would be out here so late at night?" she heard Charlie say to the boy.

"Did you love her?" Nathan asked.

Beth held her breath as she waited for Charlie's answer. "Yes, I did."

Feeling as if she'd invaded a private moment, Beth let the curtain fall back into place. She moved quickly through the salon and back down to her room. While she'd been tossing and turning, losing sleep over memories of Charlie, he'd been restless, too. Only his restlessness was because he was mourning the loss of the woman he'd loved. Nathan's mother. Even after one year, the pain of losing her hurt so much he couldn't sleep.

She took several long gulps of the mineral water. How naive she'd been to think that Charlie wouldn't have had another woman in his life at some point. As she climbed back into bed, she tried not to wonder about Nathan's mother, but the last thought on her mind before she fell asleep was that nagging question: Who was this woman who had captured Charlie's heart?

BETH WAS SURPRISED to see what time it was when she awoke the following morning. As soon as she'd showered and dressed, she went to the galley with the intention of cooking breakfast, only to have Nathan announce he and Charlie had already eaten. Nathan lay on the pull-out sofa bed watching TV. A glance outside told her Charlie was fishing off the back of the boat.

Noticing that he'd left the cell phone on the counter, she called Ed to inquire about Grace's mother. After hearing that the older woman had made it through the night without any complications, Beth assured her brother she'd stop by as soon as she was back in Riverbend.

Then she poured herself a cup of coffee and put two slices of bread in the toaster. By the time she'd finished eating, Nathan still hadn't moved off the bed. It was only when Charlie appeared at the sliding door and commented on his not being dressed that the teenager tossed the remote aside and stomped off to the bathroom, announcing he was taking a shower.

Charlie didn't say a word to Beth, but returned to

his spot on the deck. Beth took the opportunity to straighten up the living area, folding the linens for the sofa bed. Noticing Nathan's jeans crumpled in a corner, she picked them up and was about to put them next to his duffel bag when a half-empty package of cigarettes fell from the pocket.

Concern for the teenager caused her to sigh. It was not what any adult wanted to find in a fourteen year old's pockets. But then, she knew she shouldn't be in this particular boy's pocket. Feeling as if she'd invaded his privacy, she stuffed the cigarettes back into the jeans and let them fall to the floor in a heap, not wanting Nathan to notice she'd been handling his things. No sooner had she dropped them when he walked back into the room, his hair wet from the shower.

"I thought I'd make up this bed," she told him.

"Thanks." He picked up the jeans and stuffed them into his duffel bag.

"Charlie's still fishing," she told him. "Maybe you want to join him?"

"It's too hot out there. I think I'll stay in here."

She nodded, then walked into the galley and poured herself another cup of coffee. As she sat sipping it, she thought about Ed and Grace. Beth knew that recovering from a broken leg was difficult for an elderly woman, which meant her brother and sister-in-law were going to have houseguests for more than the weekend, possibly for the rest of the summer. Ed had said Grace's mother would be in the hospital several days, and after she was discharged, Beth suspected that she'd be staying with Grace and Ed until she was strong enough to make the trip home.

Taking her coffee cup, Beth went outside to find Charlie. "I need to talk to you about something," she said as she sat down on a chair beside him.

"All right," he said, glancing sideways at her. Unlike yesterday morning, his jaw was clean-shaven and Beth caught the faint scent of aftershave.

"I called Ed this morning," she told him, ignoring the physical awareness of Charlie that his scent aroused in her.

"Is everything okay with Grace's mother?" he asked, reaching into a tin can for a big, fat, juicy worm.

"She's doing well, but she'll have to be in the hospital for a while. And after she's released, she'll need physical therapy. I imagine she'll stay with Ed and Grace."

"Which means you won't have a place to stay," he concluded. "If you're worried about where you're going to sleep, you don't need to be. You can stay here on the boat." He dropped his line back into the water. "It's as much yours as it is mine."

She took a sip of coffee. "I still can't figure out why Abraham left it to the two of us."

"Guess that's a puzzle we'll never figure out."

"When Ed first told me, I thought maybe Abraham had become senile before he died and that he thought we were still married."

"Nope. He definitely was of sound mind. It was his heart that gave out, not his brain. And I've done work for him over the years. There's no way he wouldn't have known we're divorced."

She sighed. "I guess we'll never know his reasons. He left us the boat, and right now it's looking like a good thing—at least for me. Otherwise I wouldn't have a place to stay."

"Then you're going to stay here?"

"If it doesn't interfere with your plans for Nathan."

"Plans? You know me better than that," he said with a grin.

Yes, she did. Charlie took life as it happened. It was one of the ways they were complete opposites. She needed to know what was around the corner. He liked the excitement of not knowing.

"I just thought you might want to have the houseboat at your disposal so the two of you could fish or simply hang out."

"In case you haven't noticed, Nathan's not exactly crazy about the place," he said.

"I wouldn't say that. Actually he told me he thought it would be really neat if the two of you could stay on the boat the rest of the summer."

Charlie's head jerked in her direction. "He said that?"

She nodded. "I think he's enjoying it more than he's letting on."

"Must be." He jiggled his line. "So you're planning to stay in Riverbend."

"Till the end of the summer."

She nodded.

"You got a guy back there in Iowa?"

The question caught her off guard. "Nope. No guy."

"Why not?"

"That's a rather personal question, isn't it?" she asked, looking up at the patches of puffy white clouds drifting across the sky.

His voice hardened as he said, "And we wouldn't want to get personal, would we?"

She looked at him then and saw that he was staring at her, but she couldn't read what was in his eyes because of his sunglasses.

"Is there a woman in your life?" she asked.

"No."

It was the answer she expected, especially after overhearing him and Nathan last night.

"And you want to know why?" he went on, a challenge in his voice. "Because the only woman I ever wanted left me."

Amy Turner. His admission sent a tiny chill through Beth.

"So answer my question, Beth. Why isn't there a guy in your life?"

She wondered what he would say if she said, "Because the only guy I ever wanted left me, too." She thought it was better not to know the answer to that question. "I've come to the conclusion that I'm not meant to travel that road to happily-ever-after."

"Sure you are. You just had a detour along the way." Again his attention was on the fishing line.

"Is that what you think our marriage was? A detour?"

"Life's full of them," he said, reeling in the line, then casting it out again.

"In which philosophy class did you learn that?" she asked sarcastically.

"Not all education is done in school, Beth."

"So what are the next great words of wisdom going to be? 'You need to roll with the punches, Beth'?"

He grinned an annoyingly smug grin. "You said it. I didn't."

"Obviously you've steered your way through the detours. You were ready to say 'I do' all over again."

"And where would you get an idea like that?"

"Does the name Rita Dorsett ring any bells?"

"She told you I was getting married?" His voice rose in disbelief.

"I ran into her at a volleyball tournament in Nebraska about a year and a half ago. She felt it was her duty to relay the latest Riverbend gossip."

"I thought you never paid any attention to gossip."

"You're right. I don't."

"Especially when you don't care about the parties involved."

"You got it," she shot back, then immediately regretted it. She was not one to behave immaturely, and right now she felt about the emotional age of Nathan. "I'm sorry. I didn't mean that."

"You make a habit of saying things you don't mean?" He lifted one eyebrow.

A silence stretched between them and he turned his attention to the line dangling in the water. Beth found herself staring at the red-and-white fishing bobber, wondering why there had to be this tension between the two of them.

His next words told her he was having similar thoughts. "If there was a way we could clear the air between us and go back to having the kind of relationship we had as kids, I'd do it. But I don't know how to erase the past."

"It doesn't matter," she said.

"It matters to me."

"Why?"

He shrugged. "I don't know why, but it just does."

His admission was unsettling. She scraped back her chair and stood.

"I think I'll go back inside and call Ed again. Your attorney should probably let him know that it's not a problem for me to stay here. They may want to talk—you know, to make sure this is all legal."

"That's not a problem," he said.

"Good." She started for the door, but he stopped her.

"Beth, you do have a road to happily-ever-after out there. Don't let something that happened when you were young make you cynical. We were just kids, not that much older than Nathan."

And in love, she wanted to add, but couldn't. Because she wasn't sure that it had been love for Charlie. Obviously his perspective on their brief marriage was different from hers. He'd married her because they'd made a mistake the night of the spring dance. If she hadn't gotten pregnant, he probably wouldn't have even dated her again.

For her, marriage had been a dream come true. Although the timing was wrong, she'd been hoping Charlie would see her as something other than the girl next door, and when they'd made love, she'd discovered that her feelings for him were more than just infatuation.

When she'd lost the baby, there had been no mention of the possibility of the two of them staying together. She hadn't been home from the hospital but a few hours when he'd told her it was all for the best. She wouldn't have to give up her dream of going to college. They would divorce and go back to life as it had been before they'd made that one big mistake.

Mistake. That's what their relationship had been. And despite the fact that she'd earned three degrees and gone on to have a very successful career, that she'd followed her dream, it still hurt that he viewed it that way.

"We were old enough to know better, Charlie," she said quietly, then slipped inside so he wouldn't see the pain she knew was on her face.

CHAPTER SEVEN

WHEN BETH STEPPED through the patio door and saw Nathan slumped on the sofa watching a movie video, she thought again about the package of cigarettes she'd found in his jeans. Was it her responsibility to get involved in this young boy's life?

No, a tiny voice inside her cried. Nathan and Charlie were not her concern. Yet every time she looked at the teenager she felt a tug on her heart. She didn't want to care about him, but she did.

She bit down on her lip, mentally debating whether or not she should mention the cigarettes to Charlie. She glanced outside to where he sat. If she knew Charlie—and she thought she did even after fifteen years apart—he'd want to know that Nathan was choosing a path that could have serious consequences.

So she went outside and crossed to where he sat.

"You're back," he said needlessly.

"There was one more thing I wanted to talk to you about." She didn't sit, but remained standing. "It's about Nathan."

"It must not be good. I've seen that look on your face before."

His statement reminded her that he'd been very good at reading her emotions...some, not all.

"I found a pack of cigarettes this morning when

I was straightening up his bed. It fell out of a pocket of a pair of jeans I'd picked up from the floor."

He sighed. "I guess it shouldn't surprise me. Kids his age think smoking is cool."

"Then you didn't know?"

He shook his head. "I haven't spent enough time with him lately."

"It could be that he's only tried it a few times," she said, trying to sound optimistic.

"That's what all parents like to think. I'll have a talk with him about it." He started to reel in his line.

"Now?"

"Why not?"

She shifted from one foot to the other. "Well...if you do it now, he's going to know I'm the one who told you. I don't want him to think I've been digging around in his things."

"Were you?"

"No! I told you. I was putting the sofa bed back together."

"Then what's the big deal? So you found them accidentally. I'll tell him that." He pulled in the line and removed the worm from the hook.

"No, you won't." She grabbed his sleeve. "Charlie, please don't go in there and lecture him."

He leaned over the side of the boat to rinse his hands in the river. "If you didn't want me to say anything to him, then why did you tell me?"

"Because he's only fourteen and he shouldn't be smoking cigarettes."

"That's why I'm going to talk to him," Charlie said, wiping his hands on a rag. "The sooner we nip this in the bud, the better."

"You could at least wait until I'm not around," she pleaded.

"All right, I'll wait," he agreed reluctantly, "although I really don't want to. This isn't the only bad choice he's made this past year."

"You said he's having a difficult time adjusting to life without his mother," she said, her voice softening in sympathy.

"Yes, and he's at an age where his friends are a great influence. Maybe that's why he has the cigarettes—he needs to fit in." Charlie massaged the back of his neck. "I don't know why that judge thought I could help him."

"Because you can," she said without hesitation.

He looked at her then and gave a crooked little grin that made her insides tremble. "Is that a vote of confidence?"

"Yes. You've obviously been a good influence in his life up to this point. Why else would Nathan call you Dad?"

He shook his head in self-recrimination. "The kid's in tough shape if I'm the closest thing he has to a dad. I'm hardly experienced at parenting, am I?"

She almost blurted out no, but stopped herself in time. She and Charlie hadn't had the chance to discover what kind of parent either of them would have made.

"You're old enough to have learned what's right and wrong," she told him.

"Just do as my father did—is that what you're saying?"

"And remember what you were like when you were fourteen."

He raised his eyebrows. "That's what scares me. I know the kind of trouble that's out there for boys his age."

She nodded in understanding.

"I'll deal with the issue of the cigarettes once we're back at my place. So don't worry, Beth. I won't tell Nathan you found the cigarettes."

"Thank you."

"You don't need to thank me. Nathan's my responsibility, not yours. In a few hours we'll be back in Riverbend, and you won't have to be in the middle of any of this."

She knew that was true, yet that didn't stop her from caring about what happened to Nathan. Or about caring for Charlie. In just a little over twenty-four hours she'd been drawn into their lives, whether she'd wanted to be or not. It would be a relief when they could go their separate ways. The less she saw of Nathan and Charlie, the easier it would be not to think about either one of them, which was why she spent most of the trip back to Riverbend in the cuddy, reading a book.

But when the boat docked at Steele's marina, she couldn't help but notice the slouch to Nathan's shoulders as he carried his gear to Charlie's pickup. Not that she blamed him. Charlie barked out orders as if the kid was one of the carpenters on his work crew.

Although she'd vowed to stay out of their lives only hours ago, she couldn't resist stepping in front of Charlie and saying, "Haven't you heard? You catch more bees with honey than vinegar."

He stopped in his tracks and faced her, hands on his hips. "And what's that supposed to mean?"

"If you want to boost Nathan's self-esteem, you might try using a different tone," she said in a low voice, aware that the teenager could easily overhear if she wasn't careful.

"And what's wrong with my tone?" Charlie asked in an equally low controlled voice.

"Nothing, if you're a drill instructor at a boot camp," she retorted. "I've worked with kids, so I know from experience that they respond to positive reinforcement much better than they do to criticism."

"I'm not criticizing him. I'm telling him to get his things and put them in the truck."

"And you can't tell him without shouting at him?"

"I thought we agreed that Nathan is *my* responsibility," he reminded her.

She knew he was right. Whatever problems there were between her ex-husband and his ward, they were none of her business.

"Fine. You talk to him the way you think best." She started to walk back toward the truck, but his hand on her arm stopped her.

"Why do you do this, Beth?" he asked.

"Do what?"

"Make everything about the past."

She frowned. "This isn't about the past."

"Every time you open your mouth it's about the past," he said before releasing her arm.

Beth wanted to protest, but what could she say? Being on the houseboat together had proved to her that no matter how hard she and Charlie tried to get along, their short-lived mistake of a marriage would always come between them. It was probably a miracle they'd survived the weekend without anything worse happening than a few angry words.

She needed to accept that Charlie was no longer a part of her life and what he did was none of her business. It was something she repeated frequently that night as she prepared for bed in the cuddy, yet it didn't stop her from thinking about him. Long after the lights had been turned off and silence filled the boat, she didn't mentally replay the angry words they'd exchanged. She thought about the tender look that had been in his eyes when they'd been in the water, and how good it had felt to have his arms around her.

ON MONDAY MORNING, Ed picked Beth up at the marina and took her to Don's service station, where she learned that the problem with her car was located in the computer system. While Don did the repair work, Ed suggested they have a cup of coffee at the Sunnyside Café while they waited.

As much as Beth welcomed the opportunity to sit down and have coffee with her brother, she was a bit apprehensive about going to the café. For one thing, it would be full of people she hadn't seen in years. For another, Lucy Garvey worked there.

As they approached the café, she could feel her stomach muscles tense. Ed didn't seem to notice her apprehension, but held the door open for her and ushered her inside.

"This place is always busy," he said, scanning the crowded room for an empty table or booth.

"There's one in the corner, Mr. Pennington," a skinny young woman with a mop of curly brown hair told him as she hustled past with a tray of food.

"Mr. Pennington?" Beth cocked an eyebrow.

"Her husband's one of my clients." He steered Beth toward the corner, stopping to shake hands and greet several people along the way.

When they finally were able to slide into a booth, she said, "You're a popular guy."

He grinned. "Some things never change, eh?"

Within minutes the same skinny waitress set glasses of water in front of them. "And what I can do for you two on this beautiful summer morning?" she asked, a gleam of curiosity in her eyes.

Ed noticed the gleam. "Tina, this is my sister, Beth."

The young woman smiled warmly. "Hi, Beth. Can I get you some coffee this morning?"

"That would be nice. Decaf, please."

"Make that two, only I want my high octane," Ed said with a wink.

"Got it. One decaf, one regular. Will that be all?"

Ed looked inquisitively at Beth. "Want a pastry or a muffin?"

"No, just coffee for me."

"You want your usual?" Tina asked.

"If Martha did the baking, I most certainly do. The biggest one you have," he added.

"Got it," Tina said, writing their order on her notepad. "Be right back," she added cheerfully before bustling away.

"She sure is perky, and who's Martha?" Beth asked.

"The new cook. She used to work at a bakery in Chicago. Now she does all the breads and rolls for the café. You really ought to sample something. She's good."

Beth shook her head. "Maybe another time." Automatically her eyes made a survey of the room. There was no trace of Lucy.

Ed didn't miss her sweeping glance. "So what do you think? This place looks the same as it did when we were kids, doesn't it?"

"Different curtains, but the same yellow walls," Beth replied, feeling a bit nostalgic as she noticed the soda fountain was still in place. As teenagers, the River Rats often piled into the Sunnyside after basketball games on Friday nights for hamburgers and fries. "Do they still make malts from scratch?"

"Of course. The menu hasn't changed much over the years. All the comfort foods you could want—mashed potatoes and gravy, meatloaf with a baked potato, hot roast-beef sandwiches. It's why they do such a good business. Most of the single guys in town come here to get the closest thing to a home-cooked meal."

Immediately Beth remembered what Nathan had said about Charlie eating his breakfast at the restaurant every morning. Was he here now? She hadn't noticed him with her first cursory glance. This time her survey was more thorough, and to her relief, he was not in the café, probably because it was mid-morning already.

"Looking for anyone in particular?" Ed asked as he caught her surveying the room once more.

Not wanting to admit she'd been looking for Charlie, she said, "I thought Lucy might be working."

"She usually is. She must have the morning off." Ed smiled at Tina, who'd arrived with their coffee.

"Where's Lucy this morning?" he asked the waitress, much to Beth's dismay.

"She has a dentist appointment. I think she's coming in later, though," the waitress said before announcing that she'd be right back with Ed's caramel roll.

Ed reached for the sugar dispenser and poured a liberal dose into his coffee. "You do know that Grace sees Lucy regularly if you'd like to get together."

Beth almost choked on her coffee. Were men that obtuse? Grace understood why such a suggestion was better left unspoken, so why didn't Ed?

"I don't think that's a good idea," Beth told him. "Things have been awkward between me and Lucy ever since I went to the spring formal with Charlie in our senior year. And please don't say, 'Beth, that was fifteen years ago.' I know how long ago it was."

"All right, I won't say another word on the subject."

Tina returned a moment later, this time with what had to be the biggest caramel roll Beth had ever seen.

For the next half hour Ed and Beth's conversation centered on Grace's mother. When Ed had picked Beth up earlier that morning, he'd asked how the weekend had gone, but after giving him a rather stilted account, she'd changed the subject. Now the events of the weekend lurked in the back of her mind.

When Tina came by for the third refill on the coffee, Beth placed her hand over the top of her cup. "I've had enough."

Ed glanced at his watch. "We'd better get going. Don should be finished with your car by now." He left a generous tip on the table, then went to pay the cashier at the front of the store.

Evie Mazerik, an older woman with hair dyed a most unlikely shade of red, gave Beth a curious look as she said to Ed, "How was everything?"

"Great, as usual. Evie, you remember my sister, Beth, don't you?"

"Of course I do," Evie said with a friendly smile. "You and Lucy were always asking for the same thing—a root-beer float. Am I right?"

Beth smiled. "I don't think I've had one since that can compare with the Sunnyside's."

"I suppose you're back in town because of your inheritance," Evie remarked.

"Actually I'm here visiting Grace and Ed," Beth said, but the cashier's next words told her that if she'd hoped that folks in town weren't interested in her business, she was wrong.

"Have you and Charlie decided what to do about the boat?" she asked.

"Not exactly," Beth replied evasively.

When she glanced at Ed with a plea for help in her eyes, he smoothly bid the cashier goodbye and ushered Beth toward the door. Before they could make their exit, the door opened and in walked Lucy Garvey, her mouth spreading into a wide grin when she saw Ed. The grin quickly disappeared, however, when she saw who he was with.

Beth took a deep breath. "Hi, Lucy. How are you?"

"Fine. And you?" Her voice was cool, her eyes

guarded as she stepped aside to let another customer
pass.

"Great. I'm on my way to get my car from
Don's." Beth motioned with her hand in the direction of the service station. The gesture was so awkward Beth wondered if everyone in the café had
noticed.

She knew Ed had because he quickly jumped into
the conversation, making small talk about their kids'
T-ball games. Before Beth knew it, Lucy was ex-
cusing herself to go to work, and Ed was ushering
Beth out into the street.

"There. That wasn't so bad, was it?" he said as
they paused at the corner before crossing the street.

"How can you say that? It was awful." Beth
hated the tension that existed between her and her
childhood friend.

"I thought Lucy was quite friendly."

"She practically dripped ice."

"She was a little cool, but you haven't seen each
other in a long time. What did you expect? A hug?"

Beth stopped in the middle of the street. "You
guys just don't get it, do you?"

"Get what? Tim Cullin punched me in the gut
when I went out with his sister, remember? Today
he's one of my best clients."

She groaned and started walking again. "Forget
it. Women's friendships are different from men's."

"Yeah, they are. We get angry and move on. You
hold a grudge and never let it go."

"That's a ridiculous generalization," she argued.

As they passed Steele's Books, a display of children's literature caught Beth's eye. "Oh, look! I
should stop in and get the girls some books. I left

in such a rush I didn't get a chance to bring them anything."

"You don't need to bring them gifts," Ed told her.

She gave him a stern look. "Of course I do. I'm their auntie and aunties bring gifts when they visit their nieces. Can't we go inside?"

"I have an appointment. I really need to get to the office," he said with an apologetic shake of his head.

"All right. I'll come back later today."

"Thank you," he said, heaving a sigh of relief.

"I need to stop in and tell Ruth and Rachel Steele how sorry I am about the loss of their brother, Abraham. I would imagine these past few weeks have been quite difficult for them. Losing a brother must be terribly painful. At least they have the book-store."

"Abraham's death affected many people, not just the twins. That reminds me—I've already spoken to Charlie's attorney. You can stay on the houseboat for as long as you like."

"That's a relief."

"There is one condition."

"And what's that?" Her heart missed a beat as she waited for her brother to tell her the answer.

"Charlie wants Nathan to be able to use the boat before the summer's over."

Relief washed over her. "That's not a problem."

"Good. I'm glad to see everything's working out between the two of you."

"It isn't exactly working out, Ed," she said with a touch of impatience.

"You told me there weren't any problems when you shared the houseboat. Or did I misunderstand?"

No problems? If only he knew. Charlie Callahan was one big problem when it came to Beth's peace of mind, but she couldn't admit that to her brother.

"No, everything's fine. I think Charlie and I both understand the situation," she answered.

"Good. I'm glad to hear that," Ed gave her arm a squeeze. "Grace and I were worried that we'd put you in an awkward position this past weekend, so it's a relief to know that you and Charlie were able to put aside your differences."

She didn't correct her brother. If he wanted to believe that she and Charlie were back to being friends, she wasn't going to say anything to the contrary. Six weeks would pass quickly. And as long as she didn't have to see Charlie, it really didn't matter what Ed thought about her relationship with her ex-husband.

She knew the truth.

Too bad it didn't make her happy.

"How did your interview go with Dr. Bennett?" Grace asked Beth when she picked up her sister-in-law outside the entrance to the clinic.

"Good. It's all set. I'm going to work three days a week until the end of August, starting tomorrow," Beth answered. "You look tired. Are you sure you're up to going to Allison's game?"

Grace waved away her concern with a flap of her hand. "I'm fine. Sitting in the bleachers cheering on five year olds playing T-ball will do me good." She fastened her seat belt. "Let's go."

"Ed said the doctors are pleased with your mom's progress."

"They are. The physical therapist was in to see her today and told her she's doing great. Everyone's surprised at how quickly she's bouncing back from the accident."

"That's wonderful news. Do you know when she'll be released from the hospital?"

"Mom is hoping for tomorrow. She misses Dad," Grace said on a sigh.

"She's going to stay with you while she's recovering, isn't she?"

"If I get my way she will. I know Dad would take good care of her back home, but I'll feel more comfortable if she's with us."

"Of course you will. I'll do whatever I can to help," Beth offered.

"Thank you, Beth. That's very kind of you."

Beth reached across to give her hand a squeeze. "That's what family is for—to be there in times of need."

"I know, but I feel as if I've let you down. Here I invite you to come stay with us, and then this happens and you get stuck on the houseboat."

"I wouldn't exactly call staying on Abraham Steele's houseboat a punishment. Have you seen the place? It's like a plush hotel."

"But it's on the water."

"So?"

"So you never liked the water."

"Why does everyone think I have this aversion to the water?"

"Maybe because you were the one River Rat who never went swimming. And whenever anyone played down by the river, you were always shouting out warnings about the dangers of the currents. And you'd get upset when we'd climb on that big old sycamore tree that hung out over the river and use it as a diving board.''

"Yeah, and with good reason. Lily Bennett—or I guess I should say Holden—broke her foot falling from that tree.''

"Oh, speaking of Lily. When I mentioned you were coming back to Riverbend, she told me to tell you she hopes the two of you can get together.''

"I'd like that, too. I haven't spoken to her since her husband was killed in that terrible car accident. How's she doing?''

"Much better now, but when she first moved back here last spring, I was concerned about her. She spent so much time alone. I suppose that was natural, considering she was grieving, but until Abraham's bequests were made public, none of us saw much of her.''

"She was one of the beneficiaries, too?''

"Mm-hmm. He left her four paintings from his art collection.''

"That makes sense. She was the best artist in school. Does she still paint?''

"Charlie says she's been doing still lifes. I haven't seen any of them, but he says they're quite good.''

Charlie says. Beth knew that during high school Lily and Charlie had been friends, like most of the River Rats. Grace had said Lily kept mostly to herself, yet she'd shown Charlie her artwork....

"Did you know she bought that old Victorian over on East Oak Street?'' Grace rattled on, unaware of the tension Beth felt at the mention of Charlie's name. "Although I'm not sure how long she's going to be living there."

"Why is that?"

"Rumor has it that the reason she's no longer in mourning has to do with a man."

"She's in love?"

Before she could ask Grace who Lily's new love was, they had arrived at the park and her sister-in-law changed the subject.

"Oh, good. Ed's already here with Allison. I hope he remembered to bring her knee support."

"What's wrong with her knee?"

"Oh, she fell off her bike a couple of weeks ago and it's been bothering her, so Dr. Bennett suggested she wear a knee support." Any fatigue Grace may have shown earlier disappeared as she hopped out of the car and exuberantly waved at Ed and the girls.

She and Beth were heading toward the baseball diamond, when Grace said, "Look. There's Lily and Charlie."

Beth glanced at the fence separating the baseball field from the parking lot and saw her ex-husband smiling at Lily, who just happened to have her hand resting on Charlie's forearm. An emotion Beth hadn't felt for years reared its ugly head. Jealousy.

It was so unexpected that she nearly stumbled. After so many years there was no reason for her to feel anything at all when it came to her ex-husband. But she did, and she didn't like it one bit.

Beth couldn't help but ask Grace, "Why is Charlie here?"

"He often comes to watch Lucy's daughter Amber play. She's on Allison's team." She glanced over at her sister-in-law and said, "I would have told you, but I thought that after this weekend everything was okay between you two."

"It's all right, Grace. I've talked to Charlie and the awkwardness is over," she said, although that wasn't quite true. She'd gotten past the initial shock of seeing him again, but watching him with Lily Holden made her realize that there was now another reason to avoid him. She still had feelings for him.

As they approached the baseball diamond, she wished she could plead a headache and leave, but she knew that if she did she'd only call attention to herself and give people reason to wonder if she was as reconciled to her ex-husband's presence as she'd claimed she was.

Besides, Lily had already noticed her and was coming toward her. She greeted Beth with a smile so warm it seemed natural to exchange hugs, even after such a long time.

"It is so good to see you!" Lily said. "Charlie told me you were back. How are you?"

"I'm fine," she answered, then glanced at her ex-husband and knew she wasn't fine at all. She was flushed and her heart was racing, and all because he looked so attractive standing there in a pair of khaki shorts and a navy blue T-shirt. On his head was a navy baseball cap with the name of a local implement dealer embroidered in white.

"Hi, Charlie," she managed, although she wished her voice didn't sound so breathless.

"Beth." The look he gave her sent a tingling through her.

While Grace went to check in with her family, Beth, Charlie and Lily stood there making small talk. Beth could feel Charlie's eyes on her and was relieved when a shout from Ed had Charlie saying, "I think the game's going to start. We'd better sit down."

The last thing Beth wanted was to get stuck next to her ex-husband. To her dismay, Grace motioned for the three of them to come sit beside her. When Beth saw that Charlie's sister, Lucy, was on the other side of Grace, she once again wanted to turn around and flee. The only other person who looked more uncomfortable than she did was Nathan, who sat by himself at the end of the row.

Although Lily didn't appear to notice the coolness in Lucy's manner, Beth did. Except for a polite, "Hi, how are you," Lucy acted as if Beth didn't exist.

Fortunately, the action of the five and six year olds on the field was entertaining enough that anything other than casual conversation was prohibited. Beth laughed as the tiny tots dragged their bats up to the T, the baseball helmets dwarfing their small bodies. One of the children swung so hard he fell down; another hit the ball and ran to third base, instead of first.

Still, Beth was relieved when the game ended. Grace had said it was rumored that Lily had a man in her life, but other than the occasional smile at Charlie, she'd given no indication that he was anything other than a friend.

As the crowd slowly dispersed, Lily turned to Beth. "I'm so glad I came tonight. I hope we can have lunch soon."

"I'd like that, too," Beth said, noticing that Charlie stood at Lily's side, as if he was her escort.

"Come. I'll walk you home," he said to Lily, making Beth wonder if maybe the two *were* romantically linked.

Lily turned down his offer to escort her. "It's all right. I'm stopping by the school."

Charlie's grin widened. "Someone working late?"

She gave his baseball cap a tug, then said, "He's a good guy."

"I believe you."

She grinned and said another goodbye, then left Beth alone with Charlie.

He's a good guy. So it wasn't Charlie who'd captured Lily's heart. Beth wondered at the relief she felt. "Who's a good guy?" she asked.

"Aaron Mazerik."

Her mouth dropped open. "Lily's dating Aaron Mazerik—the same Aaron Mazerik we know?"

He nodded. "That's the one. He's the new coach at Riverbend High."

"What? Didn't he once get arrested?"

"Yes, but luckily Coach Drummer took him under his wing and got him into the basketball program."

"I remember. The cheerleaders used to call him the wild one."

"He wasn't that bad," Charlie said with a chuckle. "We had a lot of fun shooting hoops, but he never wanted to hang out with the River Rats."

"He must have turned his life around if he's coaching at the high school. It just seems strange to hear that someone who had such a bad reputation as a teenager is now a teacher."

"We all did things as teenagers we'd rather forget," Charlie said soberly.

Beth met his eyes. She wasn't sure what she saw there. Was it an apology? Regret?

It hurt her to think that he saw nothing good in what had happened between them, and her reply was unusually sharp. "Yes, even we made mistakes, didn't we?"

She was grateful that her niece chose that moment to fling herself at Beth. "Did you see me hit the ball?" she asked excitedly.

"Yes, I did," she said, giving Allison a hug.

Beth watched as Lucy stepped between her and Charlie. Not that it mattered. He made no attempt to speak to her again.

As she walked back to her car she wondered why every time she thought she might be able to forget the pain that loving Charlie had caused, the wound was reopened. Tonight had left her wondering if it would ever heal, because she'd made a discovery.

She was not over Charlie Callahan.

CHAPTER EIGHT

IT WAS WEDNESDAY, and as he did most mornings, Charlie stopped at the Sunnyside Café on his way to work. His sister Lucy was behind the counter.

"The usual?" she asked when he sat down on a stool. He nodded, and she said, "Good. I'll join you. I need a break."

"Isn't this your busy time?"

"Yeah, but it's slow this morning. I'll get someone to cover for me for fifteen minutes. Go sit in that booth next to the door," she told him, nodding toward the entrance, "and I'll bring the food over when it's ready."

Charlie picked up his cup and moved to the small booth with its leather bench seats. Several people stopped by to make small talk, inquiring about the health of his parents and how business was going at the construction company.

It was one of the things he liked about Riverbend. The town was small enough that people were friendly, yet not so small that everyone knew everybody else's business.

At least he didn't think they did until his sister sat down and demanded, "Why didn't you tell me Beth spent the weekend with you on the houseboat?"

"How did you hear about that?"

"You think I don't have ears?"

"Obviously other people do," he said wryly, giving the room a cursory glance.

"Yes, and you can imagine how I felt when I heard it from someone other than my brother."

"Look, it was no big deal," he answered her.

She made a sound of disbelief. "You spend the weekend with your ex-wife, and I'm supposed to believe it's no big deal?"

"It wasn't. And we didn't *spend* the weekend together. We happened to be on the same houseboat, and we had a fourteen-year-old boy with us. It was like staying at the same motel, except the motel was moving down the river."

The look she gave him left him little doubt what she thought of that analogy.

"It was." He knew she wasn't going to let the subject go until he related the entire story of their coincidental meeting, so he gave as brief and as impersonal an account as he could. "It was awkward for both of us," he concluded.

"It should have been. A guy and his ex-wife alone on a houseboat."

"We weren't alone. I already told you that Nathan was with me."

"Thank goodness."

Charlie echoed that sentiment silently. He knew that had he been alone with Beth, things might have been very different.

"Grace says Beth is going to stay on the houseboat while she's here."

He had started to eat, but paused with his fork in midair. "If you already heard the story from Grace, why did you make me repeat it?"

"Because I wanted to hear your version."

"There is only one version," he stated in no uncertain terms. He turned his attention to his bacon and eggs.

"I thought you and Nathan were going to stay on the houseboat."

"We will, if it works out with Beth." He sprinkled pepper on his eggs, then asked, "Is this why you wanted to have breakfast with me? To grill me about Beth?"

"No, I had another reason," she said with a sly smile. "I have a new neighbor."

He gave her a puzzled look. "And?"

"And she's just moved here from Covington. I thought it would be nice to throw her a small welcoming party since she's going to be teaching at Lincoln Elementary."

He tugged on his ear. "Let me guess. She's single."

Lucy grinned. "As a matter of fact she is!"

"You know I hate blind dates."

"This isn't a blind date. It's a party. Actually I'm calling it my 'goodbye to July' party, and you're not the only single guy I'm inviting."

"You going to rope Mitch Sterling into coming, too?" he asked, dipping his toast in the egg yolks.

"I'm not *roping* anyone into coming," she said defensively. "I would think most of the parents who have kids at school would like to welcome the new teacher to town. It's not going to be anything fancy. Just a summer barbecue."

"Are you inviting Beth?"

"Why would I? She doesn't live here. Besides,

you just said it was uncomfortable for both of you being together.''

It was, but that didn't stop Charlie from wanting to see her again. "I think we're over that initial discomfort," he told her, forgetting about their encounter last night at Amber's T-ball game. "I just thought that if you invited Ed and Grace, it might look strange not to invite Beth. You *are* inviting Ed and Grace?"

"Of course. And you're right. I wouldn't want to offend them, but I don't want Beth to feel out of place, either.''

Just then a waitress signaled to Lucy that she was needed. "I better get back to work. I'll think about what you said about inviting Beth, okay? In the meantime, put it on your calendar. It's a week from Saturday. And her name is Madeleine.''

BY THE END of her first full week in Riverbend, Beth had seen Charlie every day but one. Tuesday it had been the Little League game, Wednesday he'd come to the clinic to fix the entrance door, and on Thursday she'd run into him at the Sunnyside Café when she'd stopped to pick up supper on her way home from work. It was as if fate had determined their paths would cross.

Which was why on Friday she wasn't surprised to see his pickup parked out front when she stopped by her brother's house on the way home from work. She was tempted to turn around and leave, but she knew that her niece Kayla had already seen her car and was running into the house to announce her arrival. So instead of making a getaway, Beth climbed out of her car and went into the house.

Everyone was in the living room, including Grace's mother, who looked tired, but was pleased to be out of the hospital. Beth inquired as to her physical condition, then answered some of her questions regarding the rehabilitation process. When Grace suggested the girls help her get their grandmother settled in her room, Beth offered her assistance, but Grace insisted she stay and keep Charlie company.

Beth found herself alone with her ex-husband, who didn't look any more comfortable with the situation than she was.

"How's everything on the boat?" he asked politely.

"Fine. No problems at all," she replied.

Charlie asked her several questions about the boat, and they made small talk.

"Am I going to have to refill the water supply?" she asked.

"I already checked it." Seeing Beth's surprise, he added, "I stopped by while you were working at the clinic."

Her skin warmed at the thought of him being on the houseboat when she wasn't there. Even though he had every right to be there, she couldn't help but feel that he'd shared an intimacy with her she wasn't prepared to give him.

She wanted to tell him to stay away from the place, but knew that legally she couldn't. "I would appreciate it if you'd let me know when you're going to be there," she said primly.

If he sensed she was upset, he didn't show it, but simply said, "No problem."

After that the conversation became even more

stilted, which only increased Beth's discomfort. Then Ed returned and he and Charlie talked briefly. Finally Charlie excused himself, saying he needed to get home to Nathan.

"How is he?" Beth asked as he rose to his feet.

"He's fine. I took your advice and brought him to the job site with me a couple of days."

"How did that work out?"

"It didn't. I think he's a little young to be on a construction site." Not for the first time Beth noticed the calluses on his fingers. When they were married, she'd rub lotion on them when he came home from work at night. They were rough, strong, capable hands that could make her feel so good.

Annoyed by the direction of her thoughts, she looked down at her own hands, which she clutched in front of her. "Maybe he could get a job mowing lawns for your neighbors."

"Maybe he doesn't need a job, Beth," he said. pointedly.

"I think Charlie may be right," her brother interjected.

Beth felt as if Ed was siding with her ex-husband. She almost reminded him that both of them had worked every summer, once they were old enough, doing odd jobs for the neighbors. But then she realized that it really wasn't her concern.

Instead, she offered, "Nathan's welcome to come over to the houseboat anytime."

Charlie's face was blank as he said, "I'll let him know, although I'm not sure I want him there when no one's around."

"If the two of you want to use the boat, just let me know. I'll make myself scarce."

"I'd appreciate that," he said, then with a nod at Ed he left.

After he was gone, Ed looked at his sister. "You okay?"

"Yes. Why wouldn't I be?"

He nodded toward her hands. "You're clenching your fingers so tightly your knuckles are white."

Just then Grace returned. "Did Charlie leave? I thought he was staying for supper."

Beth felt even worse than she had a few minutes ago. "I'm sorry, Grace. He left because of me."

"He said he had to get home to Nathan," Ed corrected her. "You heard him, Beth. He only stopped by to give me some papers."

Beth didn't believe her brother for a minute. "Say what you want, but we all know it was uncomfortable for everyone. I'm sorry."

"Don't be silly," Grace said reassuringly, slinging her arm around her sister-in-law and giving her an affectionate squeeze. "Mom and Dad didn't notice a thing. Neither did the girls."

Just then the phone rang and Ed excused himself, saying, "I'll get it. It's probably for me."

"I thought you and Charlie behaved very cordially," Grace said when they were alone.

"You know Charlie. Always puts on a smiling face." Beth tried to make her voice sound cheerful, but failed.

"The two of you have to get used to seeing each other. You're bound to run into one another during the next few weeks."

"I know, but I didn't expect when I came home that I'd see him so often. It seems he's everywhere

I go." She shoved her hands in her pockets and went to stare out the front window. Grace followed her.

"You can tell me it's none of my business, Beth, but did something happen between you and Charlie last weekend?"

That had her turning her head with a jerk. "What do you mean?"

Grace shrugged. "It was just something about the way he kept looking at you. The minute you walked in the room I noticed it."

"It's because we're on edge when we're around each other. Can you blame us?"

"That's what you think it is? An uneasiness because you were once married?"

"What else would it be?"

Again Grace shrugged. "I don't know. Maybe it's just wishful thinking, but I'd hoped that maybe you two could, you know…"

"Get back together?" Beth asked in disbelief, then laughed. "That is wishful thinking, Grace. We were never together—at least not in the way two married people should be."

"I'm sorry. It's really none of my business," she said apologetically. "Just forget I even suggested such a thing."

"It's all right. I only hope everyone else in town isn't thinking the same thing," she said on a sigh.

"If they are, I know a way to change that."

Puzzled, Beth asked, "How?"

"How would you like to go out with a very nice man who just happens to be an old college friend of mine?"

Beth groaned. "You want to set me up with a blind date?"

"Oh, don't make a face until you've heard who it is," she pleaded.

"All right, tell me," Beth said in resignation.

"He's my college roommate's brother. He's coming to Riverbend on business, and Sally asked me if we'd entertain him while he's here."

"So I'm the entertainment?" Beth asked weakly.

"No, Ed and I plan to take him out to dinner. I thought you might like to come along, that's all." She looked at Beth with longing in her eyes. "Will you? He's a nice man and kinda cute in his own way."

"Cute?" Beth repeated.

"You just have to have dinner. Then, if that goes well, you and he can take it from there. We'll butt out." The look she gave Beth was so endearing it was almost impossible to say no. She knew her sister-in-law meant well. And the truth was, maybe it would be good to be seen with another man. Surely that would dispel any rumors that might link her and Charlie.

"I'm probably going to regret saying this, but all right. I'll do it."

"Great. He's coming next weekend, so keep Saturday night free."

CHARLIE DIDN'T WANT to be at Lucy's "goodbye to July" party. Neither did Nathan, and he wasted no time in voicing his displeasure.

"Why did we have to come to this?" he complained as soon as they had arrived for the barbecue.

Charlie was grateful the teenager had at least spoken in a low enough voice that he was the only one who'd heard. "It's a family-duty thing," he explained, which caused the boy to roll his eyes sky-ward.

"I don't know anybody here." Nathan looked around in disgust. "And the only kids are little ones."

Charlie saw his niece Amber sitting on the porch steps with two other kids comparing Pokémon trading cards. He'd hoped that Nathan would find something in common with Lucy's older daughter, but Rebecca had gone to visit her cousins in Illinois.

"We won't stay long," he assured him.

Nathan groaned and Charlie glanced around Lucy's backyard at the small gathering of familiar faces. Normally he loved Lucy's parties, but tonight he felt like a piece of meat getting ready for the barbecue spit.

As if she had radar, Lucy noticed him as soon as he arrived, and she headed toward him with a tall slender blonde in tow. Without even waiting for his sister's introduction, Charlie knew who the woman was. The new neighbor. Who just happened to be single. He wanted to groan along with Nathan.

"Here he is. My brother, Charlie," Lucy said proudly as she introduced the teacher to him. "Charlie, this is Madeleine Armstrong."

He shook the outstretched hand, returned her smile and then introduced Nathan. For the next few minutes he made small talk, trying to include Nathan as much as possible. He was relieved when Mitch Sterling arrived and Lucy took the schoolteacher over to meet him. Charlie steered Nathan to the hors d'oeuvres table, where there was an abundant supply of munchies.

Lucy had strung paper lanterns across the backyard, and when dusk settled and the lanterns glowed brightly, the party took on a more festive mood. As Charlie expected, Lucy handed him the chef's apron, urging him to take pity on her limited skills at the outdoor grill.

If Lucy's husband had been alive, he would have done the cooking, but Charlie was used to helping his sister out. Besides, it would keep him occupied and he'd have an excuse for not chatting up Madeleine Armstrong. Not that she wasn't an attractive woman. Actually she was quite charming. He simply wasn't interested.

"So what do you think of my new colleague?" Aaron Mazerik paused next to the grill. He had obviously noticed Charlie staring at Madeleine.

"Seems nice," was all Charlie said.

Aaron grinned slyly. "Rather easy on the eyes, too, wouldn't you say?"

Charlie shrugged. "She's not bad."

"Not bad? That's an understatement if I ever heard one." He eyed Charlie curiously, then turned to Nathan, extending his hand. "Hi. You must be Nathan. I'm Aaron Mazerik, also known as Maz to lots of the kids in town."

"Sorry. I thought you'd already met," Charlie apologized, grateful that Nathan's presence meant the subject of Madeleine Armstrong's attributes could be tabled. "Nathan's spending the rest of the summer with me."

Just then, Lucy returned. "I'm glad you're here, Aaron. I've been hearing a lot of good things about your summer basketball program. Do you have anything for fourteen-year-old boys?" she asked, placing her hand on Nathan's shoulder.

Aaron sized up Nathan with a friendly smile. "I have a camp for junior-high kids starting next week."

"I'm not in junior high," Nathan said with an edge to his voice. "I'm a high-school freshman."

Aaron grinned. "No problem. The high-school kids come in the mornings, the junior-high kids in the afternoon. Take your pick."

Charlie could see Nathan was not happy with what he'd heard. "What do you think, Nathan? Want to spend a week strengthening your basketball skills?"

"I don't play basketball," he said, then excused himself on the pretext of having to use the bathroom.

"He's not had an easy summer so far," Charlie told Aaron in Nathan's defense. He briefly explained what the past year had been like for the teen, and Aaron nodded in understanding.

"Don't worry about it, Charlie. If he wants to come next week, fine. I'd be happy to have him."

"I think he should try it," Lucy added. "It would be better than sitting home all day playing video games." She glanced down at the hamburgers on the grill. "As soon as the first batch is done, give me a holler," she instructed her brother, retying the apron around his waist.

A short while later she returned with a large platter.

"They're looking good," he told her, opening the cover of the grill.

"Party's a success, don't you think?" she asked as he transferred the hamburgers from the grill to the plate.

"Yeah, it's nice. I thought you said Ed and Grace were going to be here."

"They're stopping in later, after dinner."

"Beth, too?" he couldn't resist asking.

"I invited her," Lucy said in a rather defensive tone. "But I can tell you right now she won't come."

"It doesn't matter," he said, even though he secretly hoped Beth would show up. "At least you extended the invitation."

The rest of the evening, no matter how hard Charlie tried, he couldn't stop glancing toward the street, hoping to see the Penningtons arrive. When they did finally show up, Beth was not with them, as Lucy predicted.

Suddenly Charlie found himself tired of listening to Nathan ask the question, "When are we going to leave?" Despite his sister's protests, he said his goodbyes and left the party. On the way back to his place, Nathan was sullen.

"That wasn't so bad, was it?"

The boy made a sound of disgust.

"Hey. I have an idea. Maybe we should head over to the river and do a little fishing," he suggested cheerfully.

"You mean go to the houseboat?"

"Sure. What do you say?"

He could see interest flare in the boy's eyes. "What about Beth? She's living there, isn't she?"

"We can still fish off the back. She told me we could use the place whenever we wanted." He glanced again at Nathan, who was showing the most enthusiasm he'd seen all evening. "So what do you say?"

"You think she'll let me watch the music awards on TV?"

Charlie sighed. "I'm sure she will. Should we go there?"

"Well, yeah! Why not?"

Why not, indeed? Charlie asked himself as he took the river road leading to the marina. *Because you're not going so that Nathan will have something to do. You're going because you want to see Beth.*

Maybe he did want to see Beth, but he also wanted to put a smile on Nathan's face—something that hadn't been there all evening.

As he approached the marina, he saw that the lights were on in the houseboat and Beth's car was parked near the pier. She was home. His heartbeat quickened.

Driving closer, he saw there was a second car at the pier. Nathan noticed it, too.

"Looks like she's got company," he muttered, his voice losing the enthusiasm that had been there only a few moments ago.

"That doesn't mean we can't stay," Charlie said, a funny feeling unfurling in his stomach. He turned off the engine and climbed out of the truck.

Together they walked down the wooden pier to the houseboat. In the still of the night the Latin sound of mambo could be heard coming from the cabin.

"Lou Bega," Nathan said as they stepped onto the deck.

"You recognize the music?"

"Yeah. It's cool."

Charlie rapped on the metal frame of the sliding glass door. "Beth, are you here?" he called out, but there was no answer. That didn't surprise Charlie. The music was loud—too loud to hear knuckles on aluminum.

He slid the door open and stepped inside. Just then the music on the stereo ended and he heard voices.

"How's this?" he heard Beth ask.

"Ah, that's it," a man's voice responded weakly.

"Here?"

"Ooh…yes…." Sighs followed.

Charlie stopped so suddenly Nathan bumped into him.

"What's going on?" Nathan asked, then said, "Oh," when he realized the reason for Charlie's hesitation. In the living room stood a man naked to the waist. Next to him was Beth, one hand on his shoulder, the other just under his arm.

It didn't take a rocket scientist to figure out what was going on.

Upon hearing Nathan's voice, Beth pushed herself away from the man. "Charlie! What are you doing here?"

"Just checking up on my property," he answered.

CHAPTER NINE

BETH COULD SEE by the look on Charlie's face that he had misread the situation. He was staring at her as if she'd been seducing Howard Fishburn, rather than trying to evaluate his shoulder sprain. She didn't quite understand how anyone could aggravate a shoulder injury by demonstrating the mambo, but then Howard had been dancing rather exuberantly when he'd cried out in pain.

"Nathan, wait for me in the truck," Charlie ordered the teenager.

"We're not leaving already, are we?" he protested.

"You don't have to leave," Beth spoke up, but Charlie paid no attention.

"Just wait in the truck, Nathan."

"But you said I could watch the music video awards," the boy reminded him.

"I said wait in the truck," Charlie repeated sternly.

With a dejected "all right," the teenager dragged his feet and retraced his steps back to the pickup.

Beth glanced from Charlie to Howard and saw both men regarding the other suspiciously. Howard had a sheepish look on his face as he reached for the plaid sports shirt draped over the arm of the sofa.

"If I thought you needed privacy, I wouldn't have

brought Nathan over.'' Charlie's voice was curt as he watched Howard button his shirt.

Howard gave Beth a puzzled look. ''I'm sorry. Did I miss something here?'' He extended a hand to Charlie saying, ''I'm Howard Fishburn, and you are…?''

''Charlie Callahan. Beth's ex-husband.''

Beth could see that Charlie's words took Howard by surprise. They hadn't gotten around to discussing previous relationships, and she'd allowed him to assume that she'd never been married. To his credit, he retained his composure as he said, ''It's nice to meet you.''

Charlie shook his hand, but said nothing. The way he stood there with that grim look on his face gave the impression that he felt he had been wronged.

Beth felt compelled to clarify the situation. ''We divorced fifteen years ago,'' she told Howard. ''And until we inherited this boat this summer, we hadn't seen or talked to each other since.'' She glared at Charlie, wondering what he hoped to accomplish with his Sly Stallone stance.

Standing next to her ex-husband, Howard looked puny. Beth immediately chastised herself for even comparing the two men. What did she expect? Howard sat at a desk all day while Charlie did physical labor.

''Well, it's obvious you two need to talk and I really should be going,'' Howard announced, looking rather uncomfortable. Not that Beth blamed him. The proprietary way Charlie was standing on the boat would have made any man uneasy.

''We haven't had our coffee,'' Beth said, hoping

her date for the evening would stay and Charlie would leave. It didn't work that way.

"Maybe next time," Howard said with a smile of regret. "Thank you for a lovely evening. And for taking a look at my shoulder."

"Does it feel better?"

"Yes, much. You have a gentle touch," he said, then took her hands in his and raised one of them to his lips. "I'd like to do this again next time I'm in Riverbend. The dinner part, I mean."

Out of the corner of her eye Beth could see Charlie's face tighten in disapproval. What did he think? That she wasn't entitled to a social life?

"That would be nice," she told Howard, even though she really shouldn't give him any encouragement. She wasn't interested in him as anything other than Grace's college roommate's brother. Yet she found herself smiling warmly.

"Good. I'll give you a call next time I'm passing through Riverbend. Only I think we'd better skip the mambo," he said with a flirtatious grin. Beth retrieved the CD from the stereo and handed it to him.

She ignored the look of disgust on Charlie's face and showed Howard the door. As soon as he was gone, she turned to Charlie, who stood there like a sentinel, his arms folded across his chest.

Annoyed by his attitude, she asked, "Would you mind telling me what that was all about?"

"What what was all about?" he asked with mock innocence.

"You barging in here acting as if you have a right to be here. *I'm her ex-husband,*" she mimicked. "Just because you've consented to let me use the boat doesn't entitle you to disrupt my evening."

"I *am* your ex-husband," he said. "And this is my boat, too, in case you've forgotten."

"I'm not likely to forget when you keep showing up here, am I?" She faced him squarely. "And just what *are* you doing here? I thought you and Nathan were going to Lucy's party."

"And that you'd have the boat all to yourself so that you and Howie could mambo your way into the bedroom?" he sneered.

She gasped. "We were not going into the bedroom, but even if we were, it's none of your business what I do with my guests."

"Yes, it is, if you're doing it on my boat."

"It's my boat, too."

"That doesn't mean you can use it as a love nest."

"I wasn't using it as a love nest," she denied indignantly. "Howard is a friend of Grace's and he's in town on business. We went out to dinner and then he drove me home. He loves mambo music, so I put on the CD he'd brought and—"

"And poor Howie mamboed so vigorously he injured his shoulder, and you, being the kind soul you are, offered to put it right again, so he took off his shirt and all that moaning and groaning we heard when we walked onto the boat was the grateful sound of pain relief," he said in exaggerated disbelief.

She held up her hands. "Just stop. Do you know how ridiculous you sound?"

"Do you know how ridiculous you looked?" he countered. "I happen to be responsible for a fourteen-year-old boy this summer, and I don't need him to see that kind of stuff happening on my boat."

"The *stuff* was an examination, and you wouldn't have seen it had you called first, which is what common courtesy requires in this case," she retaliated, her voice rising in frustration.

"He had his shirt off so I could examine his shoulder." She threw up her hands, asking herself the rhetorical question, "Why am I bothering to try to explain this to you?" She took a deep breath to calm herself. "You're acting as if Nathan walked in on me having sex with some guy."

"You better make sure *that* never happens," he warned.

She stared at him. "Good grief, Charlie. Is that the kind of woman you think I've become?"

He raked a hand through his hair. "No." He was silent, as if collecting his thoughts. Then he turned to her and said, "I'm sorry. I overreacted, but I didn't expect you to be entertaining men on this boat."

She dropped onto the sofa and sank against the cushions. She didn't want to argue with Charlie. "I don't plan to entertain men," she said wearily.

"You told Howie to come back."

"If I didn't know better, I'd say you were jealous," she said.

"Maybe I am."

It wasn't what she expected to hear. Nor did she think he'd sit down beside her on the sofa, so close that his thigh touched hers. Then he leaned closer and picked up her hands in his. "I'm not used to seeing you with another man."

She wanted to tug her hands out of his grasp, but his touch sent tremors of pleasure through her. She swallowed with difficulty before saying, "You gave up your right to be jealous fifteen years ago."

"Doesn't matter. Part of you will always belong to me, Beth."

"What's that supposed to mean?" she asked with an uneasy laugh.

"I have memories that won't let me forget what it was like to be with you."

When she would have eased herself away from him, he moved closer until his face was just inches from hers. He placed his fingers on her jaw and forced her to look at him. "You remember, too, don't you?"

She couldn't deny it, and she lowered her eyes, not wanting him to see what was in them. "That's all past."

"Is it? Then why is it that every time I see you, I think about what it was like to wake up with you in my arms?"

"Charlie, don't," she begged, not wanting the rush of memories his words produced.

"Don't what? Remind you of how good it was between us? It *was* good, Beth." As if to prove his point, he placed his lips over hers. They were warm, moist and a bit unsteady, as if he wasn't sure he should be kissing her. But then they became commanding and insistent, coaxing a response from her.

She groaned and gave in to the temptation to kiss him with the same urgency he was kissing her. Her lips parted, allowing his tongue to push its way into her mouth. Just as he had in the past, he took charge, sweeping her off her feet, making her feel alive, exuberant, in need of his touch.

"Mmm, you taste so sweet," he murmured

against her lips, easing her down onto the sofa so that she was no longer sitting but lying beneath him. Beth lost all sense of time. It was as if they were the same two teenagers who'd made love on this very boat the night of the spring dance. He was Charlie, the boy of her dreams, the guy who made her feel special, the only one she'd ever wanted to share her life with. And it felt wonderful to have his mouth on hers, to have his tongue caress hers, to feel his hands on her flesh.

"Hey! Are we going home or aren't we?"

Nathan's voice had them scrambling apart. They quickly sat up and tried to act as if nothing had happened, but Beth knew that her face wore the same look of guilt as Charlie's.

"Yeah. We're going," he told Nathan, jumping to his feet.

"You don't have to," Beth told them, then immediately felt stupid. It sounded as if she was telling Charlie that she had wanted what had happened between them only a few moments ago.

She didn't know whether she should feel relieved or disappointed when he said, "No, it's late. We'll go."

Nathan didn't say anything, but stood there looking at the two of them curiously, which made Beth wonder if he'd seen them kissing. They made polite small talk as Beth walked them out to Charlie's truck.

"Anytime you want to come visit, Nathan, you're welcome," she told the boy as he climbed into the passenger side. "I work at the clinic three days a week, and the days sometimes vary, but I'd be happy to have some company when I'm not working. That is, if it's all right with Charlie,'' she added.

Charlie had climbed behind the steering wheel, and in the darkness, it was difficult for Beth to see his face clearly. "It's okay by me," he told the two of them.

"Good. Then why don't you come over on Monday?" Beth suggested.

"All right." Nathan gave her a weak smile.

Then Charlie said, "Not this Monday. I've signed him up for Aaron Mazerik's basketball camp."

Nathan didn't comment, but Beth suspected by the way he slouched lower in the cab that he wasn't exactly happy with the news. She wondered if Charlie had thought to ask the boy if he wanted to attend the camp.

Beth watched the pickup disappear into the darkness, wondering why it seemed that everything Charlie tried to do for Nathan met with the boy's disapproval. But it wasn't the troubled teenager who was in her thoughts as she prepared for bed later than evening. It was Charlie.

No matter how hard she tried, she couldn't stop feeling his lips on hers. Tremors of delight echoed through her body as she remembered what it had been like to be in his arms. And as she fell asleep, there was only one question on her mind. Would it happen again?

SUNDAY AFTERNOON the entire Pennington family, including Grace's mother in her wheelchair, went for a picnic in the park, where they watched an outdoor performance of *Annie* by a traveling theater group. It was a wonderful way to spend a summer afternoon, and Beth returned to the houseboat feeling a bit nostalgic. As a child she'd loved Sunday afternoons at Riverside Park, which on summer weekends became a beehive of activity.

"It's good to see that someone's using Mom's picnic hamper," Beth told Grace as they'd picked up the remains of their lunch.

"Ed and I agreed that Sundays in the park were a tradition we wanted to preserve," Grace answered.

Beth found herself a bit envious of her brother. Until this summer, she hadn't realized how much she'd missed family traditions.

If there was one thing she'd noticed since her return to Riverbend, it was the sense of community that existed in the town. Even though Grace's parents had moved away more than ten years ago, people still treated them as if they were neighbors. In the two weeks since Grace's mother had fallen, the Pennington house had been like the town square—full of people coming and going, all of them stopping with get well wishes that often included gifts of food. There was no shortage of kindhearted volunteers asking if there was anything they could do to help out.

Beth, too, wanted to relieve her sister-in-law of some of the everyday chores so that she could nurse her mother without any unnecessary stress. That was why she offered to take her nieces to visit the dentist the following Monday morning for their semiannual checkups.

The last time Beth had visited Dr. Freeman's office, she'd been seventeen. Although the waiting room had been updated, her dentist still looked the same, except his head was now a bald dome.

"Beth, it's good to see you. Let me see that smile," he commanded.

She obeyed.

"Beautiful. What brings you to my office?"

Beth used her thumb to point behind her. "My nieces. They need to get their teeth checked before they go back to school."

He looked over her shoulder at the three little girls huddled in the corner. "Who wants to go first?" he asked.

Kayla was the one who stood. "I will. Then I'll be the first one done," she said as she cautiously walked toward the open door.

As soon as all three girls had had their teeth cleaned, been given new toothbrushes and sent off with the good news that not one of them had a cavity, Beth announced that she had a surprise for them. Since they'd been such model patients at Dr. Freeman's office, she would take them to the bookstore and they could each pick out something new to read.

While the girls perused the children's section, Beth browsed through the new arrivals in the hope she'd find something appropriate for Grace's mother.

"Can I help?" she heard someone say over her shoulder.

Beth turned to see a woman with big hazel eyes and reddish-brown hair standing beside her, a friendly smile on her face.

"I'm looking for a gift for someone who's going to be limited in her physical activity for a while. Something cheery, but not necessarily screaming 'Get well.' You know what I mean?"

The woman thought for a moment, then said, "I

think I have something that might work.'' She disappeared into the office, only to return shortly with a large square box. ''These came in this morning and I haven't had time to look at them yet.''

Beth watched as she set the box on the counter, then opened it and pulled out a floral package encased in plastic. Inside was a china teacup, several pouches of imported tea and a small book containing meditations for teatime. ''What do you think?''

Carefully Beth examined the rose-patterned teacup, then paged through the tiny book filled with quotations. ''I think this may be just what she needs to cheer her.''

''I can giftwrap it for you if you like,'' the woman offered.

''Thank you. That would be lovely.'' Just then Beth felt a tug on her shirtsleeve. ''Auntie Beth, I found the most beautiful book. Can I have it, please?''

''I'll take a look at it in just a minute,'' she told her niece, who went scrambling back to the children's section.

''Allison Pennington is your niece?'' the store clerk inquired.

Beth nodded. ''You know her?''

The clerk smiled. ''She's in the same Sunday-school class as my twins, Hannah and Hope. I'm Kate McMann.''

''Beth Pennington,'' she said with a warm smile.

''I thought you looked familiar, but I couldn't quite place you until I saw Allison,'' Kate said. ''Grace mentioned you were coming home for the summer.''

''You know Grace?''

"And your brother, Ed, too. When you have five-year-old twins, you meet the parents of other five year olds," she said with a smile.

As Beth stared at the woman behind the counter, she had the feeling they'd met before. "You look familiar. Did you grow up in Riverbend?"

"Yes, but I was a couple of years behind you in school. I do remember seeing you when I first started working here at the bookstore, though. You were one of the regulars."

Beth recalled seeing Kate, who at the time had been very shy and seldom said a word to anyone, other than the necessary business exchanges. Quite different from the self-confident woman running the bookstore today.

"I always did like coming here," Beth admitted, glancing around the store with an appreciative eye. "Guess it's because I love books."

"Me, too," Kate said with a gleam in her eye. "That's why this job is so right for me. I get to spend my days helping people choose good books."

"Speaking of which, I'd better go see if I can get my nieces to make a decision. Otherwise we might be here all day."

"That's fine with me," Kate said. "I'll get this wrapped, so it'll be ready for you."

By the time the three little girls had made their selections, several more bookstore customers had come and gone. As Beth's nieces placed their books on the counter, Kate smiled at Allison, who beamed up at the freckle-faced woman and said a shy "Hi," then giggled.

"Is this your book?" Kate asked as she picked up a picture book with a dog on the cover. Seeing the little girl nod, she said, "Hope and Hannah like this one, too."

"Can I have a cookie?" Allison asked.

"Of course you can," Kate answered. "You know where they are."

Beth watched as the three girls ran over to a ceramic cookie jar in the shape of a house. They lifted one peak of the roof and reached inside.

"You want one, Auntie Beth?" Kayla called out.

"None for me, thanks," she answered.

"They're really good," Kayla said as she skipped back to the counter.

"Why, thank you," Kate said with a wide grin.

"You bake them yourself?" Beth asked.

"I love baking almost as much as I love books," she answered. "In fact... Excuse me a minute." She again disappeared into the office briefly, this time returning with a small white box, which she handed to Beth. "Here. These are for Grace's mother. Cookies to go with the tea."

Kayla's eyes widened. "We get a whole box?"

"To help cheer up your grandma," Beth told her niece. "Thanks, Kate. I know these will be appreciated."

Kate finished ringing up their order, giving each of the girls their own sack to carry. Then she handed Beth a beautifully wrapped package with the teacup inside. "Tell Grace I've been thinking about her, will you?"

Beth nodded and said goodbye, shepherding the three little girls out of the store. As they walked to the car, Allison said, "I wish I had another cookie."

"Me, too," little Cierra seconded. "I'm hungry."

Beth glanced at her watch. No wonder the girls

wanted more to eat. It was already past noon. "How about if we go to the Burger Barn?"

"Can we?" they asked excitedly.

"Sure. Let me call your mom and tell her where we'll be, okay?"

It had been years since Beth had been in the Burger Barn. The smell of hamburgers cooking on the grill teased her nostrils as soon as she pulled into the parking lot. Inside the restaurant, she ordered three kids' meals and a cheeseburger and fries for herself, then found an empty booth for the four of them.

They'd just sat down when she heard Kayla say, "Look. There's Charlie."

Beth turned to see her ex-husband placing an order at the counter. She knew there was little hope that he wouldn't see the four of them, not when they were sitting so close to the exit. It didn't help that the girls were doing everything short of rushing up to the counter to get his attention.

When he did finally glance in their direction, he smiled, the flirting kind of smile that used to make Beth's heart beat faster. She discovered it still did. The girls waved and he waved back. As soon as he was given his order of take-out food, he walked toward them.

"Well, hello, you sweet things," he said with a grin that could stop even the youngest of hearts.

It made Beth's nieces giggle and caused her own face to color as if she wasn't much older than the girls. It didn't help that all she seemed able to think about was the last time she'd seen him and how they'd kissed as if...

She pushed those memories aside and concentrated on sorting through the food the waitress had just brought.

"Wanna eat lunch with us?" Allison's question caused Beth to look up.

"Charlie ordered his lunch to go," she pointed out. "He probably needs to take it back to work to eat."

"Do you?" the five year old asked him.

"I had planned on eating in the truck," he answered.

Allison clicked her tongue reprovingly. "You're not supposed to eat in the truck because you'll get your greasy fingerprints all over everything. That's why they have tables in here," she explained, sounding very much like a miniature Ed.

"You can eat your food in here even if it's in a bag," Kayla added.

"You can sit by me. There's room." Allison squeezed in closer to her sister and patted the bench beside her. She batted her eyelashes at Charlie in an endearing display of affection any man would have had difficulty ignoring.

"You talked me into it," he said, sliding in beside the two of them.

"It didn't take much talking," Beth said under her breath, but she could see that Charlie had heard.

"Nope, it didn't," he agreed with his infuriatingly handsome grin. He leaned across the table and said to her, "Some guys might be a little uncomfortable having lunch with four beautiful women. I'm not one of them."

"Obviously," was all she managed to say. She concentrated on the food in front of her. She had to. Otherwise she'd end up staring at Charlie. Dressed in a white T-shirt, a pair of jeans and work boots, he looked as if he'd stepped off the pages of a "Construction Men at Work" calendar.

Fortunately the girls' lively chatter made it unnecessary for her to say much. They talked about the play they'd seen at the park and their favorite foods at the Burger Barn, then debated which was scarier—going to the dentist or the doctor. Beth appreciated the way Charlie listened to their fears without trying to persuade them they were unfounded.

She found herself surprised at how easily he related to the children. She realized that this was actually the first time she'd seen him with young kids.

He was great with them. He didn't seem to mind that Allison clung to his side or that all three of them wanted his attention. Patiently he listened as they talked to him as if he were a dear uncle, and Beth could see that, despite what Ed had told her, Charlie was a close friend of the entire family.

As she always did, Beth had removed the pickles from her burger before biting into it. They sat on the edge of the wrapper and on more than one occasion she'd noticed Charlie eyeing them.

Finally he said, "You gonna eat those?"

She slid the wrapper in his direction. "Be my guest."

He scooped up the pickles and popped them into his mouth. The result was a feeling of déjà vu for Beth. How many times had he done that very thing when they were teens? His eyes met hers, and she wondered if he was having the same thought.

Allison broke the moment by announcing, "I like pickles, too. See?" She pulled one off her hamburger and dangled it over her mouth before chomping on it.

A discussion of food likes and dislikes followed and again Beth remembered her short marriage. During their brief time together, she'd learned a lot about Charlie's preferences. To her surprise, he'd eaten everything she'd put on the table without a complaint.

Once again his eyes met hers, and she wondered if he was remembering those days, as well.

The time passed quickly and before long Charlie said, "I've got to get back to work." As he rose to his feet, there were several groans, followed by a plea from Allison.

"Can't you stay a little bit longer?"

As if reminding him of his responsibility, his cell phone rang. He pulled it out of his pocket, flipped it open and answered the call. After a brief conversation he snapped it shut again.

"Gotta go, girls." He put his empty wrappers in the sack and crumpled it between his hands. "This was fun. We'll have to do it again sometime." His comment was directed at Beth and caused her stomach to flutter at the thought that he wanted to spend more time with her.

He started to walk away, then backtracked. "Oh—I almost forgot. I told Nathan I'd bring him over one night so he could watch some rock-music show on TV. Is that going to be a problem?"

"Not at all. As I told you the other night, he's welcome anytime. I'm working at the clinic tomorrow, but I'll be home all day Wednesday if he's interested in coming by in the afternoon."

''Can't. He's at basketball camp all this week,'' he told her.

''Oh, that's right. Then bring him over in the evening.''

Allison, intensely interested in their conversation, piped up with, ''Did you know Auntie Beth is going to let us sleep over one night on the boat? We're going to make popcorn and watch a movie and paint our toenails. Wanna come?''

''Allison!'' Beth chided gently. ''Pajama parties are for girls only.''

''Darn,'' Charlie said with a mischievous twinkle in his eye. ''Nothing I'd like better than to have my toenails painted.'' The girls burst into giggles and even Beth couldn't suppress a grin. ''Well, I better go,'' Charlie said at last. ''You girls be good, okay?'' With a wave, he headed for the exit.

Allison watched him walk away, standing up so she could follow his progress through the crowd. ''Charlie didn't go out the door. He went back to order more food,'' she reported.

Beth didn't turn around but said, ''He's probably getting a soda to take with him back to work. Finish your lunch,'' she ordered the little girl, but Allison wasn't about to sit back down as long as Charlie was in the restaurant.

She gasped and wiggled excitedly. ''He's buying ice cream!''

Kayla and little Cierra turned around to check it out. ''Alli's right,'' Kayla announced. ''He's got four ice-cream cones. One for each of us!''

That had Beth twisting her head for a peek. As she did, her eyes met Charlie's. The message she saw there made her breath catch in her throat. There was no mistaking the flirtatious glint, and he didn't break eye contact with her until he was back at their table.

As he set the tray down in front of the girls, he said, "Everybody like ice cream?"

Squeals of delight could be heard as small hands grabbed the cones. As the three girls licked their cones with great pleasure, Beth just sat there.

"There's one for you, too," Charlie said with a sparkle in his eyes.

"Thank you," she finally said. The ice cream had started to melt and was dripping down the side of the cone. She tipped her head to catch the drizzle with her tongue, aware that Charlie was watching her with great interest. "Why are you looking at me like that?" she asked, wondering if she had ice cream on her chin.

He shrugged. "No particular reason. I just like watching you eat ice cream."

Whether or not it was his intention, Beth felt her cheeks warm at the provocative statement. She was grateful the girls once more broke the tension with effusive thanks for their dear sweet Charlie. And then he was gone and this time he didn't return.

"Isn't Charlie fun?" Allison said as he walked away.

"Yes, he is," Beth agreed, wishing she didn't have to admit that, like Allison, she didn't want him to leave, either.

CHAPTER TEN

BY THE TIME Beth had dropped off her nieces and made her way back to the houseboat, she felt as if she'd run a couple of miles. Keeping up with three energetic girls was no easy task. She looked forward to a tall glass of iced tea then kicking off her shoes and putting her feet up on a deck chair.

The thought of peace and quiet with nothing but Mother Nature for a companion was a welcome one. Only she soon discovered she wasn't going to be alone on the houseboat.

As she stepped onto the pier, she saw Nathan at the opposite end, his feet dangling in the river. With his head bent, he didn't see her approach. Once she got closer, she realized it was because he was pre-occupied. On his lap was a sketch pad and in his fingers a pencil. He was drawing.

"Ahoy, there," she called out, not wanting to startle him.

His head jerked around, then he immediately reached for the backpack at his side and shoved the sketch pad into it.

"I didn't expect you to be here. I thought Charlie said you were at basketball camp," she said when she'd reached the end of the pier.

"Naw, I didn't go."

"So how did you get here?" she asked. "Did Charlie drop you off?"

"No. I got a ride from some guy in a delivery truck."

The thought of a fourteen year old hitchhiking brought a frown to her face. That, plus the fact that Charlie obviously didn't know he was here, gave her an uneasy feeling.

"Did you tell Charlie you were coming here?" she asked, although she was certain she knew the answer.

"No. He was at work."

Beth knew Charlie had a cell phone, which meant Nathan had chosen not to notify him. Her uneasiness grew.

"You said I could hang out here with you," he reminded her.

"I know I did, and you can. It's just that I'm a little concerned Charlie might be worried about you. You should probably let him know you're here."

"Why? He's busy at work."

"He still needs to know where you are."

Nathan pulled his feet from the water and stood. He bent to pick up the backpack, then walked straight past her and toward the riverbank.

"Wait. Where are you going?" she called.

"If you're going to phone Charlie, I might as well go home right now. He's not going to let me stay here."

"Sure he will if I tell him I want you to stay. He's one of the good guys," she said, finding it rather ironic that she was defending her ex-husband.

"You'd really tell him that you want me to stay?"

"Sure. Come." She motioned for him to follow her. "I'll unlock the door and we'll go inside." He walked back toward her, standing beside her as she inserted her key in the door. "I'm sorry I wasn't here when you arrived, but I spent the day with my nieces."

He shrugged. "It's all right. Just sitting on the dock is better than being stuck in some gym."

Again a shaft of uneasiness went through Beth. She wondered if Charlie knew that Nathan wasn't at Aaron Mazerik's camp. "Charlie thought you'd enjoy the basketball camp."

"I told him I didn't want to go, but Lucy talked him into it." As they stepped into the cabin, he asked, "Do you think it would be all right if I watched TV?"

"I think so."

"Cool." For the first time since they'd been talking he smiled. He made a beeline for the remote control and plopped himself down on the sofa.

Beth offered him a soda, then pulled her cell phone from her purse. "Do you want to call Charlie or should I?"

She could see he didn't want either of them to make the call, but reluctantly he took the phone and dialed Charlie's number. From the brevity of the responses on Nathan's end, Beth concluded that Charlie had reacted just as she'd expected.

As soon as the conversation ended, she asked, "Is he coming over?"

"Yeah, but he said it'll be a while. He's on some important job he has to finish."

"That's good. It means you can hang around here for the rest of the day."

"I don't want to bother you."

"You're not bothering me," she assured him, and she wondered if it was Charlie who put that possibility in his head. "Now, how about if I get you a snack? Are you hungry?"

"A little."

"What would you like? Chips, salsa, ice cream, a sandwich?"

"I could go for a sandwich."

Beth suspected that he might not have had any lunch, so she made him a ham and cheese sandwich, sprinkled some chips on the plate and took it to him.

"Thanks. This looks good."

By the way he devoured the food, she was convinced he hadn't eaten lunch. When he'd finished, she made him a second sandwich, handed him the bag of chips and told him she was going to grab a book and sit outside on the deck.

That was where she was when Charlie arrived. He'd changed out of the T-shirt and jeans he'd had on when she'd seen him earlier that day. It was obvious he'd gone home and showered before coming to pick up Nathan. He wore a pair of khaki shorts and a hunter-green polo shirt. And he smelled wonderful. Beth's heart fluttered as the scent of his aftershave wafted on the summer breeze.

He didn't greet her, but simply said, "Is he inside?"

"You look upset," she answered.

"Of course I'm upset. When he didn't show up at the basketball camp, Aaron Mazerik phoned me. I've been driving all over town looking for him."

Worry lined his face, tugging on Beth's emotions. She sat forward, dropping her legs so that she was no longer stretched out on the lounger, but straddling it. "He doesn't want to play basketball," she said softly.

He chuckled. "What do you mean? Every kid in Indiana wants to play basketball."

"Not that kid. Did you ask him if he wanted to play?"

"I didn't have to ask him. He and I used to shoot hoops all the time," he said, grabbing a deck chair and sitting on it backward. "Lucy said it's a great camp."

"Then maybe she should send her kids," Beth retorted.

"Don't blame Lucy for trying to help out."

Beth didn't want Lucy in their conversation, so she said nothing.

"Nathan is a natural when it comes to basketball," Charlie went on. "He's got a great jump shot."

"He doesn't seem to think so."

Charlie sighed. "That's why he needs someone like Aaron Mazerik. Aaron understands kids like Nathan, and this camp will give him an opportunity to see boys from his old school."

Beth could see that his intentions were good, but the fact remained that Nathan didn't want to go to the camp. "I think you need to reconsider sending him, Charlie."

"You think he doesn't want to play, don't you?"

She nodded.

"If that's the case, why didn't he tell me?"

"Maybe he didn't want you to be disappointed in him."

He rubbed a hand across a jaw that was beginning

to darken with shadow. "And what do you suggest I do with the kid? Leave him home all day by himself so he can get into more trouble, break a few more windows?"

Beth knew she should keep her nose out of it, but she found herself saying, "He could stay here with me on the days I'm home."

"And what about the three days you work?"

"There must be something else in town for him to do. I know in Iowa they have summer drama programs for teens. Last year they put on a production of *Romeo and Juliet,* which was a lot of fun for the kids. Maybe there's something similar here."

"You think he's going to want to act in a play?" He stared at her in disbelief.

"You could ask him and see."

He chuckled derisively. "I don't need to ask him. I know what he'd say."

His cocky attitude annoyed her. "Wouldn't it be better than forcing him to go to a camp where he feels out of place?"

"He hasn't even given basketball a try. He never showed up today, so he doesn't know whether or not he'll like it." With one hand he reached up to massage the back of his neck.

"Just forget everything I said, then," Beth told him, annoyed by his attitude.

"I don't want to argue with you about this. Nathan's my concern, not yours."

He'd told her as much on several occasions, a polite way of saying, "Butt out."

He got to his feet in a way that said the discussion was over. "Thank you for letting him stay here this afternoon."

"As I said, he can come anytime I'm here."

Without another word, Charlie went inside. When he came out again, Nathan was with him.

"Thanks, Beth, for making me the sandwiches," he said. Something in the way he stood there in his baggy shorts and baggy shirt, the backpack slung over his shoulder, made her want to give him a hug. Maybe it was the fact that he had no mother to fuss over him. Or maybe it was because she knew Charlie was relentless about the camp and this fourteen year old looked very much like a kid who needed a little tender loving care.

"Come anytime, Nathan. Just make sure you let Charlie know, okay?"

"Okay," he said with the briefest of smiles. He walked away, his shoulders slumped, and Beth felt an odd little pain in her chest.

She wished that Charlie would put a hand on Nathan's shoulder or show some sign of affection. He didn't. They looked like two men at odds with each other, and Beth found herself wanting to be the peacemaker.

But it wasn't her job and she knew it. That didn't stop her from wishing things could be different, though, or from wondering what it would be like if the three of them were to spend the evening together.

BETH THOUGHT ABOUT Charlie and Nathan often the following day. She wondered if Charlie had reconsidered his decision to send the teenager to basketball camp. If Julian Bennett hadn't needed her to come in for a sick employee, she would have called

Charlie's home and invited Nathan to spend the day at the houseboat.

Instead, she found herself stuck at the clinic, wondering how the teenager was spending his time. By the end of the afternoon, she had her answer.

Shortly before the clinic closed, Nathan walked into the waiting room, holding a wet cloth to his mouth.

"What happened?" Beth asked when she saw him at the registration desk.

"He fell playing basketball and cut his lip." It was Lucy Garvey who answered for him. She'd been sitting on one of the waiting-room chairs, but upon seeing Beth rose to her feet and came up to the counter. "Aaron thought he might need stitches."

"Does Charlie know about this?" Beth asked.

"I called him, but he was over in Covington, so I thought I'd better not wait for him to get back. I brought him right in."

"Smart decision," Beth said with a critical eye on Nathan. Judging by the amount of blood on the cloth he held against his mouth, the injury needed immediate attention.

"I'd like you to come this way, Nathan," one of the nurses said, gesturing for him to follow her.

"I'll wait out here," Lucy told him as he headed for the door leading to the examination rooms.

A surge of annoyance had Beth wanting to march right over to Lucy and tell her what she thought of her insistence that Nathan play basketball. But then she noticed Lucy's daughter Amber was with her, and she saw the concern on Lucy's face at the sight of Nathan disappearing into the doctor's office.

"I'm sure he'll be fine," she told her old friend, her professional side taking over.

Lucy simply nodded, then sat down, pulling Amber onto her lap. The little girl had a book in her hand, which she opened, then she tugged on her mother's arm.

Watching Lucy read to her daughter, Beth remembered how her friend used to take the younger kids in the neighborhood to the park. She had a way with kids, and Beth had never understood why she hadn't gone to college and become a teacher. That was all she'd ever talked about doing when they were growing up.

By the time Beth had finished with her patients for the day, she noticed that Lucy was the only person left in the waiting room. Amber had fallen asleep, her body sprawled across her mother's lap and the chair next to her. It was such a serene picture of mother and child, and Beth found herself wishing she could get rid of the awkwardness that existed between her and her childhood friend.

Except for a few words of acknowledgment at the T-ball game and small talk exchanged at the café, the two of them hadn't spoken since Christmas of her freshman year in college.

It was a day she wanted to forget, yet she could still remember the confrontation she'd had with Lucy. It had been ugly—even uglier than what she and Charlie had said to each other. They'd said things no best friends should ever say to each other, shutting a door Beth wasn't sure could be reopened.

Just thinking about it caused Beth pain. The friend who'd been there for her in her darkest moments had deserted her at the most painful time in her life.

Instead of getting Lucy's understanding and support, all she'd gotten was her anger.

Beth had been so empty at the time that she hadn't bothered trying to set things right with Lucy. Divorce left casualties in its wake, and she'd accepted that their friendship was one of them.

She'd gone away to school, determined to make a fresh start. Totally focused, she'd buried herself in her studies, carrying as many credits as the university would allow, and working part-time besides. Although she'd made new friends, none was as close to her as Lucy had been.

They had been the best of friends. Sharing dreams and disappointments. Laughing and crying together. Beth could still remember the poem Lucy had given her the day of her mother's funeral. It wasn't one she'd written herself—Lucy didn't like poetry. She knew that Beth did, though, which was why she'd spent a whole afternoon at the library looking through books to find the right one to give Beth on such a sad occasion.

Memories of their childhood flashed in Beth's mind. She and Lucy riding their bikes with the summer breeze in their faces. Lucy reading teen magazines out loud and giggling over the questions about boys. The two of them making a bed in the garage so the stray cat would have a place to give birth to her kittens.

It was those memories that Beth wanted to share again. They gave her the courage to walk out into the waiting room and sit down on the chair next to Lucy.

"Dr. Bennett's just finishing up stitching Nathan's lip," she said in a low voice so as not to wake

Lucy's daughter. "It took him a little longer than he'd expected, but he'll be ready to go home in a few minutes."

"So he had to have stitches?"

Beth nodded. "A few."

Lucy shivered. "It makes me queasy just thinking about it."

"You looked pretty calm when you brought him in."

"I wasn't. I just didn't want to make a scene in front of Amber." She paused and nodded toward her daughter. "She thinks I've got my act together."

"She's a beautiful child, Lucy. She looks a lot like you."

"She's got the Garvey nose," Lucy said with affection, her eyes lovingly examining the sleeping girl on her lap.

"Judging by the way she hit that ball off the T last week, I'd say she's got your athletic ability. Ed tells me the River Rats have been after you to join in their pickup game on Wednesday nights."

"So I've heard, but I don't think the guys really want a woman crashing their night out."

"Then they're fools. Nobody can hit those long jumpers with as much accuracy as you do." She said it because it was true, not because she wanted to flatter Lucy.

But Lucy's expression became guarded. "That was a long time ago. I'm older. Fatter. Slower."

"Aren't we all?" Beth quipped, although Lucy was by no means fat.

She eyed Beth enviously. "You look as if you haven't gained a pound since high school."

"That's what's great about wearing a lab coat. You can hide the extra bulges."

"You never did have to worry about your weight. Can you still eat anything you want and never gain a pound?" Before she could answer, Lucy held up her hand. "No, don't answer that. It's better I don't know."

It was the closest they'd come to having a normal conversation, and Beth didn't want to break the fragile truce. "I'd probably still flunk the physical-fitness test at Riverbend High. I never was as coordinated as you."

"But look at you now. You're working here and I'm at the diner." There was a self-deprecating ring in the words.

"It isn't that great, Lucy. The only people who need me are injured or sick. Look at what you have—a beautiful daughter." She glanced at the sleeping Amber.

Before Beth could say another word, the door leading to the examination rooms opened, and Nathan emerged, followed by Dr. Bennett.

"He's going to have a little difficulty eating tonight, but after the swelling goes down, he should be okay." The doctor explained to Lucy what they'd done and gave her instructions for follow-up care.

"Are you okay?" Lucy asked Nathan after Dr. Bennett had gone.

The boy shrugged. "I guess. It just feels numb right now."

"You heard what Dr. Bennett said—it'll be sore tomorrow," Beth said.

"I hope that means I don't have to go to basketball camp."

Beth wanted to say no, he could stay home, but knew that it wasn't her decision to make. "You'll have to talk to Charlie about that."

He didn't look pleased with the answer and Lucy noticed. "It's a good camp, Nathan."

"Yeah, well, if Charlie hadn't made me go today, I wouldn't have all these stitches in my lip," he complained.

That brought a furrow to Lucy's brow. "It's not Charlie's fault that you fell, Nathan," she said in defense of her brother. Beth could see that one thing hadn't changed. Lucy was still protective of Charlie.

The child on her lap stirred and Lucy said, "Come on, sweetie. Time to wake up." As the little girl opened her eyes, she had that startled look on her face children have when they wake up in a strange place.

Noticing Nathan's presence, she asked sleepily, "Did you see the doctor?"

"Yes, he did, and he's going to be fine." Lucy helped the little girl stand, then looked up at the teenager at her side. "He'll be back playing ball tomorrow as if nothing happened, won't you, big guy?"

Beth could see that Lucy definitely shared Charlie's opinion on the value of the summer program, and Beth felt a need to defend Nathan. "Maybe it would be wise to keep him home tomorrow, Lucy. I know he's got great athletic ability and he probably won't fall again, but just to be safe..." She trailed off, not wanting to sound as if she was interfering, but she was genuinely concerned for him.

To Beth's relief, Lucy noticed the way the teenager's face lit up at her suggestion. She lifted Nathan's chin with her finger and examined the stitches with a critical eye. "I think Beth is right. You'd hate to crack that thing open again."

As the three of them headed for the exit, Beth said goodbye to them, then added, "It was good to see you, Lucy."

Her only response was a lukewarm smile. It bothered Beth that at one time they'd been the best of friends and now they were no more than polite strangers. She missed the girl who'd lived next door to her for the first seventeen years of her life.

Lucy must have been thinking the same thing, because to Beth's surprise she paused at the door and said, "It was good talking to you, too, Beth. If you're in town, stop in at the Sunnyside and we'll have coffee."

"Thanks, I will," Beth managed to say, despite being caught off guard.

"Good. I usually take a break around nine-thirty—that's when it slows a bit."

Beth nodded. "I'll remember that."

BECAUSE SHE'D WORKED an extra day at the clinic, Julian Bennett suggested Beth take Wednesday off. By the time she arrived at the houseboat that evening, she'd already decided that she was going to call Charlie after dinner and suggest that he bring Nathan over the following morning so that he could spend the day with her. But before she had a chance to phone him, the sound of tires on gravel alerted her that someone had come down the road leading to the pier. A glance out the window revealed it was Charlie, and Nathan was with him. Expecting them to come onto the houseboat, she was puzzled when they both climbed out of the cab and stood leaning up against the pickup.

Beth slipped on her sandals and walked out to greet them.

"Hi. I didn't expect to see either of you," she said as she approached the truck. "Is everything all right?" she asked Nathan, wondering if Charlie had brought him over because he had a question about the stitches.

"Everything's fine. We just had something to eat at the Burger Barn and thought we'd stop in for a bit," Charlie answered for both of them.

"Were you able to eat with your mouth like that?" she asked Nathan.

He shrugged. "A little. Mostly I just drank a malt."

Beth gave his arm a reassuring pat. "Today will be the most difficult day, but it'll get easier. Want to come inside?" The invitation was issued to both of them.

"Nathan does, but I don't." Again it was Charlie who answered.

His words produced a little stab of disappointment that she didn't want him to see, so she made her voice extra perky as she said to Nathan, "Good. It gets pretty quiet here in the evening. I could use some company."

"I was hoping you'd say that," Charlie said with a rather furtive grin. Then he turned to Nathan. "Grab your bag and go on inside. I'm going to take Beth for a ride."

A ride? She lifted one eyebrow and stared at him.

Nathan grabbed his backpack from the truck and started up the pier. "Take your time," he said.

Beth faced Charlie and informed him tersely, "You're not taking me anywhere, Charlie Callahan."

"You don't even know where it is I want to take you or how," he argued.

She gave him a suspicious look. "What do you mean, how?"

He crooked his finger and motioned for her to follow him to the back of the pickup. Once there, he opened the tailgate to reveal a bicycle. As Charlie pulled it out, she could see that it was built for not one, but two riders.

"Where did you get that?" she asked as he set it on the ground.

"I'm doing some remodeling work for this guy who owns a bicycle shop. When I told him I needed a peace offering, he suggested this."

"A peace offering?"

"I was wrong about the basketball camp," he told her. "I should have listened to you—and Nathan. If I had, he wouldn't have needed stitches today."

There was no mistaking the guilt in his voice. "He could just as easily have fallen here or anywhere else," she reminded him.

"He could have, but he didn't." His eyes held hers with an unwavering sincerity that made her breath catch in her throat. He was the first one to look away, patting the second seat on the bicycle. "So what do you say? Can I take you for a ride and make up for Saturday night?"

She eyed the tandem cycle. "You really want to go for a ride on this?"

"Why not?"

"Because maybe you don't know how to ride a bike, for one thing."

He chuckled. "Of course I know how. Why would you think I didn't?"

"Because you seldom rode anything but that motorized bike you and Ed were always working on in the garage. You thought you were too cool for 'wheels with no engine,' remember?" she reminded him.

"What? You think that because Ed and I spent every penny of our allowances to buy that moped that we never learned how to pedal a bike? Have you forgotten about that little dirt bike I had—the purple one with all those yellow-and-orange flames painted on the fenders?"

She had forgotten, but now that he'd reminded her, the memory returned and was crystal clear. "Didn't you leave it too close to the street and the garbage truck backed over it?"

"Yes, which is why I never had another bike. My parents refused to buy me one after that fiasco. They said I'd been careless, and if I was going to get a new one, I'd have to buy it myself."

"And so you bought the motorbike."

He smiled wistfully. "Ed talked me into it."

"I'm sure," she retorted with a healthy dose of sarcasm. She studied the tandem bicycle. "So this is your idea of a peace offering?"

"I remember how you and Lucy used to love riding bikes when you were kids."

She smiled at the memory. "We did. We used to have a contest to see who could ride the farthest without hands."

"And who'd win?"

"Who do you think?"

He grinned and her heart flipped over. "Lucy. She always was more athletic than you."

"You mean I was always the uncoordinated one," she retorted.

"No, you're weren't. You ever been on one of these things before?" he asked, turning the bicycle around so that it was facing the road.

"No."

"Me, neither. You willing to give it a try?" He straddled the front portion of the bike.

She glanced up at the road. "It's not easy to pedal on a gravel road."

"We can do it," he said confidently. "Come on."

"You expect me to sit behind you?" She could hardly believe she was considering going for a ride with him.

He lifted his leg away from the frame and positioned himself next to the rear seat. "You can have the front. But that means you'll be responsible for steering," he warned.

When she hesitated, he cajoled her again. "Come on. It'll be fun."

She knew he was right. It would be fun. So she grabbed the handlebars, lifted her leg over the center bar and said, "Okay. We're going to have to start at the same time or this isn't going to work."

"I'm ready when you are," he said from over her shoulder.

"All right. On three. One, two…" She sat on the leather seat, kept one foot on the ground and placed the other on the pedal. On three she pushed on both of the pedals. Their start was a bit wobbly, but to her surprise, after only a few jiggly moments, the bike moved smoothly. She narrowly missed a huge oak on the way out of the drive, but once they hit the gravel road, she managed to keep them on a straight path.

"Hey—I think we've got it!" he declared with an enthusiasm she shared.

"This is great. Where are we going?"

"Turn right at the fork in the road up ahead," he instructed. "I want to show you something."

"Isn't this a private road?" she asked as she followed his instructions.

"Yes, but I know the owner. He won't mind if we use it."

They rode past fields of corn ready to be harvested, the silks gleaming like gold in the setting sunlight. Beth loved the month of August when the crops were fully grown and standing majestically in the fields.

"Can we stop?" Without waiting for a reply, she squeezed the handbrakes.

"Stop for what?" Charlie asked when she put her feet on the ground.

"I just want to look at the corn. Isn't it incredible?" She pointed at what seemed to be endless rows of stalks.

Charlie leaned forward, resting his arms on the handlebars. "Wasn't your grandfather a farmer?"

"Mm-hm." She stood there gazing at the fields, thinking back to her childhood and those visits to the farm. "I remember he used to say to me, 'If you think you're a big shot, all you have to do is stand next to the corn at harvest time and you'll see what a little shot you really are.'"

"You never thought you were a big shot, did you?"

"Not me," she said with a sly grin. She shaded her eyes with her hand and turned to the west. "It looks like a great crop this year, doesn't it?"

"The weather's been good." He let her stand there for a while longer before saying, "So, have we admired the corn long enough—can we continue our journey now?"

"Where exactly is this journey taking us?" she asked as they started pedaling again.

"I told you. I want to show you something."

They continued down the road until they came to a wooded area she recognized as the Duncan homestead. When they'd been in high school, the place had been owned by an old farmer named Otis Duncan, but he'd died shortly after her graduation, and the house had been abandoned.

"It's just on the other side of these trees," Charlie told her, instructing her to keep going.

The road curved around the trees to the spot where the Duncan farmhouse had stood. In place of the ramshackle building was a beautiful modern two-story brick house with a porch that ran the length of the front.

"Did you build this?" she asked as they rolled to a stop.

"Unfortunately I can't take credit for this." They dismounted and he propped the bike against a tree. "It belongs to a guy named Hargraves who flew in an architect from Chicago to create his ideal country home."

"No kidding," Beth said, admiring the exquisitely carved railings on the porch. "Should we be here? I mean, it is his home.'' She glanced nervously about to see if anyone was there.

''Relax. He and his wife are on vacation.''

''At this time of year?''

''He's not a farmer.''

''But the corn on the way in here...''

''...is somebody else's. He rents out the land. But this house isn't why I brought you here. Come.'' He waved for her to follow him around to the back of the house. ''*That* is what I've been building for him.'' He pointed.

Beth gasped. ''Omigosh! It's adorable.'' Sitting next to wooden playground equipment was a playhouse that was a replica of the Hargraveses' farmhouse. From the gabled cedar roof to the carvings on the porch railings, nearly every detail was the same.

''I take it Hargraves has a daughter,'' Beth said as she stepped onto the miniature wooden porch and peered in the windows.

''Isabelle.'' He dug into his pocket for a set of keys. ''Come on. You can have a mini-tour.''

Beth felt like a child herself when she entered the tiny house. Everything inside was in miniature, from the fireplace in the family room to the built-in hutch in the dining area. Although Beth and Charlie could walk inside, the house was designed for people half their size.

''Electric lights,'' Charlie announced, flipping a switch that made the tiny brass chandelier glow. ''And we wouldn't want Isabelle to catch cold.'' He pointed to a thermostat on the wall.

''Does she have air-conditioning, too?''

''No, just heat.'' He shoved his hands into his

jeans pockets. "I guess Mr. Hargraves figures she can open the windows if she gets warm."

"This is incredible." Beth ran her fingers over the marble countertop in the kitchen. "I wonder if Isabelle will appreciate this."

"We'll soon find out. I just need to varnish some of the woodwork and finish putting up a few trim boards, and it'll be all hers," Charlie told her. "The plan is to have it done by the time they return from their holiday next week."

Beth gave the little place one final appraisal, then stepped back outside. "You do beautiful work, Charlie."

"You think so?"

"Of course I think so." She waved her hand to encompass the house. "Just look at this." She shook her head in amazement. "I would have loved a house like this when I was a kid."

"You mean, instead of the blankets and cushions you and Lucy used to build your playhouse?" he said with a half smile.

"I'm surprised you remember that."

"I remember a lot of stuff about you, Beth. We were pretty close when we were kids."

The way he was looking at her made her pulse flutter. "That's what happens when you're next-door neighbors," she said lightly. Feeling uncomfortable, she stepped down off the porch and surveyed the view of the river. "I can see why Mr. Hargraves likes it here. It's peaceful, isn't it?"

"Yes, it is. That's why I brought you here." She knew he had walked up behind her and stood close to her, but she didn't turn around.

"The peace offering," she murmured in acknowledgment.

"Beth, I'm sorry." His voice was as smooth as velvet and sent little prickles of awareness up and down her flesh.

"It's all right. I know you meant well with Nathan. You hoped he would take to basketball the way most of the River Rats did," she said, not wanting to make any more out of this moment than what it was—an apology for their argument on Saturday night.

But then he said, "I am sorry about that, but it's not why I'm apologizing."

Puzzled, she turned to face him.

"I'm sorry for what happened to us. It was all my fault and I want to apologize."

CHAPTER ELEVEN

"YOU DON'T OWE ME any apologies, Charlie."

"Then why is it that every time we're together, I get the feeling I should be doing something to make up for the pain I caused you?"

"Is that the real reason you keep coming around? To appease your guilty conscience?" she demanded, her eyes darkening with emotion.

Charlie never expected that she'd make his apology seem like an insult. "No, I don't have a guilty conscience about us."

"Well, good. Because I don't, either," she said sharply, much too sharply for Charlie not to question whether it was the truth.

It annoyed him that he couldn't even apologize to her without having tension between them. "Did you ever think that maybe I come around simply because I like to talk to the girl who lived next door to me for most of my life?"

"That girl is gone, Charlie," she said quietly, turning away from him.

He could see she was extremely ill at ease with the conversation. She kept shifting from foot to foot and rubbing her elbow. He knew from experience that whenever she was nervous, her right hand found her left elbow and slowly massaged it.

Reaching for her shoulders, he turned her around to face him again. "I don't think she is."

"You're wrong. The thing that happened between us that summer? That was the end of the girl next door." She took a step back, and this time her hands clutched both elbows.

"It wasn't a *thing*, Beth. It was a marriage."

"No. We were just kids who got caught doing something we shouldn't have been doing." She paused. "And I really don't want to talk about this." She started walking around to the front of the Hargraveses' house.

"Maybe circumstances forced us to get married, but it was a marriage," he argued, following her. "We had a wedding ceremony and we lived together as husband and wife for four weeks, which was why we had a divorce. We were legally married."

"All right, so it was a marriage," she shot back, but she kept on marching.

Annoyed by her attitude, he grabbed her arm. "Will you stop running away from any discussion about us?"

She stopped and faced him. "Us? There is no *us*, Charlie."

He should have shown her just what *us* there was still between them. If he kissed her right now, he knew she'd respond the same way she had on Saturday night. As much as she wanted to deny there was anything between them, he knew he could prove her wrong. And he was tempted to do just that. She'd never looked more alluring than she did at that moment, her cheeks rosy, her dark curls in disarray.

Before she could blink an eye, he could cover those beautiful bow-shaped lips with his mouth and kiss her until she wanted him as much as he wanted her. And he did want her.

But something stopped him. Pride. He knew he could kiss her, even make love to her, and it wouldn't change a thing. She'd still say there was nothing between them. She'd leave at the end of summer and forget that anything had happened between them, just as she'd done fifteen years ago.

It was a sobering thought.

Ever since Beth had returned to Riverbend, he'd been tormented by memories of the good times they'd shared. And each time he saw her, a little ray of hope encouraged him to forget that the only reason they'd gotten married was that she'd been pregnant. When that reason no longer existed, she'd wanted to leave. Instead of staying together and trying to work things out, she'd gone away to school. To pursue her dreams.

That was what had hurt him the most. Her dreams hadn't included him.

And they still didn't. If he was foolish enough to think they might, her actions right now were enough to convince him he was only asking for trouble. She'd given him plenty of indications that the only thing the two of them were ever going to share was the houseboat—and even that partnership she wanted to end.

Feeling defeated, he let go of her arm. ''It'll be getting dark soon. We should head back.''

She didn't disagree, but continued heading to the front of the house and the tandem bicycle. The ride back to the houseboat had none of the laughter they'd shared on the way out. No stopping to gaze at the majestic cornfields, no teasing glances.

When they reached the marina, he loaded the bike into the pickup. Just as she was about to step onto the pier, he said, "Beth, before you go inside, I'd like to talk to you."

Wearily she asked, "What is it?"

"It's about Nathan. I'm worried about him being home alone during the day while I'm at work. I know you've offered to have him come here."

"Yes, on the days I'm not working at the clinic," she confirmed. "Do you want him to come tomorrow? Normally I work Wednesdays, but because I worked today, I'm off tomorrow."

"If it's not a problem for you, I'd appreciate it. I'm going to be working on Isabelle's playhouse, and I could drop him off in the morning."

"It's no problem at all," she told him. "Does this mean you're not going to make him go back to the basketball camp?"

Charlie shoved his hands in his pockets. "There doesn't seem to be any point, does there? It's really a shame, because Aaron Mazerik is running a great program."

"I don't doubt that he is."

"Maybe after the lip heals Nathan'll want to go back."

"Maybe," she said noncommittally.

He smiled and shook his head. "Who am I kidding? He doesn't want to play basketball." He sighed. "Maybe I'll have to give work another try. I'll bring him to the job site with me."

"Is there a reason he can't stay alone? He is fourteen, and it's not as though he's gotten into any trouble since he's been here, has he? Don't you feel you can trust him on his own?''

''I do think I can trust him, but I still believe he needs to get involved with something, hang out with kids his own age.''

She smiled then for the first time since they'd left the playhouse. ''That sounds like Charlie the extrovert talking. You always did like a crowd.''

''Is there something wrong with that?''

''No, but not everyone wants to be with people all the time. Some of us prefer our own company or that of a few close friends.''

''Nathan has his own company an awful lot of the time. That's one of the reasons I pushed the basketball camp.''

''I understand your concern. There must be someone here in Riverbend he wants to spend time with.''

''Well, there is. You. He told me so.''

''Really?'' She looked surprised. ''I'm amazed he told you that after I called you and reported that he'd skipped out on camp yesterday.''

''It's true.''

She turned and glanced at the houseboat, perhaps thinking about the teenager inside. ''He's not a bad kid, Charlie.''

''I know that. I've known him for four years, and I can honestly say he's a great kid. This is just a difficult time in his life right now.''

She nodded. ''It's like he's adrift, floating on the river but not sure where the current is taking him. I don't think he knows if he should get out of the water, try to go back upstream, look for another boat...'' She seemed embarrassed all of a sudden. ''Probably not the greatest metaphor.''

"I think it's an appropriate one. Nathan *is* adrift, and I guess my job is to see if he can put his feet on solid ground."

"I'd like to help if I can."

He wanted to ask why, but thought it better not to question her motives. "Thank you. I appreciate that. So...shall I drop him off tomorrow morning?"

"Sure. That'll be fine. I'm up early, so don't worry about the time."

He chuckled. "I'll be lucky if I can get him out of bed by eight."

"Maybe he should spend the night here. It would eliminate that problem."

"Are you sure you wouldn't mind?"

"I wouldn't have suggested it if I did," she answered.

He knew that was the truth. Beth was forthright. "I wouldn't be a humane individual if I didn't tell you that having a fourteen year old in the house can be damaging to your sanity," he warned.

"I think if my sanity can survive working with college kids, it can take one teenager overnight," she assured him. "I suppose we should ask Nathan if he wants to sleep here," she added.

Charlie grinned. "Do you think there's a chance he won't want to watch nonstop music videos till the wee hours of the morning?"

"Hey—even I have my limit," she replied, a smile in her voice. She turned again to look at the houseboat. "I'm surprised we can't hear the music out here."

"Maybe he's reading a book," Charlie suggested facetiously.

She waved her arm. "Come on in. We'll find out."

As Charlie followed her down the pier, he thought about how good it felt to be with her. It was as if they were kids again, enjoying the friendly camaraderie they'd always shared.

Only, he wanted more than camaraderie with Beth. And this evening had shown him just how unlikely a possibility that was.

BETH DECIDED that having a fourteen year old in the house wasn't nearly as dangerous to her mental health as Charlie had warned. Contrary to what they both thought, Nathan did not stay up half the night watching music videos. What kept him up late was the video game Charlie had rented for him. He spent hours killing space aliens, and Beth helped him.

Normally video games didn't interest her, but she was feeling extremely sympathetic toward Nathan because of his stitches. When he said there were only two things he wanted before he went to bed—a bowl of ice cream and a chance to play his video game with a partner—Beth couldn't say no to either request.

She hadn't played any electronic games since she was a teenager, and as a result was a bit overwhelmed by the technology and graphics. Being a novice, she found her reaction skills were much slower than Nathan's, which meant he crushed her character in nearly every game they played. She knew, however, that experience didn't always provide the edge in annihilating the opponent. Bike races with Lucy had taught her that.

Sometimes luck played a part in a victory, along

with a desire to win. Always a fierce competitor, Beth rose to the challenge and gave the game her undivided attention. As her losses mounted in the early games, she became more determined to win at least one contest.

By the time she finally was able to declare victory, it was past one o'clock in the morning. She should have felt guilty for keeping Nathan up so late, but judging by the color on his cheeks and the sparkle in his eyes, it had been a therapeutic night.

As Charlie predicted, Nathan slept in the following morning. Beth was about to make herself some breakfast when she decided she'd accept the challenge Lucy had issued—and challenge was exactly the way she saw her childhood friend's invitation. After a quick shower, she dressed and left Nathan a note, telling him she'd be back around noon.

All the way to the Sunnyside Café she was filled with apprehension, wondering if she wasn't making a mistake thinking she could renew a friendship that had self-destructed so many years ago. But then she remembered the warm feeling she'd had when she'd talked with Lucy at the clinic, and she knew in her heart that if she didn't give it a try, she'd never know if their friendship was truly dead and buried.

Outside the café door Beth hesitated, but Lucy chose that moment to glance toward the entrance. When she noticed Beth, she waved for her to come inside. With a deep breath, Beth pushed open the door and crossed to the counter.

"Hi. Is this a good time for you to take a break?" she asked in a nervous rush.

"It's fine. If you want to sit down, I'll be right over. Are you ordering any food?"

Beth didn't feel much like eating anything. "Maybe just some toast. Whole wheat. And a cup of coffee—decaf."

Lucy grinned. "Got it." She tended to a customer at the counter and Beth searched for a vacant booth. There was one close to the cashier.

As she sat down, Evie Mazerik leaned over and said, "How are you doing, Beth?"

"I'm doing fine, thank you," she answered, setting her purse beside her on the bench seat. "How about you?"

"I'm good. How's Grace's mother?"

"She's getting better. Thanks for asking."

The redhead went on to tell Beth about a friend of hers who'd broken her leg and was recovering nicely. It was only when a customer came to pay a check that Evie had to return to her spot behind the cash register.

It wasn't long before Lucy was setting two cups of coffee down on the table.

"Tina will bring out our food when it's ready," she said, sliding onto the seat across from Beth. She took a sip of coffee and sighed. "It's been a busy morning. I didn't expect to see you here."

Beth was caught off guard by Lucy's straightforwardness, but she could see that Lucy was as nervous as she was. It was there in the brisk actions of her hands as she lifted her cup and played with the spoon on the saucer.

The best approach, Beth decided, was to simply be honest. She was not one to play games or beat around the bush.

"We used to be good friends, Lucy. Really good friends," she began.

"That was when we were kids," Lucy said, avoiding her eyes as she spoke.

"Yes, it was, and I know that a lot has happened since then, and not all of it good." She put her hands in her lap so Lucy wouldn't see that she had to clasp them to keep them from trembling. "The last time we talked—that Christmas I came home from college—we both said things I wish we hadn't."

Lucy didn't respond, but sat staring into her coffee cup as if the dark brown liquid held the words she needed. Beth waited for her to make some comment—any comment—but none was forthcoming.

"I went through some pretty heavy stuff that summer after graduation," Beth continued, "and I know it wasn't easy for us to talk about it...because of Charlie."

"He *is* my brother," Lucy said defensively.

Beth forced a smile. "And that's not going to change. But this isn't about Charlie, Lucy. Don't you ever wish things could be different between us?"

"You're making this really awkward, Beth." Lucy glanced around nervously, as if worried others might overhear their conversation.

"I'm sorry, I'm not trying to make you uncomfortable. I'm trying to apologize and to tell you that I don't like it that we can't be in the same room together without feeling we should run in opposite directions."

Lucy continued to fidget with her cup and spoon. "But after everything that's happened..."

Lucy met her eyes then, and Beth saw the same uncertainty she knew was in her own. "Fifteen years is a long time to be angry, Lucy."

"I'm not angry anymore, Beth."

"Good, because Charlie and I have come to terms with what happened. Don't you think *we* should be able to?"

"You and Charlie have been seeing each other?" The defensiveness crept back into Lucy's voice.

"Only because of the boat. And then there's Nathan. You probably heard that the day he skipped basketball he came to the *Queen Mary*."

"That's Charlie's fault. He should make it perfectly clear the boat's off-limits unless he's with him." She took a sip of her coffee and for once didn't fidget with her spoon. "I do think that Nathan should go to Aaron's camp, though. One of my neighbors has both of her sons enrolled and she's had nothing but good things to say about it."

"I'm sure it's a great camp, but Nathan doesn't want to go," Beth said.

Lucy sighed. "I guess there's no sense pushing a kid into sports if he doesn't want to participate, is there," she stated soberly. "Remember Janey Lipitz?"

"The one whose mom was determined to make her the star center on the JV basketball team?"

"The poor thing was a nervous wreck. She hated coming to practice."

"Yeah, she'd always complain of a sore ankle or a sore knee or a sore something. I spent more time helping her with her noninjuries than I did with the girls who really needed attention," Beth reflected.

"You always did like taking care of people. Even back in grade school you were the first one to the rescue when kids fell in the playground." There was a hint of admiration in her voice, and Beth felt the first stirrings of hope.

"Thank goodness I was good at something. I never would have made it on my athletic ability. Remember how long it took me to learn how to dribble and run?"

Lucy grinned. "I do recall a few nosebleeds on the way to success."

"I should have known it was a sign I should learn how to sit on the bench without getting a sore rear end."

That caused Lucy to laugh outright. "You weren't that bad."

"Yes, I was. Don't you remember the free-throw contest they had when we were in fifth grade? That one shot I threw hit the teacher in the face."

Lucy gasped in delight. "That's right! You did! I had forgotten about that. That was so funny."

"For the other kids in school maybe, but for me it was embarrassing."

"Is that why you don't think Nathan should have to go to basketball camp? Are you worried he'll embarrass himself?"

"Not really. Charlie says he's a natural." Just then the waitress arrived with their food.

When she'd gone, Lucy said, "I thought someone like you who worked in athletics would encourage a talented kid to go to camp."

"That's just it. I've worked in athletics long enough to know that if the desire to play isn't there, it doesn't matter how much talent someone has. And it sounds like Nathan's troubles won't be solved by going to a basketball camp."

Lucy's brow wrinkled. "You know about that?"

"Only that he lost his mother last year and he's been struggling at school." As Beth spread strawberry jam on her toast, she took the opportunity to ask about Nathan's background. "Lucy, you've known Nathan for a while. Charlie said he and his mother lived here before she died. He must have made friends then, didn't he?"

Lucy reached for the syrup to pour over her French toast. "He was always on the quiet side. He and my Rebecca are in the same grade. She was in his sixth-grade class. Said he pretty much kept to himself at school."

"It's hard to believe you have a daughter who's fourteen," Beth said.

"Actually, she's thirteen. She was born the summer after Michael and I were married," she said, her face losing some of its glow.

"I'm sorry about Michael," Beth said quietly. "Ed told me he was awarded a commendation of bravery posthumously."

She nodded. "He died trying to protect a woman from her abusive husband, but you knew Michael. That's the kind of guy he was. Always thinking about others first and always trying to protect women. That's why I loved him."

"It must have been a difficult time for you."

She sighed again. "It was, but everyone in Riverbend was so supportive. People I hardly knew sent cards and money and flowers...I guess because he was a cop."

"He was a good man."

Lucy's eyes had a faraway look as she said, "It seems so long ago, as if it happened in another lifetime, yet I can still remember what he said to me that last morning I saw him.''

"What was that?''

Lucy didn't answer, but sat staring out the window, as if lost in her thoughts.

"Lucy, are you all right?'' Beth finally asked.

She jerked her head. "Yeah, I'm fine.'' Then she returned the subject to Nathan. "Fourteen can be a difficult age for boys. They're too old to be with the little kids, but not old enough to hang out with the older teens. Charlie's got his hands full, that's for sure.''

Beth nodded. "I've offered to help out but I'm not sure what I can do.''

Lucy swallowed a bite of French toast, then said, "He's really not your responsibility, is he?''

"No, you're right. He's not, but...'' Beth wasn't sure how to explain the way she felt.

And Lucy didn't appear interested in understanding the situation, for out of the blue she asked, "How long are you planning to stay in Riverbend?''

"I told Dr. Bennett I'd fill in at the clinic until the end of the month.''

They chatted about people in the town while they finished their breakfast. It wasn't an uncomfortable atmosphere, but Beth felt as if the warmth that had sparked when they'd been talking about their youth was gone.

When Lucy announced she'd better finish her coffee and get back to work, Beth said, "I'm glad we had this chance to talk.''

"Yeah, me, too. It was nice.''

Not wanting to lose what little camaraderie they'd

found, she added, "We share a lot of good memories, Lucy."

Her friend didn't contradict her. "I know. It's just that we're not the same people we were fifteen years ago."

"You're right, we're not. You're a mother—"

"—and you're a career woman," she finished for Beth, as if that put them on different planets.

Beth sensed it was a criticism, but tried to dismiss it with a smile. "I always was a workaholic, wasn't I?"

"You had different goals than I did, Beth, which is probably the real reason our friendship came apart." This wasn't said with bitterness, just matter-of-factly.

"Does it have to be apart? I know we can't pretend that everything is like it was when we lived next door to each other, but isn't it worth trying to see if the people we are today can't have just as much fun?"

Lucy eyed her curiously. "Why is this so important to you?"

"Because yesterday when I saw you at the clinic and we started talking, I realized that I've missed my friend Lucy."

Just then one of the waitresses called out, "Hey, Lucy, we could use you up here."

Lucy glanced toward the kitchen, then did a quick survey of the café. "I've got to get back to work. Midmorning crowd is here." She stood and automatically cleared the dishes.

"Will you think about what I said?" Beth asked.

"Sure." Before leaving she smiled and said, "I miss my friend Beth, too."

BETH EXPECTED Nathan would be sitting in front of the big-screen TV when she got back to the houseboat. He wasn't. Nor was he outside. It was only when she saw the note on the counter that she realized he was gone.

It read: ''Went with Charlie. Be home after lunch.''

Beth frowned. Had Charlie come and taken Nathan to help him work at the playhouse?

Deciding to take advantage of her free time, Beth ran a few errands in town. This time when she returned, Nathan was home. He was outside lying facedown on the dock, his arms and head extending out over the water.

It was only as she got closer that she realized what he was doing. In his hands was the end of a loaf of bread. He was crumbling it into little pieces and feeding the ducks that swam next to the dock.

''Looks like you have some visitors,'' Beth said when she spotted the mama and her ducklings.

''They like bread. My grandpa told me.''

''Looks like your grandpa knows what he's talking about,'' Beth said as the tiny beaks plucked the bread crumbs from the water. ''I have a question for you.''

''Shoot,'' he said without looking up at her.

''Is there anybody you'd like to see in Riverbend? Any friends?''

''You sound like Charlie. He thinks I should hang out with the kids from my old school.''

''Would that be such a bad idea?''

He shrugged. ''It depends on who they are.''

He continued feeding the ducks and seemed in no

hurry to tell Beth where he'd been. Finally she asked, "I saw your note. You went with Charlie?"

"Yeah. It was really cool. He wanted to show me this brand-new video arcade that just opened."

"Charlie took you to play video games in the middle of the day?"

"Yeah. He said he needed a break from work. He told me he used to do that all the time when he was younger—you know, stop working in the middle of the day to have some fun."

Beth smiled. That sounded more like the Charlie she used to know. "So who won?"

"I did mostly, but I let him win a couple," Nathan said with a sly grin. "And Eric won a couple, too."

"Eric?"

"Yeah, he's this kid who was in my sixth-grade class. He used to be a geek, but he's pretty cool now. Charlie took us to lunch at the Burger Barn."

"Sounds like you had fun."

"Yup." He jumped up and brushed the crumbs from his jeans. "Would you care if I took more bread for the ducks?"

"No, go ahead," she said, still mulling over the fact that Charlie had stopped work to spend time with Nathan.

When he came to pick the teenager up that evening, Beth and Nathan were in the midst of dinner preparations.

"We're having pizza. Want some?" Nathan asked, his fingers buried in the lump of dough.

"You're welcome to stay for dinner," Beth seconded.

"I'm dirty," Charlie answered, glancing down at his work clothes.

"Take a shower here," Nathan suggested.

"You can," Beth added. "It *is* your shower, too."

"That would be great except I don't have any clean clothes," Charlie said. "Why don't I go home, get cleaned up and come back? That won't be done for a while, will it?"

"At the rate we're going, I'd say you've got plenty of time," Beth replied.

"Yeah. We haven't even chopped the veggies for the topping," Nathan added.

"All right. I'll go home, shower and come right back."

"Could I talk to you for a minute before you go?" Beth asked, then followed him out onto the deck.

"What is it?"

"Nathan told me about your trip to the video arcade."

"And you disapprove. I know, he should be working," Charlie said, not allowing her to finish.

"I didn't say that."

"But it's what you're thinking, right?"

She glared at him. "You've learned mind reading along with carpentry since I've been gone?"

"I've always been able to read your mind," he shot back.

"This time you're reading the wrong page, Charlie. Taking Nathan to the video arcade was a good idea, and I know why you did it."

"Because I like having fun," he answered for her.

"Because you wanted him to meet up with some of his old friends. And it worked, didn't it?"

"He did see one boy from his sixth-grade class," Charlie admitted.

Just then Nathan called, "Beth, the timer's buzzing."

"I've got to go. You go shower and come back. We'll talk later."

Beth and Nathan were outside on the deck when Charlie returned. As soon as she heard his truck, Beth slipped inside to stick the pizza in the oven. She thought she could make it back outside before he reached the houseboat, but she was wrong. When she turned around, he was right behind her in the tiny kitchen. In his hand he carried a bunch of flowers.

"For you."

"What for?" she asked ungraciously.

"For baby-sitting Nathan today," he told her.

Nathan, who'd been fishing off the rear deck, had come in right behind him. "I don't need a baby-sitter."

Beth sniffed the flowers appreciatively. "Nathan's right. He doesn't need a baby-sitter."

"All right. Poor choice of words. Thank you for teaching Nathan how to make pizza." He looked at the boy and said, "There. Is that better?"

During dinner Nathan told Beth how much fun he'd had with Charlie at the arcade, and then divulged to Charlie how he and Beth had stayed up past one in the morning playing video games. When he offered to do the dishes after they'd finished eating, Beth accepted graciously.

Charlie suggested he and Beth sit outside, since

it was such a beautiful summer evening. As soon as they were alone, he commented on the video games.

"You were up until one in the morning playing video games?"

"I knew his mouth was hurting," she explained.

Charlie grinned. "You can't fool me. I remember playing games with you and Lucy. You like to win."

"Yes, I do," she confessed with a matching grin.

He reached for her hand. "It's very sweet of you to care about him. I know you didn't come to Riverbend to look after a kid you hardly know."

She pulled her hand away. "He's a good kid. He really likes it here on the boat. Actually I think the boat's the reason for the change in him. You two are the ones who should be staying here, not me."

"It's funny you should mention it, because that's exactly what I've been thinking."

She frowned. "You want me to move out?"

"No. Don't be silly. I wouldn't ask you to do that, not with Ed and Grace's situation being what it is. I have another idea."

Beth felt little shivers of apprehension travel up her spine. "You have?"

"Yes. What would you think about Nathan and me moving onto the houseboat with you?"

CHAPTER TWELVE

"YOU'RE JOKING, right?" Beth asked, although judging by the look on Charlie's face, he was dead serious.

"This is my houseboat, too," he reminded her.

"Yes, but...but...we *both* can't stay here at the same time!"

"Why not? You and I managed to spend a weekend here without any fur flying."

It wasn't the fur flying she was worried about. Quite the opposite. It was the kissing and the fact that whenever she was with him, she wanted to revive those girlish dreams....

She shook her head. "It's not a good idea."

"You just said it would be great for Nathan."

"For Nathan, yes. For us, no."

"What are you afraid of, Beth?"

"I'm not afraid," she lied. "We *can't* live together, Charlie. It wouldn't be right."

"We wouldn't be *living* together. We'd be sharing living quarters."

She shook her head. "It wouldn't work. Look, if you and Nathan want to use the boat, I'll find another place to live."

"No, you have just as much right to stay here as I have," he argued. "It would only be for a few weeks. Nathan goes back to West Lafayette at the end of August. When you think about it, there'll be little time for us to even be on the boat together. I spend a lot of hours working, and you spend most of your free time with Ed and Grace.''

She knew he was right. They'd hardly see each other. She could make sure she was gone by the time he arrived home each night. Except she'd have to sleep there. They both would. *But so would Nathan,* a little voice reminded her.

''I wouldn't expect you to cook for us,'' he added. ''We could pretty much go our separate ways. You do your thing. We do ours.''

Beth glanced back at the houseboat and saw Nathan's head through the window. He was at the sink rinsing the dishes. There was no doubt in her mind that he would jump at the chance to move on board. She also knew that staying on the houseboat would be good for him.

Charlie noticed the direction of her glance. ''I wouldn't ask except you saw the way Nathan was when I first brought him to Riverbend. He was sullen and distant. Now look at him. He finally seems to be fitting in around here.''

Beth couldn't argue that. The only alternative she could offer was, ''He could stay with me.''

Charlie shook his head. ''That's not a good idea. The judge made me responsible for him, not you. And it rather defeats the point of his coming to Riverbend if I don't ever see him. I'm trying to rebuild the relationship I had with him before he moved to West Lafayette.''

She turned and stared out at the river. It crept past serenely in the twilight, giving the false impression that it was harmless. Beth thought that Charlie was a lot like the river. When he spoke to her in that quiet smooth tone, she tended to believe he was safe, but she knew he was a threat to her heart.

She wanted to say no to his suggestion. She knew she should say no, but she found herself saying, "All right. We'll share the boat."

His delighted grin made her feel as if that was the only answer she could have given.

"Thanks, Beth. It'll work out. You'll see."

TO BETH'S AMAZEMENT, it did work. As Charlie predicted, their paths seldom crossed. Nathan, on the other hand, was always around. Beth was glad. The better she got to know the teenager, the more facets of his personality she discovered. And liked. He was a special kid.

On several occasions Beth had seen him sketching, but every time he noticed her interest, he'd shoved the pad out of sight. Not wanting to intrude on his personal space, she hadn't asked him about his artwork.

Then one afternoon, when she came home from visiting Grace, she found him sitting on the dock sketching. This time when she approached, he didn't put his paper and pencil away.

That gave her the courage to ask, "What are you drawing?"

Automatically he hunkered over his paper, shielding it, but after only a couple of seconds he lifted the sketch pad for her appraisal. It was the river, with reeds and low-growing shrubs in the background, but it was the creature in the center that caught Beth's eye. It looked to be half human, half amphibian.

"It's going to be a cartoon," he told her.

"Nathan, this is very good," she said. "The detail is exceptional."

He looked a bit self-conscious. "Lots of kids draw cartoons."

"I'm sure they do, but I don't think many of them are as good as this. Do you take art in school?"

"Yeah, but I'm not very good. I got a C last semester because I didn't get all my work done on time."

Beth found it unbelievable that someone with such talent could get a C in art class. "Do you have more drawings?"

He nodded and took the sketch pad from her. "They start here," he said, flipping back the pages.

As Beth studied the drawings, she realized that he had created a story. Captions beneath the pictures told the tale of a creature who'd been living at the bottom of the river since prehistoric times. Beth read with fascination, amazed that Nathan could not only draw so well, but compose such a compelling story.

"Nathan, these are wonderful. Have you shown them to anyone else?"

"Just some of my friends," he said with an awkward shrug.

"You haven't shown them to Charlie?"

"Uh-uh. He thinks art is for sissies."

"What makes you say that?"

He shrugged. "I just know he does."

Beth couldn't imagine what Charlie could have said or done to give the boy such an impression, but she found herself defending her ex-husband. "I don't think you're right about that, Nathan. A good friend of his is an artist, and I've never heard him say anything negative about her work.''

''Yeah, *her* work. It's different if the artist's a girl.''

''Have you met Lily Holden?''

''I don't think so.''

''Maybe you should,'' she suggested, an idea forming in her head. ''I'll tell you what, Nathan. I won't say anything to Charlie about your artwork, but I do want to talk to Lily.''

''Why?''

''Because she understands what it means to be an artist. Would it be all right if I called and invited her over?''

He looked uneasy. ''She might think these are dumb.''

''If I thought that was true, I certainly wouldn't ask her to look at them, would I? I think she's going to be as impressed as I am.''

He hesitated, seeming very unsure of himself. ''You really think they're good?''

''Yes, I do,'' she answered honestly. ''Would you mind if I called Lily?''

He looked as if he wanted to say no, but finally he shrugged and said, ''I guess it's okay.''

''Great. I'll go see if I can find her number.''

It took only a few minutes for Beth to track down Lily's phone number. A quick call produced the desired results. When Beth asked Lily if she would come to the houseboat to see Nathan's work, Lily said she'd be happy to oblige, but suggested it might be better for Nathan to visit her. That way he could see what an artist's studio looked like and also view some of her work.

Beth knew Nathan was apprehensive about the visit. All the way to Lily's he fidgeted in the seat next to Beth, asking the same question over and over again. "What if she says it's bad?"

"It's not bad," Beth told him each time he asked, knowing that until he'd received Lily's approval, it really didn't matter what she said.

Lily was waiting for them on the veranda of her Victorian home on East Oak Street. As Beth parked out front, she waved a welcome.

"Beth, hi." Lily gave her a warm smile and a hug. Then she turned to Nathan and said, "Hi, Nathan, remember me?"

"Oh, yeah. Hi, Lily." Nathan seemed a little less nervous.

"You two know each other?" Beth asked.

"We met at the ball park that night Lucy's daughter was playing T-ball," Lily replied.

They chatted on the sidewalk a few minutes until Lily said, "Let's go inside and I can give Nathan a tour of my studio."

Beth was grateful Lily didn't press Nathan to show her his drawings—not that she'd expected she would. Anyone could see from the way he was clutching his sketch pad that he was feeling uncertain about allowing anyone to look at his work.

Lily's studio was on the second floor. Light and airy with lots of windows, it did more to make Nathan feel at ease than any words either Beth or Lily could say.

"You painted that?" Nathan stood in front of an easel, admiring an acrylic painting of a river.

"It's a view of the Sycamore from Riverside Park," Lily explained.

"I know. I've been there and seen that tree," he said, referring to an oak that had been split in two by lightning.

"These are some that are a little more abstract," she said, indicating a collection of finished canvasses. "I've been matting them and getting them ready for the art show."

"You're having an exhibit of your work?" Beth asked.

Lily nodded. "Kate McMann has offered to let me show some of my work at the bookstore. The date's not firm yet, but when it is, I hope you'll come." The invitation was extended to both of them.

"I'd like that," Beth told her.

"Yeah, me, too," Nathan said.

Lily talked about how she'd always wanted to be an art teacher when she was younger, but it wasn't until a few months ago that she'd actually started painting again. She didn't press Nathan to show her his work, but gave him time to relax, encouraging him to talk about the kind of art he enjoyed.

Eventually he opened his sketchbook. Beth stepped back and allowed the two of them to talk. Hearing the way Lily spoke to Nathan, Beth knew that the woman would make a wonderful teacher; it was no surprise to her that Nathan responded the way he did.

Finally Lily said, "Well, I think we've bored Beth long enough with our art talk. Why don't we go downstairs and I'll get us some lemonade?" Noticing that Nathan's eyes were on her bookcase, she said, "Would you like to take a couple of those books with you?"

"You wouldn't mind?"

"No. Here. Let me show you a few I think you'd enjoy." She bent to look at the books, pulling several out and handing them to Nathan. "These are some of my favorites and this…" She drew out one more. "This is a good basic book on the principles of art."

Nathan eyed them apprehensively. "They look awfully expensive."

"You'll be good to them," Lily said with confidence.

Nathan nodded. "When do you want them back?"

"When you've finished with them. Now, let me help you carry them downstairs and we'll have something cool to drink." She took several of the books from his hands.

Once they were back on the main floor, Nathan went out to sit on the porch while Beth offered to help Lily with the lemonade.

"Well, what did you think?" Beth asked when they were alone in the kitchen.

"He's very good," Lily confirmed. "Right now he thinks he wants to do comic-book art, but if you notice the background in his drawings, you'll see that he's very good with landscapes."

"I'm so glad you said that. I thought so, too, but then I've never had any training in art. Thank you so much for taking the time to encourage him. He needed to hear that."

"It was my pleasure. Hasn't he been getting any support?" she asked, pulling a glass pitcher from the refrigerator.

"I think it's more a case of him not showing anyone his work." Feeling at ease with Lily, she asked, "You know Charlie. Would he discourage Nathan from working at his art?"

"Charlie? No, why would he?"

"That's what I'm wondering. Nathan seems to think Charlie believes art is for sissies."

"That doesn't sound like the Charlie I know," Lily said as she set three crystal glasses on a silver tray.

"You're right. It doesn't."

Lily moved gracefully about the kitchen. "So how is Charlie?"

Beth watched Lily's long delicate finger arrange cookies on the cut-glass plate as if she was creating a work of art. "Is there a reason you're asking me that question?"

Lily had the grace to blush. "I heard he had moved onto the houseboat."

"Is everybody in town talking about us?" When Lily looked uneasy with the question, Beth added, "You can tell me the truth, Lily. I'm sure ever since people heard that Abraham Steele had left us the houseboat together, they've been speculating as to the reasons. And now that I'm here in Riverbend, it's probably only adding to the rumor mill."

"Actually I heard it from Charlie. And to be honest, I don't think many people know he's staying on the houseboat."

"Maybe not yet, but once the news does leak out, it'll be all over town before you know it," Beth predicted with a sigh.

"And would that be so bad?"

"No, because there really is no news to get out.

We're sharing the houseboat, but there's nothing going on between us.''

"There isn't?"

Beth could hear the skepticism in her voice. "No. Did Charlie imply there was?"

"No," Lily denied quickly. "It's just that I know both of you, and I guess I was hoping that since neither one of you had remarried in all these years, maybe it meant that..." She left the sentence unfinished.

"No." Beth spoke more abruptly than she intended. Even though Lily had articulated what she'd been secretly hoping would happen, it didn't mean she wanted to hear it.

"I'm sorry, Beth. I shouldn't have even brought it up."

Beth raised her hand to wave off the apology. "No, it's all right. I know you and Charlie are good friends and you wouldn't mention it if you didn't care about him."

"I do care, and to be perfectly honest, Beth, from the way he's been acting lately, I did suspect there was more to your relationship than sharing a boat."

Beth couldn't help but recall the times Charlie had kissed her recently. She was tempted to confide in Lily, to confess that she was beginning to think of him as more than a boat mate, too. But if she did that, she'd have to examine her feelings for Charlie more closely and decide what to do about the situation. And she wasn't quite ready for that.

"Ah, yes, the boat," Beth said on another sigh. "Abraham Steele certainly stirred things up with his last will and testament, didn't he?"

"Yes, he did," Lily agreed soberly. "He didn't

just bequeath gifts, he changed people's lives forever.''

"You mean Aaron's, don't you."

Lily nodded. "I don't understand why Abraham didn't tell Aaron he was his father. Instead, he kept silent. It was easier to give Evie Mazerik money than to admit he'd made a mistake.'' She shook her head. "It's really sad. Boys need fathers."

Beth thought about Nathan. He was growing up without either parent. Charlie was doing his best to fill the void left by his father, but who would fill the void left by Nathan's mother?

Not you, she told herself. She was grateful when Lily changed the subject and asked about Grace's mother. There was no point in fantasizing about what could be if she and Charlie were to reconcile.

As she'd told Lily, they shared a houseboat. That was all. In a few more weeks she'd be leaving Riverbend. Charlie and Nathan would no longer be a part of her life. It should have brought her peace of mind, but it didn't. It only made her heart ache.

DR. BENNETT WAS a kind soul. Working at the clinic with him was an experience Beth would remember long after she'd left Riverbend. In a world full of stressed-out, overworked physicians who often found there was never enough time to get to know patients, Julian Bennett made an effort to talk to each and every one. And not just about their health.

It came as no surprise to Beth that most patients were willing to wait an extra fifteen or twenty minutes if it meant they could see Dr. Bennett. Nor did she find it unusual that he did whatever he could to help those less fortunate, so when he asked her to do an act of kindness for him, she readily said yes.

He wanted her to take some medication to a patient who was housebound. Beth didn't question why, but simply took the bag of pharmaceutical samples he gave her and the slip of paper with the address on it and headed out the door. As she walked toward her car, she glanced at the numbers.

It was 1377 Jefferson St., Apt. 4. Beth stopped in her tracks and reread it. Just as she'd thought. Dr. Bennett had sent her to the very spot she and Charlie had lived during their brief marriage.

When Beth pulled up in front of the wooden fourplex, her heart beat in her throat. It looked nearly the same as it had fifteen years ago. It was still a dull shade of green with yellow shutters framing the windows. The porch no longer held a wooden swing, as it had when she and Charlie had lived there, but an old washing machine and dryer. Toys littered the yard, and a round "kiddy" pool sat smack-dab in the middle of the lawn. The same Beware of Dog sign hung on the fence gate, which made Beth wonder if Barney Brose was still the landlord.

Carefully she opened the gate and entered the yard. Hearing no animal sounds, she walked up the steps to the front porch and entered the building. As she climbed the stairs to the second story, she remembered the first time she and Charlie had come to look at the apartment.

She'd been full of dreams. Even though she and Charlie were getting married because she was pregnant, she felt sure that once they set up housekeeping, everything would turn out the way she'd always dreamed it would be. He'd fall madly in love with her and become a wonderful father to their child. Little did she know that only a month later their marriage would be over and he'd be gone from her life.

She had to shake her head to clear it of the memories. At the top of the stairs she turned to the right and knocked on the door. At first no one answered, so Beth knocked again. Finally the door swung open and Beth stood face-to-face with a very young, and very pregnant, teenage girl.

"Hi. I'm Beth Pennington from the clinic. Dr. Bennett sent this over for you." She handed the girl the sack with the medication.

"Oh, please. You must come inside," the girl said, pulling Beth by the hand into the tiny apartment. "It's so hot outside today. Let me get you something cold to drink."

Beth wanted to say no, that she really had to leave, but something compelled her to enter the apartment she'd once called home. Except for the kitchen, which still had the small apartment-size stove and the yellowed aging refrigerator, nothing else in the place looked familiar.

"You'll have to excuse the mess. The apartment is so small and Marcus wants all his toys out." She gave Beth an apologetic shrug.

A baby cried and Beth noticed the high chair in the corner of the kitchen. There sat Marcus, tugging on his ear. He appeared to be around nine months old.

His mother lifted him out of the chair and said, "Look. This nice lady brought you your medicine. Now you're going to start feeling better," she cooed, the baby on her hip. She peered into the sack and pulled out a small bottle of medicine.

"Would you like me to open that for you?" Beth offered as she saw her struggle with the cap.

She smiled at Beth. "That would be nice. Thank you."

Beth opened the bottle, then read the instructions. "You need to fill the dropper to the halfway mark. The medication must be kept in the refrigerator. Shall I?" she asked, motioning toward the refrigerator.

"Please. And take out something cold to drink."

Beth slipped the bag with the other sample bottles into the refrigerator, but declined the offer of a beverage. "No, thanks, I really need to get back to work," she said, then headed for the door.

It felt strange to be in the apartment where she and Charlie had spent their entire married life. The sofa that had pulled out into a bed was gone, but she hadn't forgotten how the springs had squeaked every time one of them had rolled over. Nor had she forgotten how Charlie had looked that first morning they'd woken up as husband and wife. He'd smiled at her, brushed her hair away from her cheek and told her he didn't take wedding vows lightly. He'd told her not to look so scared, then kissed her and promised they'd make their marriage work.

"It's so nice of you to bring the medicine to me," the young woman said, interrupting her musings. "Dr. Bennett knows it's hard for me to get out to the clinic, so he stopped by here on his way to work this morning and told me he had some samples he could give me free of charge."

Beth listened as the young woman extolled the

virtues of Julian Bennett. The longer she stayed in the apartment, the more memories flashed in her mind. Feeling short of breath and extremely hot, she said, "I really must get going. Be sure to call the clinic if Marcus doesn't improve."

As Beth made her way down the steps, the heat felt stifling. The first thing she did when she climbed into the car was turn on her air-conditioning. Still, she had to reach into her purse for a tissue to wipe the perspiration from her brow. On her way back to the clinic she stopped at the Burger Barn to get a cold drink.

She intended to make a quick trip in and out of the restaurant, but just as she was about to leave the counter, she heard someone call her name. She turned around and saw Lucy. Beside her was her daughter Amber, wearing a sundress and a paper crown on her head.

"Hi. I thought you'd be at the clinic," she said to Beth.

"I had to run an errand for Dr. Bennett, so I stopped to get something to drink." She held up her soda. "It's so darn hot today."

"Isn't it awful?" Lucy agreed. "Thank goodness for air-conditioning."

"It looks like it's a special day," Beth remarked, glancing toward the rear of the restaurant, where balloons and crepe paper decorated a small section.

"It's Amber's birthday, so we're having the party here," Lucy announced, giving her daughter a hug.

"Happy birthday, Amber," Beth said with a smile.

"Do you want to come to my party?" the little girl asked.

"I wish I could, but I have to go back to work," Beth answered. "I bet you're going to have a lot of fun."

Just then Amber recognized a couple of friends who'd arrived. She raced over to greet them.

"Looks like you're going to have your hands full," Beth remarked as the little girls skipped and giggled their way back to the party section.

"I have help." She turned and motioned for a young girl with blond hair to join them. "This is my daughter Rebecca," Lucy announced when the girl was at her side.

"It's Becky. Mom's the only one who calls me Rebecca." She gave her mother an admonishing look.

"You can go by whatever name you like but you're always going to be Rebecca to me," her mother said with a maternal pride which caused Becky to roll her eyes.

"It's nice to meet you," Beth said with a warm smile. "I'm Beth."

That caused the girl's eyes to widen. "The Beth who owns the houseboat with Uncle Charlie?"

"Yes. You've probably heard your mom talk about me." And in a not-so-nice way, Beth surmised from the look on Becky's face. Determined not to let anything deter the progress she'd made in mending her friendship with Lucy, she said, "We were friends when we were kids."

Beth didn't miss the glance Becky shot her mother, as if seeking confirmation that the statement was true. To Beth's relief Lucy said, "Good friends. I think hardly a Friday went by when one of us didn't spend the night at the other's house."

Becky looked a bit surprised by her mother's words, but quickly smiled and offered Beth her hand. "It's nice to meet you. It must be neat living on the houseboat. Uncle Charlie took us for ride a while back and it was fun."

"Yes, it's a pretty nice place."

"It'd be great on a day like today. I mean, when you get home, you can just jump in the river and go swimming."

Noise could be heard coming from the party section, prompting Lucy to say, "You'd better go keep an eye on things back there."

"Sure, Mom."

"She's a lovely girl, Lucy," Beth said when the teenager was gone. "She looks a lot like you. And I'll bet she's as independent as you were at her age."

"She is," Lucy agreed with pride in her voice. "She's much more self-confident than I was at thirteen, though. And she's strong. She's had to be. We all have had to be since Michael died."

Beth nodded in understanding. "I should get going. I have to get back to work, and you have a birthday to celebrate."

"Before you go, I want to talk to you about something," Lucy said.

Beth's stomach muscles tensed. Lucy must have heard about Charlie moving onto the houseboat with Nathan and was going to let Beth know exactly what she thought about it.

But her next words had nothing to do with her brother. "I'm planning a small get-together for Lily Holden in a few weeks or so, and I thought you might like to come."

Beth hoped her mouth didn't drop open, but the invitation was so unexpected, she was speechless for a moment. Finally she asked, "What's the occasion?"

"It's an unofficial bachelorette party."

"Does that mean that Lily and Aaron Mazerik are getting married?" Beth knew the two of them had been dating and things appeared to be serious, but this was the first she'd heard of an engagement.

"They've kept the news rather quiet and want the ceremony to be small, which is why I thought I'd keep the bachelorette party limited to a group of her close friends. Basically we just want a chance to tell her how happy we are for her and celebrate her good news."

"It sounds like a great idea."

"Then you'd be interested in coming?"

"Sure, if I'm still here. You do know I'm going back to Iowa at the end of the month?"

"Grace told me, but I thought maybe your plans had changed."

When Beth told her they hadn't, she wasn't sure if she'd imagined the look of relief on Lucy's face. But then Lucy said, "Maybe if we plan it far enough in advance, you could come home for the party."

"If it's at all possible, I'd like to," Beth found herself saying.

"Good. I'll let you know when I have a definite date." Amber raced to her mother's side and tugged on her shirt.

"Hurry up, Mommy. We want to start the party."

Lucy gave her a gentle shove. "All right. Go sit. Mommy will be right there." To Beth she said, "You should give me your phone number."

"Sure." Beth dug in her purse for a scrap of paper and a pen. She pulled out an old grocery receipt and wrote her number on the back. "This is my cell phone."

Lucy glanced at it before tucking it into the pocket of her shorts. "I'm glad you want to come to Lily's party, Beth." The birthday celebrants were beginning to sound rambunctious again. "I better go."

Beth wished her luck and said goodbye. As she stepped out into the sweltering heat, she saw Charlie's pickup pull into the parking lot. When he stopped in the spot next to hers, she knew there was no way she was going to avoid seeing him.

It was not what she wanted, not after visiting the apartment where they'd lived together as husband and wife. She felt vulnerable and exposed, and when he stepped out of the pickup and smiled at her, she felt like a young girl again. Her knees wanted to buckle, and her face flushed.

She tried to tell herself it was the heat, but she knew it was Charlie. He'd always had that effect on her. Even though she knew it was foolish, the attraction she felt for him now was no less than it had been fifteen years ago.

"Hi. You're leaving?" he asked, seeing the paper cup in her hand.

"Yes. I have to go back to the clinic."

"We're here for Amber's birthday." He nodded toward Nathan, who'd climbed out of the pickup and carried a large box wrapped in bright-colored paper.

"Lucy's inside," she said, stating the obvious. "I think the party's ready to begin. Have a good time." She opened the door of her car.

Before she could get inside, Charlie said, "Beth, wait." He told Nathan to go ahead, then came around to her side of the car. He wore his work clothes—jeans, white T-shirt and leather boots—but to Beth he'd never looked better.

"I spoke to Lily," he said. "She told me you and Nathan stopped over."

She felt defensive. Why, she didn't know, but her voice had an edge as she said, "He wants to draw, Charlie."

"Yes, I know, and I hear he's very good." He pinned her with his gaze. "I don't think art is for sissies."

"Nathan seems to think you do."

"Not anymore. I talked to him about it."

The tension drained from her. "I'm glad to hear that, Charlie."

"You also might be interested in hearing that Lily's going to give Nathan art lessons."

It was the best news Beth had heard all day. "That's great!"

"Yes, which is why I wanted to talk to you. I wanted to say thank-you for everything you've done for Nathan. I'm not sure he would have told me about his interest in art if you hadn't encouraged him."

"I'm surprised you didn't see him drawing."

"I obviously wasn't paying as much attention as I should have been. You're the one who's made a difference in his life this summer, not me."

The way he was looking at her made her feel extremely self-conscious. "I didn't do that much."

"Yes, you did. And I'm not sure why. He sure

didn't welcome anyone taking an interest in him, yet you kept reaching out to him. Why, Beth?''

She looked away from his penetrating gaze and stared out at the traffic on the highway. ''Maybe because I saw in him...'' She couldn't finish. She couldn't tell him that since the first day she'd met Nathan and learned he was fourteen, the same age their child would have been, that she'd felt this connection to him.

''Saw what?'' Charlie probed.

He was studying her curiously when she turned back to him, and though she wanted to tell him the truth, something stopped her. ''I guess I just saw a need in him and wanted to do what I could to help,'' she replied lamely, then climbed into her car and closed the door.

As she drove out of the parking lot, she had to clasp her hands tightly on the steering wheel to keep them from trembling. When she paused at the exit and glanced back, Charlie still stood in the lot watching her drive away.

How could she tell him that Nathan made her dream of the child she'd never had a chance to know. She thought she'd managed to forget about that lost child, yet for the past few weeks the memories had haunted her every single day.

At the time of her miscarriage she'd dealt with the pain by telling herself it was a pregnancy that never should have happened. If she'd had the baby, it would have been raised by parents who were only together because of a mistake. If she and Charlie had stayed married, it would have been for their child's sake, not because of love. And that was not the right sort of home for *any* child.

Yet now, when she looked at Nathan, she wondered if it might have worked. If their child been born healthy and strong, maybe she and Charlie would still be married.

The realization caused tears to well up and stream down her cheeks. She'd thought she was finished grieving for the loss of her baby, but coming home to Riverbend and seeing Charlie again had made her realize that the pain would never go away. She would carry it with her forever.

It was a pain that should have been shared. If Charlie had loved her, he would have stayed with her. She wouldn't be alone today.

But he didn't love her. And all the crying in the world wasn't going to change that. She'd just have to live with the fact that Charlie Callahan had a piece of her heart and always would.

CHAPTER THIRTEEN

WHEN BETH ARRIVED home from work, Charlie's pickup was parked next to the pier. Still feeling raw from their earlier encounter in the parking lot, she decided to change her clothes and head over to Ed's, rather than spend the evening on the boat.

As she entered the air-conditioned cabin, she saw that Charlie and Nathan were in the galley. As usual, a tiny shiver of pleasure traveled through her at the sight of Charlie. He looked as if he'd just taken a shower. His dark hair was still wet, and she imagined his scrubbed clean skin smelled of soap and aftershave.

When he saw her, he said, "You're just in time. Nathan's making dinner."

Beth looked at the boy. He wore a chef's apron over his shirt and shorts, but what was really remarkable was his hair. The blue streak was gone. And the gold ring that usually adorned his nostril was gone, as well.

"You like tacos, don't you, Beth?" he asked, hope lighting his eyes.

"Yes, but—"

He didn't let her finish. "See, Charlie? I told you she'd like them." Fluttering about the kitchen like a nervous cook, he said, "Do you think that's brown enough?'' He pointed to the crumbled hamburger meat sizzling in a frying pan on the stove.

''It looks good to me, but maybe we should ask Beth,'' Charlie suggested.

''No!'' Nathan looked at Beth, who'd started toward them, and held up his hands. ''You can't do anything. I'm making dinner for you.''

The thought of eating dinner with Charlie made Beth's stomach tense, yet what choice did she have? If she said no, she'd disappoint Nathan, and he was obviously trying very hard to please her.

So instead of saying she was going to change her clothes and go have supper at Ed's, she asked, ''Are you sure there isn't something I can do to help?''

''No, everything's cool. I know what I'm doing.''

Beth wasn't totally convinced, especially when she heard him mumble to Charlie, ''I hope I do this right. I haven't made these since before Mom died.''

''You're doing fine,'' Charlie replied in a low voice, then glanced at Beth to see if she'd heard.

She pretended she hadn't. ''If you two don't need me, I think I'll take a quick shower and change— that is, if there's time....''

''Yeah, sure,'' said Charlie, glancing at Nathan for affirmation, ''but be quick.''

Beth hoped the cool shower would ease the tension that seemed to have every muscle in her body in its grip. Ever since she'd run into Charlie at the Burger Barn, she'd been confronted with the realization that she was still in love with him.

She closed her eyes and let the water stream over her face, regretting that she had agreed to let him share the boat. But then again, she had to admit that they'd manage to avoid each other quite well up to this point. There was no reason they couldn't continue to do so for the rest of her stay in Riverbend. All she had to do was get through this one taco dinner....

It wasn't going to be easy. As she dressed, she wondered if she should make up an excuse. She could tell Nathan that Grace had called her and she was needed there. But the minute she returned to the salon, she knew she couldn't lie to Nathan.

"I made iced tea," he said. "You want some?"

"That would be nice," she told him, sitting on the sofa.

"I'll get it for her," Charlie offered.

Beth would have preferred to get the tea herself, rather than have Charlie wait on her. When he brought it to her, she caught a whiff of his aftershave. It acted like an aphrodisiac, reminding her of the nights they'd spent making love on that squeaky old sofa bed in the apartment. And when his fingers brushed hers as he handed her the glass, pleasure tingled through her.

She took a deep breath, causing Charlie to ask, "Are you all right?"

"Oh, it's just the heat," she responded lamely, then took a sip of the tea.

"It does feel warm in here. I'll check the air-conditioning and see if it's working properly." He disappeared for a few minutes, giving Beth time to collect herself.

Again she asked Nathan if he needed any help, but he proudly told her he was doing okay. When he announced it was time to eat, Beth deliberately took a seat at the end of the breakfast bar, hoping that Nathan would take the chair next to hers.

He didn't. He waited until Charlie returned, ordered him to sit next to Beth, then served dinner.

What she thought was going to be an awkward experience turned into one of the most pleasant evenings Beth had had since she'd returned to Riverbend. Tonight there was no TV blaring or video games buzzing, just good food, good conversation and lots of laughter.

They had dessert—a frozen chocolate-cream pie—outside on the deck beneath a summer sky sprinkled with stars. Charlie looked totally relaxed, listening with a smile on his face as Nathan reminisced about their early experiences in the Big Brothers program.

When Nathan asked Beth to tell him what Charlie was like as a kid, she found herself laughing frequently as she recounted tales from their youth. Before long, Charlie was telling stories, too, and as Beth met his eyes, she knew that although the anecdotes were of their childhood, the reminiscing had brought back memories of their marriage for him, just as it had for her.

When Charlie pointed out that it was already past eleven, Beth sighed. She hated to see the evening end, and apparently she wasn't the only one.

"You're not going to bed already, are you?" Nathan asked as both adults commented about having to get up for work in the morning.

"I'm pretty tired," Beth said, realizing it was true.

Nathan groaned. "I was hoping we could go swimming. I bet the water's really warm."

"Sorry," Beth replied with an apologetic smile, "but I'm going to have to pass. I want to thank you for making dinner, Nathan. The tacos were great.'' When she went to pick up the empty dishes from the picnic table, Charlie stopped her.

''You go on in, Beth. Nathan and I will clean up out here.''

She didn't argue, and said good-night. As she did every night before she went to bed, she pulled out the clothes she would wear to work the following morning and made sure her alarm was set. She was just about to get undressed when she realized she'd left her watch next to the sink. She went back upstairs and found it just where she had left it. As she reached for it, she glanced outside and saw two bodies splashing in the water.

Nathan and Charlie had gone for that late-night swim. She couldn't resist watching the two of them. As quietly as possible, she slipped outside, inching her way along the deck and staying close to the cabin in order to be in its shadow.

In the still of the night, sound carried with remarkable clarity. Not only could she see Nathan and Charlie playing in the water, she could hear them, and what she heard had her ducking around the corner to make sure she wasn't seen.

''How come you don't ask her out?'' the fourteen year old wanted to know.

''How come you don't mind your own business?'' Charlie retorted good naturedly.

''She's hot. You really should ask her out,'' Nathan persisted.

''And I think you should stop trying to find me a woman.''

''Someone has to.''

"No, someone doesn't. I'm perfectly capable of finding my own."

"Doesn't look like it to me."

A flurry of splashing told Beth they were having a waterfight. She crept back inside and down the steps to the cuddy, one question on her mind. Was she the one Nathan had referred to as being hot?

If she was, it wasn't a good sign. Charlie had more or less told Nathan he wasn't interested in her. And from what Charlie said, this wasn't the first time Nathan had tried to get Charlie to start dating.

Ed had said Charlie was single, not that he was a hermit, she thought with self-derision. Why wouldn't there be a woman in Charlie's life? He was handsome, virile...

His love life was not a subject she wanted to dwell on, but as she lay in bed that night, she couldn't stop thinking about Charlie. He didn't seem to have a girlfriend. Had he been so in love with Nathan's mother that he hadn't wanted to date since she'd died?

There was only one woman she wanted to see in his life and it was her. She punched her pillow in frustration.

This was all Abraham Steele's fault. If she hadn't inherited half the boat, she wouldn't be lying here thinking such thoughts, and she wouldn't care about Charlie Callahan's love life.

But she *had* inherited the boat and she *did* care. Now she had to figure out how to change that.

WHEN BETH WENT UP to the kitchen the following morning, Charlie was already there. He wasn't eating and he hadn't made any coffee. He was simply sitting at the counter staring into space.

"Good morning," she said as she walked into the salon.

He turned around and smiled. "Hi."

"Is everything all right?"

"Everything's great."

"Good." She opened the cupboard to get the coffee.

"I was thinking…"

"Then you're ahead of me. My brain doesn't work in the morning until I've had my coffee." She filled the glass pot from the coffeemaker with water.

"I was thinking about us," he said. "And if you try to tell me there is no *us,* I'm going to come over there and prove to you there is."

Her hands trembled as she measured the coffee grounds to put into the basket. Without turning around, she asked, "What were you thinking about us?"

"That I'd like to take you to the Sycamore County Fair on Saturday."

The county fair. She didn't say a word. She couldn't, because her mind was filled with images. Tractor pulls and demolition derbies. Corn dogs and cotton candy. Sitting at the top of the Ferris wheel watching the fireworks explode over the grandstand.

"Well? Will you go with me to the fair on Saturday?" he repeated.

Words of the conversation she'd overheard last night flashed in her memory. *How come you don't ask her out?* Could Nathan have meant her? Or maybe this didn't constitute a real date.

"You want me to go with you and Nathan, right?" she asked, spinning around to face him.

"No, I want you to go with me. Nathan's going with Lucy and her girls."

"Lucy? Why would he go with them?"

"Maybe because Rebecca's thirteen and has big blue eyes."

Beth's mouth fell open. "Since when?"

"Since she's been born, I guess."

"No, I mean, since when has Nathan been interested in Rebecca?"

"Since he went to Amber's birthday party at the Burger Barn," Charlie said with a knowing grin.

"So *that's* the reason he washed the blue out of his hair."

"And got rid of the nose ring. He's gone preppie, like Rebecca."

Beth shook her head in amazement. "Well, isn't that interesting."

"Yes, isn't it?" he said with amusement. "So you see, Nathan doesn't need a date for the fair. I do."

"You're asking me out on a date?"

"Yes. Are you going to accept, or do you need some special convincing?"

His meaning was clear. "I accept," she said quickly, enjoying the banter but not wanting it to become any more than that.

"Good. It'll be like old times."

"I'm not sixteen," she reminded him.

He got up from the stool and came up behind her to whisper in her ear, "That doesn't mean I can't kiss you at the top of the Ferris wheel." His breath was warm against her cheek and she was tempted to turn and capture his lips with hers, but he was gone before she had a chance to do anything so foolish.

Old times. Was that the reason he'd asked her to the fair? She decided it didn't make a difference, because she wanted to go with him no matter what the reason.

BECAUSE LUCY LIVED ONLY a couple of blocks from Charlie's house in town, Charlie and Nathan decided to spend Friday night at his house so that he could drop Nathan off at Lucy's first thing in the morning.

When Charlie picked Beth up the following afternoon, she thought it was a good thing he hadn't been at the houseboat overnight. Otherwise, this morning he would have seen how nervous she was about their date. Despite telling herself she wasn't going to analyze why he'd asked her to the fair, she'd thought of little else all morning, and it was only when she saw him that she had her answer.

He was taking her to the fair because he wanted to be with her. It was there in his eyes and in his smile. And in the tone of his voice when he said, "You ready to have some fun?"

"I am," she answered truthfully. She wanted to be with Charlie and she couldn't think of a better place to be with him than at the fair.

As soon as she saw the white grandstand with its flags flying along the roof, she was filled with nostalgia. The Sycamore County Fair had been one of the things she loved most about summer in Indiana. For the rest of the year the fairgrounds were deserted, but during the middle of August they came alive with vendors selling everything from tractors and combines to kitchen utensils and household cleaners.

As a 4-H kid, Beth had spent long hours at the fairgrounds. If she wasn't giving a speech or demonstrating some sewing technique, she was cooking a meal or giving tips on animal care. She'd entered every competition open in her age group and displayed her blue ribbons with pride. And when she'd gone back to school in the fall and the teacher had asked what she'd liked best about the summer, she'd always had the same answer. Fair week.

As she climbed out of Charlie's truck, she took a deep breath. "Don't you just love the smell of the fair?"

"Is that a hint that you're hungry?" he asked with a grin as the breeze carried the aroma of food from the various concessions. "What do you want? Minidoughnuts? Corn dog? Cotton candy?"

"I can wait. We need to get a schedule of events so we don't miss anything," she told him, steering him toward the entrance gates.

As the crowds of people grew denser, Charlie reached for her hand. "I better hang on to you so you won't get lost."

Beth didn't bother to pull her hand out of his grasp. She liked the warmth and strength of his hand around hers. As he gave their tickets to the man at the gate, she knew that no matter what happened after tomorrow, today she was going to have a great time.

And she did. They walked from one end of the fairgrounds to the other, taking in every possible sight. They ate corn dogs smothered in mustard and

French fries dripping with ketchup, then washed them down with fresh-squeezed lemonade.

They walked past tables filled with blue-ribbon pies, cakes and jams, and stood in line to get a peek at a woman who could make her entire body fit into a small box not much bigger than a peach crate. They listened to a country-and-western singer perform in the shade of the bandshell, and sat on bleachers to watch the tractor pull.

By the time the sun was sinking in the sky, they'd been through every barn, viewed all the arts-and-crafts exhibits, and heard enough sales pitches to last until the next August.

"I think there's only one thing we haven't done," Charlie announced as Beth checked the map in her hands.

"The rides."

"If we time it right, we'll be able to see the fireworks from the top of the Ferris wheel. You do want to ride the Ferris wheel, don't you?" he asked, his eyes twinkling flirtatiously.

"Isn't that why we came?" she returned coyly.

He squeezed her hand before dropping it. "You wait here and I'll be right back with the tickets."

Beth watched him work his way through the crowd to the ticket booth a short distance away. She was right outside a small roped-off section called Kiddyland, where tamer versions of the adult rides had children's eyes widening in excitement. Beth took a seat on a bench, content to watch as moms pushed strollers and dads carried kids on their shoulders.

She hadn't been there but a few seconds when she heard a voice call, "Where's Charlie?"

Beth glanced to her left and saw Lucy coming toward her, Amber at her side. The little girl had a mound of cotton candy in a plastic bag, which she clutched in her fist.

"Hi. He went to get tickets for the rides. He should be right back," Beth answered, giving Amber a smile.

"I hope you know what you're doing." Lucy's voice had an ominous ring to it.

"Oh, I'm not going on any of those thrill-seeking rides. Just the Ferris wheel," Beth said, sliding over to make a place for Lucy to sit.

But Lucy remained standing. "I'm not talking about the rides, Beth. I mean Charlie."

Beth's stomach roiled.

"Nathan told me Charlie brought you to the fair." It was more of an accusation than a statement, and Beth shifted uncomfortably on the bench.

So Lucy didn't like that her brother was with her. She hadn't come right out and said it, but Beth could tell by the way she stood, the tightness of her mouth, the narrowing of her eyes.

"We're having a good time," Beth said quietly, wishing she didn't feel the need to defend herself. She sensed the fragile bond of friendship she'd been fighting so hard to reconstruct breaking apart again.

Amber broke the tension between them by asking if she could go on the carousel. Lucy looked as if she wanted to say no, but reluctantly pulled a ticket out of her pocket.

"All right. Mommy'll take you," she told the little girl, her voice softening.

Just then Nathan and Rebecca came running over to them. "Look what Nathan won for me at the hoop shoot!'' Rebecca exclaimed, proudly holding an enormous stuffed lion.

Lucy gave him a high five and a sly smile. ''Way to go, Nathan. And you said you couldn't shoot hoops.''

He acted a bit embarrassed, but Beth could see he was pleased to have won the stuffed animal for Rebecca.

''Hey—now that you're here, would you two take Amber on the carousel?'' Lucy asked.

''Sure, Mom,'' Rebecca answered, taking the tickets from her mother and grabbing Amber's hand.

Which left Beth alone with Lucy. She looked anxiously toward the ticket booth, wondering what had happened to Charlie.

Please come back, Charlie, she silently prayed, but he was nowhere in sight.

As soon as the kids were gone, Lucy returned to the subject of her brother, just as Beth had expected. ''Do you really think it's a good idea to date your ex-husband?''

Feeling at a disadvantage sitting on the bench, Beth stood. ''I think it's a good idea *not* to be having this conversation.'' She knew that unless she did some fast talking, they could end up arguing over Charlie, just as they had fifteen years ago. ''Look. Isn't it better that Charlie and I try to have a friendly relationship, rather than a hostile one?''

''But is that all you want, Beth? To be friends with Charlie? Is that why you suggested he and Nathan move onto the houseboat with you?''

Suddenly Beth understood the reason for Lucy's animosity. Nathan hadn't simply told her that Charlie had taken her to the fair. He'd revealed their living arrangements. Well, what did she expect? It was hardly a secret—nor was there any need for it to be one.

"It's for convenience's sake, nothing else. And if you'd asked your brother, he'd have told you it was his idea, not mine," she told Lucy, wondering why she had to explain. Charlie should be dealing with his sister.

"You're divorced."

"I know that, Lucy." Beth could feel her control slipping away, yet was powerless to stop it.

"It's foolish to think you have any more in common now than you did fifteen years ago," Lucy warned. "You're a career woman, Beth. Why don't you just leave him alone so he can find someone who wants the same things he does?"

Beth knew she shouldn't rise to the bait, but she couldn't stop herself. "And what makes you think I don't want the same things he does?"

"Do you honestly think you and Charlie would still be married if you hadn't lost the baby?"

Beth could feel the blood pounding in her ears. She knew she should end the conversation and walk away, yet she couldn't. Things she should have said fifteen years ago needed to be said.

With an amazing calmness she looked Lucy straight in the eye. "We'll never know, will we? But one thing I do know that you don't is that I wanted my baby. The reason you didn't know that is because you weren't my best friend then. If you had been, you would have known that nothing—not going away to college, not getting a great job, *nothing*—could ever make up for what I lost.

"So in the future when you feel this need to presume to know what I want, I would appreciate you keeping your opinions to yourself. Because, Lucy, you don't know me very well at all.''

Before Lucy could respond, Beth hurried away.

''Beth, wait,'' Lucy called, but Beth kept on walking.

Actually, her walk was more like a run as she pushed her way through the crowd, her heart palpitating. Suddenly she felt a pair of arms around her.

''Whoa! What are you doing? Running out on me?''

She turned around and saw Charlie. He was looking at her with such a tender expression she took comfort in his arms and buried her face against his shoulder.

''You're trembling. What happened?'' he asked.

She didn't say anything, just soaked up his strength until her trembling stopped. Then she gently pushed him away. ''It's nothing. Really.''

He studied her flushed face. ''It sure doesn't seem like nothing.''

''I know.'' She linked her arm through his and entwined their fingers. ''But it's over now.''

His gaze swept the crowd. ''Did some guy hit on you or something?''

''No. I told you it was nothing.'' She needed to forget about Lucy and try to recapture some of the magic she'd felt earlier. ''Did you get the tickets for the Ferris wheel?''

He patted his pocket. ''And two for the bungee jump.''

She stopped. ''You're kidding, right?''

He grinned then, a wonderful heart-stopping grin

that made Beth forget everything else. "That's a little more fun than even I can handle," he confessed.

As twilight faded to darkness, the fairgrounds sparkled with the brightly colored lights of the amusement rides and the concession stands. Barns closed their doors and vendors packed away their goods, while visitors headed for the parking lot or the carnival attractions.

Just as they had done when they were teenagers, Beth and Charlie rode the Ferris wheel while fireworks burst in the sky. And once again, when they stopped at the top, Charlie kissed her. Not the way a teenage boy kisses a girl who's just turned sixteen, but the way a man kisses the woman he loves.

Beth forgot all about her confrontation with Lucy. She forgot that she was only in Riverbend for a visit. And she forgot that she'd promised herself she wouldn't let Charlie Callahan back into her life.

She'd let him in and she wanted him to stay there. And that was the message she gave him as her lips coaxed his into an intimate kiss that had him saying afterward, "Now do you believe there is an *us?*"

For an answer she kissed him. Then the Ferris wheel jerked into motion again and they reluctantly let go of each other as the ride carried them to the ground.

Beth hated to see the day come to an end. They made their way back to the parking lot, fingers entwined. In her other hand she clutched the tiny stuffed dog Charlie had won for her at the coin toss. He'd spent a small fortune trying to win a huge stuffed gorilla, but had finally had to settle for a miniature dog.

Although the gorilla had been adorable, Beth wouldn't have traded the tiny dog for anything. She'd treasure it—a symbol of the wonderful day they'd spent together.

When they reached the pickup he pulled her into his arms. "I enjoyed today."

"Me, too," she said, her breath catching in her throat at the look in his eyes.

"How would you like to have a real date?"

"Today wasn't real?"

"I mean, an evening out. Dinner for two, some quiet conversation with soft music in the background."

"That sounds nice, but what about Nathan?"

"He's a big boy. He can make himself a pizza. How about tomorrow night?"

With the colored lights twinkling in the background, the moment seemed magical, and Beth saw no reason not to say, "All right. I accept."

"Good. Now I need to kiss you good-night."

"Good-night? Aren't you giving me a ride home?"

"Yes, but in about five minutes Lucy and her gang are going to be here, and there'll be no more of this." He pulled her into his arms and kissed her with the same passion he'd shown at the top of the Ferris wheel. A deep intimate kiss that Beth would normally have responded to with an equal fervor, but the mention of Lucy reminded her of the unpleasant scene they'd had. She suddenly felt cautious.

Charlie noticed. "I hope you meant what you said up on that wheel and it wasn't just the altitude making you dizzy."

"And what was that?" she asked, even though she knew.

"That there is an *us*." He pushed an errant curl away from her face with his fingertip. When she didn't answer right away, he said, "You're not going to try to deny it, are you?"

"No. There wouldn't be much point, would there?"

Her answer had the desired effect. He smiled a slow sexy smile, nuzzled her neck with kisses, then released her when she reminded him, "This is a public place and you're expecting company."

Within a few minutes Nathan came walking toward them. Alone.

"Where's Lucy?" Charlie asked.

"Amber had a stomachache, so I told Lucy I could find my way to your truck myself," Nathan answered.

"Okay. Let's go home," Charlie said, holding the door open for Beth to climb inside.

As she slid into the middle of the bench seat, she thought how natural it felt for the three of them to be going back to the houseboat together. Three tired but content fair-goers.

Everything felt right in Beth's world. Nathan was happy. Charlie was happy. And she was not about to say or do anything to change that. She didn't want to think about what would happen at the end of the summer. For now she'd be content to enjoy her last two weeks in Riverbend.

SUNDAY MORNING Beth awoke to discover she was alone on the houseboat. On the counter was a note from Charlie explaining that he'd received a call from Nathan's grandfather asking if his grandson could come for a visit. He'd taken the teenager back to West Lafayette for the day and they would return that evening—after dinner.

Beth couldn't help but feel disappointed that she wouldn't be having dinner with Charlie. Not wanting to think about what might have been had he taken her out again, she called Grace and offered to have the girls for the afternoon. She took them to the movies and then back to the houseboat, where they made pizza.

There was still no sign of Nathan and Charlie. It wasn't until after she'd taken the girls home and the sun had sunk low in the sky that his pickup pulled into the drive. As much as she wanted to wait outside on the deck for him, she remained in the salon, not wanting to look anxious to see him.

But she was. Every nerve in her body was in a heightened state of alert at the sound of his shoes clomping on the dock. When he appeared at the door, her breath caught in her throat.

"Hi. Where's Nathan?" she asked when he stepped inside and she saw he was alone.

"With his grandparents. He's going to stay the night."

"Is everything all right?"

"Yes. Everything's fine. Actually it's great. Nathan's grandparents were tickled pink to have him spend the night, and I think he needed a little of his grandmother's TLC."

Beth smiled in understanding.

"I'll pick him up tomorrow after work. I'm sorry it's so late. I didn't expect there to be so much traffic."

"It's all right. I was just sitting here listening to some music," she said, walking over to turn down the stereo.

"I promised you dinner," he said with an apologetic grin.

"We can do it another night."

"Have you eaten?"

"I had pizza with Ed's girls, but I could make you something if you're hungry," she offered.

"I am, but I don't want to make you work. Come. I'll take you to a favorite spot of mine," he told her.

"I should change," she said, glancing down at her jeans and T-shirt.

"Uh-uh. You'll fit in just fine with what you're wearing."

Beth understood what he meant when he pulled up outside a small building that had a single neon light over the door that said Dick's Bar. There wasn't much atmosphere—just a jukebox in the corner that continuously played country-and-western music. Everybody seemed to know everybody else, including Charlie, and Beth soon discovered why he liked the place. They made great hamburgers.

Which was what Charlie ended up ordering, not that there was anything else on the menu. Beth had to agree with him that whoever was cooking in Dick's kitchen earned every penny he was paid.

It wasn't exactly the quiet dinner he'd promised, yet the bar did have a rather intimate atmosphere. The booths had high backs, making Beth feel as if she and Charlie were isolated from the rest of the room. Charlie didn't sit across from her, but slid in beside her, leaving her no doubt as to how he felt about her.

It was there in his eyes every time he looked at her, and in his touch as he bent close to her, and their shoulders and thighs rubbed. She felt as if they were two lovers, sharing the most intimate of details, yet they hadn't made love yet.

Without Charlie saying a word, Beth knew exactly what was on his mind, because it was the same thing that was on hers. They might have been eating hamburgers and talking about recent movies they'd seen, but they both knew their being together now was about one thing—their attraction to each other.

All evening long it had been growing, creating an anticipation that practically crackled in the air. Of what would come after dinner. Or tomorrow.

As they drove back to the houseboat, she wondered how she ever could have thought she was over him. She would never be over Charlie. Since he'd kissed her on her sixteenth birthday, she'd been in love with him, and no amount of running away was going to change that.

When they got back to the houseboat, he flipped on the stereo. He pulled a tape from his pocket and slid it into the cassette player.

"Is this the soft background music you promised?" she asked as they waited for the tape to begin playing.

His smile was secretive. Then the song began, and Beth's eyes met his. It was a hit from the '80s, and just happened to be the first song they'd danced to at the spring formal their senior year in high school.

"Sound familiar?" he asked as her eyes misted over at the memories it stirred.

"You remembered," she said, her voice sounding breathless.

"It was our first dance." He stood several feet away from her as if unsure of himself.

"Where did you find a copy?"

"Remember the guy who used to do the PA announcements at school? He has a huge collection of music from the '80s, so I asked if I could tape this song."

She wrinkled her nose. "It's really not very good, is it?"

He smiled. "That's what I thought when I heard it again, but I didn't want to say so."

"I remember how grateful I was that the first dance was a slow song. I was so nervous, especially since the only other person I'd ever danced with was Ed," she reflected wistfully.

"You didn't look nervous."

"I was."

"You're not nervous now, are you?"

"A little," she confessed.

"Do you remember what I said to you while we danced that first dance?" he asked close to her ear.

"I believe it was that famous line all senior boys say to their dates at the senior formal," she quipped, trying to make light of his declaration of love. "'You look so gorgeous I do believe I am falling in love,'" she quoted.

"You do remember."

"And what did I say?"

"That you'd been in love with me since you were thirteen." He chuckled. "Not exactly words a guy wants to hear."

She stepped back from him. "Why not?"

"It made it sound like you had a crush on me."

"I did."

"I know, but I wanted more than that." The song came to an end and they stopped dancing.

"Music's over," she stated inanely.

He didn't release her, but stood staring into her eyes. "I really put that song on because I thought it would make good background music for me to tell you what I have to say, and now the song's over."

"So tell me, anyway," she said, her heart pounding.

"Ever since you walked back into my life, I haven't been able to stop thinking about you," he admitted.

"You haven't?"

He shook his head. "When I'm with you I remember how it was to lie with you in my arms at night, to feel your heart beating beneath my hand, to hear those little noises you make when you sleep, to see your hair spread across my pillow—"

She put a finger against his lips. "Don't say any more. Show me."

He pulled her into his arms and kissed her long and hard. But kissing wasn't enough for either of them. Beth's hands slipped inside his shirt, loving the feel of the solid warm muscles beneath her fingers.

Quickly he found the hem of her T-shirt and slid his hand beneath the cotton. It had been a long time since she'd let a man get so close, and the sensations he aroused when his palm brushed the silky fabric of her bra caused her to quiver with desire.

This was the reason she'd come back to Riverbend. To feel his whisper on her skin, to know the ache of longing his touch created in her.

She didn't want anyone's kiss but his. She didn't

want any other hands caressing her breasts, no other arms holding her.

"Oh, Charlie, no one's ever been able to make me feel the way you do," she said as he moved his mouth from hers and began to trail kisses down her throat.

"It's good between us. It always has been," he said huskily, his eyes dark with passion.

Pressed close to him, she could feel his need for her. When he saw the look in her eyes, he grinned and said, "See what you do to me?"

She pulled his mouth back to hers and pushed her body as close to his as possible. When she started to unbutton his shirt, he stopped her.

"We can't do this just yet."

Beth stared at him in bewilderment.

"It's not that I don't want you." He kissed again, and she was breathless by the time he lifted his mouth from hers.

"Then what?"

"I just hadn't planned this to happen *tonight*."

"Charlie, I don't care about the romantic dinner. I—"

Now it was his turn to place a finger over her lips. "That's not what I mean. We need to be responsible. Take the necessary precautions."

"Oh." He was talking about safe sex. She stepped back and giggled nervously. "I have to confess, it's been a long time since I've had this discussion. Actually I've never had this discussion."

He moved closer to her. "There hasn't been anyone since…?"

She shook her head. "Since you? No."

He pulled her to him and hugged her tightly.

''That makes it all the harder for me to wait, but it's also the reason we can't go any further.'' When she looked up at him, confusion in her eyes, he said, ''You're not on birth control, right?''

''No.''

''Then we have to wait.''

Beth nodded because she did understand. The night of the spring dance they'd made love, without using any protection, and the result had been an unwanted pregnancy.

He lifted her chin and said, ''But I'm warning you. I won't wait long.''

''You won't have to,'' she promised.

CHAPTER FOURTEEN

BETH DIDN'T WANT to wait long to make love to Charlie, either. That was why on Monday morning she took the necessary steps to make sure that the next time they were together there would be no fear of an unplanned pregnancy to interrupt their night of passion.

Only, when she dropped in at Grace and Ed's that afternoon, she discovered there was something else that might stand in their way.

"Hey! I'm glad you stopped by. I was just going to call you," Grace said as she welcomed her into the house. "I have a surprise for you. Wait right here."

She disappeared for a minute, and Beth could hear her hollering up the stairs for her daughters. It wasn't long before the three girls came bouncing down the steps, delighted to see their auntie Beth.

"She's here, she's here!" they chanted, circling her legs.

Beth gave them a group hug. "How nice to be loved!"

"We've got a surprise for you," Allison boasted with a huge grin.

"Come with us," Kayla said, pulling her by the hand up the stairs to the second floor, where their rooms were located.

"Look!" Kayla said, urging her to step into the guest bedroom.

Beth hesitated, not wanting to intrude on Grace's mother's privacy. "Where's your grandma?"

"She went home. Go inside," Kayla urged her again, giving her a gentle push.

Beth did as she was told and saw that the three of them had made a colorful banner, which hung on the wall. It read Welcome, Auntie Beth.

"Isn't it great? You can stay with us now 'cause Grandma felt good enough to go home," Allison said happily.

Beth turned to see Grace enter the room. "It's all they've been talking about since my mom left yesterday. They're so excited that you'll be able to spend at least part of your summer vacation here."

"You want me to move in here," Beth said weakly.

"It's going to be so much fun, Auntie Beth. We can make cookies and eat breakfast together and watch Barney videos," Allison told her.

"That does sound like fun," Beth managed to say with a smile, although it was nothing compared to the pleasure she had hoped to share with Charlie.

Grace put a hand on her arm. "I'm just sorry it took this long. I know how awkward it's been for you having to stay on the houseboat with Charlie."

"It hasn't been that bad," Beth told her, wondering how she could convince her family that it wasn't bad at all, that it was just the opposite. Exactly where she wanted to be.

She wanted to tell Grace that another houseguest was exactly what she didn't need after nursing her mother back to health. Yet she knew that if she expressed that sentiment to her sister-in-law, she'd dismiss it with a toss of her hand. So Beth waited until Ed stopped home for lunch to discuss the matter with him.

When they had a few minutes of privacy she said, "I'm worried about Grace. Do you think it's a good idea that I stay here? After everything she's been through with her mother, she needs rest, not an extra person to feed."

"You're right," Ed told her. "That's why I want you here."

Beth frowned. He wasn't making any sense. He'd just admitted Grace didn't need another houseguest, but he wanted her to stay with them? Suddenly, warning bells went off in Beth's brain.

"You know what Gracie's been through this past month," he said, and Beth nodded. "She's tired. Really tired. And what she needs is a couple of days of peace and quiet—you know, just the two of us."

Beth swallowed with difficulty. "And you want me to watch the girls while you go away for a few days?"

"We won't be gone long. I thought maybe I'd take her to that nice inn in Billie Creek Village. She loves those covered bridges and all the shops. Give her a few days to relax and regroup. What do you think? Can you help out your brother out for a few days?"

Beth wished she could say no, but knew she wouldn't. "Of course. I think it's a good idea. Grace has been a rock throughout this whole ordeal with her mother, but she does need some downtime." Beth only wished that her sister-in-law's downtime didn't have to come at the expense of her love life. "When do you want to leave?"

"The day after tomorrow. But hey—move in today. You've seen how excited the girls are to have you."

To Beth's relief, she was able to convince her nieces that she needed one more day to pack up her things before moving into the guest bedroom. If Grace suspected the reason had more to do with Charlie than with packing, she didn't say anything.

Beth was just about to leave Ed's to return to the boat when she had another unexpected conversation. A clinic in Iowa phoned to offer her a position as a physician's assistant.

"Hey, congratulations, sis. Didn't I tell you you wouldn't be unemployed for long?" Ed said as she told him about the position she'd been offered at a highly respected clinic.

Adding her congratulations, Grace said, "It sounds like they're offering you the kind of job you want."

Yes, they were. Last month when Beth had interviewed for the position, she'd hoped that by September she'd be working at the clinic. It was more money than she'd ever made, a good location, and hours that couldn't be matched by any of the other places where she'd interviewed. So why wasn't she more excited about it?

She knew the answer. Because of Charlie. Until the clinic had called, she'd been conveniently forgetting that she was only in Riverbend temporarily. Her home was in Iowa, not Indiana.

With one phone call, she'd been jerked back to the real world. Her relationship with Charlie was suddenly much more complicated than it had been last night. She needed to talk to him—the sooner, the better.

When she returned to the houseboat that afternoon, she learned that Charlie was not going to be around all evening. After picking up Nathan in West Lafayette and dropping him off at the boat, he'd gone out on a job, leaving Beth a note that said he wasn't sure what time he'd be back, but that she shouldn't wait up for him.

"Don't wait up for him?" she repeated aloud, which had Nathan looking at her rather curiously.

"Somebody screwed something up," Nathan told her. "Charlie has to straighten it out, that's why he's working so late."

"I see," Beth said, although she really didn't. What she had with Charlie was too new to be facing such tests as job offers in other parts of the country and working late at night.

She didn't go to bed, but sat up with Nathan. After packing her things, she read a book while he played a video game. Not that she could concentrate on the story. She kept glancing out the window, hoping to see the truck's headlights coming through the trees.

She didn't, and finally she got tired of waiting and went to bed, leaving Charlie a note that said she needed to speak to him as soon as possible. As usual, she slept without waking. The next morning, as she headed for the shower, she saw that Charlie's door was open, his bed made. If it hadn't been for the wet towel in the bathroom, she'd have thought he hadn't come home.

But he had been home, which was evidenced by

the note left for her on the counter. It simply said, "Sorry I missed you last night. Have a good day. We'll talk tonight. Love, Charlie."

Love, Charlie. It was the first time he'd signed a note that way, and she liked the way it looked. It was the "We'll talk tonight" that had her frowning. She'd told Ed and Grace she'd move back to the house this evening so they could leave for their brief vacation, yet she hadn't had a chance to tell any of this to Charlie.

As she drove to work, she wished she didn't feel as if a dark cloud waited to drop its nasty rain on her parade. Yet considering her past and everything that had happened since she'd been in Riverbend, was there really any reason to believe there was a rainbow above?

"Be here by seven."

Beth had received strict orders from Grace that unless she wanted to miss Kayla's dance recital, she needed to arrive on time at the Pennington house.

After coming home from work and finding neither Charlie nor Nathan there, she took a quick shower, loaded her suitcases into the car and left for Ed's. She tried not to be angry with Charlie as she drove into town, but she knew any hope that the two of them could get together to discuss whether or not they would share a future was growing dim.

Subsequently Beth was not in the best of moods when she arrived at Ed's. It didn't help that when she rang the bell, there was no answer. Thinking they were probably in the backyard, she walked around the side of the house and opened the gate, only to be nearly startled out of her mind.

"Surprise!" a chorus of voices rang out.

At least a dozen people jumped up and said "Happy birthday" as a flabbergasted Beth stood rooted to the spot. Included in the bunch was Charlie, who waited patiently as the others greeted Beth with hugs.

When it was his turn to wish her a happy birthday, he didn't kiss her on the mouth, but on the cheek, hugging her tightly and whispering in her ear. "I'll have to give you my present in private."

The secret message he conveyed with one single look had Beth smiling inwardly. "I'll look forward to it," she said, then was nearly knocked off her feet as her three nieces grabbed her.

"What about this dance recital I was supposed to see?" she said, giving Kayla's ponytail an affectionate tug.

"We made it up," the eight year old confessed. "My dance recital is always in the spring. Mom said you wouldn't know the difference."

"And mom was right," Grace said coming up to give Beth a hug. "Happy birthday. Like your surprise party?"

"Yes, it's wonderful." To Ed, who was right behind Grace, she said, "You didn't make anything else up, did you? Like the trip to Billie Creek Village?"

"No, that's on. You did bring your suitcases, didn't you?"

"They're in the car."

"Why are your suitcases in your car?" Charlie asked from behind her, overhearing the tail end of her conversation with Ed.

She spun around and said, "I'm moving into the guest bedroom now that Grace's mother is gone."

That had the smile on his face fading, so she quickly added, "Ed is taking Grace away for a few days of R and R."

"And you're baby-sitting?"

"Yes."

As if to confirm to her story, Allison brought her a glass of lemonade and said, "Can we make pizza when Mom and Dad are gone?"

Beth gave Charlie a look as if to say, *See. I told you.*

Nathan came over to give Beth a package wrapped in blue-and-white paper.

"What's this?" she asked, shaking the box.

Grace took the package out of her hands. "Uh-uh. No opening of presents until after we've had cake and ice cream."

Which Beth's nieces insisted be immediately since they were all anxious to see what Beth had gotten for her birthday. Grace lit thirty-two candles on the cake, then everyone sang the birthday song before Beth was instructed to make a wish before blowing them out.

She looked directly at Charlie and wished that this time their affair wouldn't be just a summer thing. Then she took a deep breath and, with the help of Cierra and Allison, managed to blow out every candle on the cake.

"I hope you made it a good one," Ed remarked.

Again Beth's eyes met Charlie's and they shared a knowing smile.

It was the perfect evening for a party. By the time all the presents had been opened, the sun was sinking into the horizon. Beth wanted nothing more than to go back to the houseboat with Nathan and Charlie, but she knew she couldn't.

"Isn't this a great August night?" she said as she helped Grace clear away the wrapping paper and ribbons.

"It is," Grace agreed on a sigh. "I always get a little nostalgic this time of year. I think it's the back-to-school sentiment."

"I know. It's hard to believe in a couple of weeks it'll be September," she said, tossing a curly ribbon into the bag of trash.

"And you'll be back in Iowa. I wish the summer wouldn't have been so hectic. I'd hoped we'd get to spend a lot more time together than we did," Grace told her, scooping up plastic forks and paper plates from the table.

"About Iowa—" she began, but Grace didn't let her finish.

"I bet you're excited about that new job, aren't you? Do you know when you start?"

The last thing Beth wanted to talk about was leaving Riverbend. Before she could tell Grace that she hadn't made a decision yet about the job, Cierra fell off the swing and needed her mother's attention.

While Ed and Grace hovered over the three year old, Charlie pulled Beth aside. "Can I talk to you alone?"

"Sure." She followed him around the side of the house, thinking he wanted to give her the birthday present he'd told her needed to be delivered in privacy. Only she soon discovered he hadn't wanted to get her alone to kiss her, but because he was angry.

"Did you forget to tell me something?"

She thought his anger had to do with moving back to Ed's without telling him. "I just found out about this baby-sitting thing yesterday—"

"I'm not talking about your moving back here," he said impatiently. "You told me you didn't have a job waiting for you in Iowa."

"I didn't…at least, I didn't until yesterday." She explained about the position she'd been offered.

"Ed said it's a done deal."

"Well, Ed doesn't know everything. He doesn't know about us, for one thing. But then, how would he? You wouldn't even kiss me at my own birthday party," she shot back at him. "Were you afraid people might think you're interested in me?"

"If I was worried about that I wouldn't have moved onto the houseboat this summer."

"Why are you so angry? I just told you I haven't accepted the job yet."

"But you didn't turn it down, either, did you?"

She couldn't lie. "No, but even if I had, there are still two weeks of summer left before I'd have to leave."

"Is that what you want us to be—a summer romance?"

"How do we know if it can be anything else?"

"We won't know if you go back to Iowa," he argued. "Is the position really that lucrative?"

"No, it's…" *It's what?* she asked herself. She wasn't sure why she suddenly found it difficult to tell him she had second thoughts about their relationship. Because that's exactly what she was feeling—uncertainty about letting herself get seriously involved with him again.

"Is that what you really want, Beth? To go back

to Iowa?'' he asked, the look in his eyes pleading with her to say it wasn't.

"No... Yes... I don't know,'' she answered honestly, rubbing two fingers across her forehead.

Her confusion caused his brow to furrow. "Well, when you make up your mind, be sure to let me know.'' If there was one thing Charlie seldom was, it was sarcastic. But there was no mistaking the tone of his voice. With an "I'm leaving,'' he started to walk away.

She went after him. "Charlie, wait. Don't you think we should discuss this...discuss us?''

"It's difficult for there to be an us when you're going to be hundreds of miles away.''

"Then you want me to stay?''

He chuckled sardonically. "You need to even ask?''

She could see the longing in his eyes. It stirred such an intense response in her that she was frightened. "I want to stay, but...''

"But what?'' His eyes held hers.

"Iowa's my home,'' she told him, trying to steady her voice.

"So is Riverbend—at least, it used to be.'' He sighed and looked out at the horizon, before turning back to her to say, "What do you want me to do, Beth? Beg you to stay?''

"No, but it would be nice if you tried to understand—''

Again he interrupted her. "Understand what? Two nights ago we were making plans for a future together and nearly made love. Now, without a word, you move off the houseboat and are considering a job offer that will take you away from me.

What were you going to do? Leave Riverbend without telling me?''

''No, I wouldn't do that to you,'' she said quietly.

''You did it fifteen years ago,'' he said soberly, then turned and walked away.

Speechless, she could only stare at him. She watched him thank Ed and Grace, give each of the girls a hug, then grab Nathan and head for his pickup.

Although it was a warm evening, Beth felt chilled. He had acted as if she were the one who'd left him that summer. Didn't he realize that she hadn't wanted their marriage to end? That if he hadn't suggested they get a divorce, she would have stayed married to him forever?

Because that's what his love had been to her—something she wanted to hang on to forever. Yet here they were fifteen years later, hurting each other again.

Pain caused tears to well in her throat, but she swallowed back the emotion and forced herself to rejoin the others, determined not to let her argument with Charlie spoil her birthday. But long after she went to bed that night, she replayed his words in her mind. With them came a familiar pain, one that went back fifteen years and she was afraid that it would never go away.

As CHARMING AS Kayla, Allison and Cierra were, they couldn't take Beth's mind off her troubles with Charlie. She hated the way their relationship had gone from ''on the brink of something wonderful'' to ''near disaster'' in less than forty-eight hours.

Although during the day the girls were a pleasant

distraction that kept her from obsessing about Charlie, at night she couldn't help but think about him and ponder what would happen if she were to move back to Riverbend. She was fairly certain Dr. Bennett would welcome her as a full-time employee at the clinic, but a job wasn't the issue that was causing her uncertainty. It was her relationship with Charlie.

They'd been married and had lost a baby, yet she didn't feel as if they'd ever been truly intimate. It was true they'd always been friends, and physically there was no denying their attraction to each other, but love was supposed to be more than sex. Love meant you were there for each other in good times and bad, even when things got so bad the pain of living threatened to suck you right down into a black hole of despair.

Fifteen years ago Charlie had told her he loved her, yet he hadn't been there for her when she needed him most. Was it any wonder she was having trouble deciding whether to stay or leave?

Not that he was trying to persuade her to stay. He'd made it clear the night of the party that she would have to go to him. That's why she was surprised to see his pickup pull into Ed and Grace's driveway the third night she was there.

When she opened the door to him, he shoved a paper bag at her.

"What's this?" she asked.

"Stuff you left behind on the boat. I thought you might need it."

His coolness angered her. Only a few days ago they'd nearly made love together. Now he looked at her as if she'd simply been a houseguest who'd outstayed her welcome. "So this is how it ends, Charlie? With you shoving a paper bag in my direction?'' she challenged him.

''I don't think we ever started, Beth,'' he said flatly.

She wanted to prove to him that he was wrong. And there was only one way to do that. She threw her arms around him and kissed him.

As she had hoped, he couldn't resist the provocative move. His lips caressed hers with such exquisite tenderness she whimpered.

While his tongue explored her mouth, his fingers fumbled with the buttons on her blouse.

''This doesn't feel like it's over to me,'' she said between kisses that left her breathless.

Suddenly he went still.

''Charlie?''

He shook his head, then stepped back, shoving his hands into his pockets.

''You make me crazy with wanting you, Beth,'' he said soberly. ''We both know that. But that's not going to solve our problems.''

His tone frightened her. ''What *is* keeping us apart, Charlie?''

''I think you're the only one who can answer that question.''

''Me?'' Confused, she stared at him, her eyes pleading for an explanation.

''I'm not the one thinking about leaving,'' he reminded her.

Again he was making her responsible for the trouble between them. ''You want me to give up everything, my job, my home, yet you've made me no promises.''

''I will make you promises, Beth. All you have

to do is stay and give me a chance. Give *us* a chance.''

''I want to, but…''

''But what?'' He raked a hand over his hair. ''You know what I think? Fifteen years may have passed, but nothing's changed.''

''And what's that supposed to mean?''

''Love isn't enough for you. You've set some big goals for yourself. There's always going to be another degree to be earned, another job to land. It's why you left Riverbend in the first place.''

''I left because you didn't want to make our marriage work!''

He held up both hands. ''Wait a minute. You're not going to blame our divorce on me. You were the one who wanted to go off to college, not me.''

''I wouldn't have gone if we'd had the baby.''

''But you didn't want the baby, Beth.''

Before she knew it, her hand had connected with his cheek. ''Don't you ever say that again, Charlie. I did want my baby,'' she said, her voice quivering with emotion.

''But Lucy said—''

She cut him off. ''Don't talk to me about what Lucy said. She didn't know what I was going through. No one did. My God, Charlie! Why do you think I cried for days?''

''I thought you were unhappy because you were stuck in a marriage when you really wanted to be away at college,'' he said quietly.

Tears that had been pooling in her eyes began to trickle down her cheeks. ''Losing that baby was the worst experience of my life. I felt so alone…'' Unable to hold back the tears, she began to sob. "I *was* alone...so alone."

"You weren't. You had me," he said, pulling her into his arms and cradling her head against his chest.

But she didn't want his comfort and pushed him away. "No, I didn't have you, Charlie. You were gone, always gone—off having fun with the guys, or whatever it was you did when you weren't with me."

"Because I didn't know what to say, Beth."

She swiped at the tears with the back of her hands. "It doesn't matter. It's o-over." She said with a hiccup.

"It matters to me, Beth." Again he tried to take her into his arms but she flinched at his touch and he dropped his hands to his sides. "I didn't realize what you were going through."

"Because we weren't a real married couple."

"Yes, we were."

"You didn't want to be married. You didn't want a baby," she said accusingly.

He frowned. "Is that what you think?"

"It's the truth, isn't it?"

"I wasn't unhappy being married to you, Beth. I thought I showed you that every night when we went to bed."

She didn't respond, but stood perfectly still, her arms wrapped around her chest.

"I'm sorry, Beth. I've hurt you, and I didn't even realize it was happening," he said, resignation in his voice. "We can't undo the mistakes we made as kids, and if you're not able to forgive me..." He didn't finish, but looked at her expectantly.

He was waiting for her to say that she could forgive him, and she wanted to say the words, but they stuck in her throat.

After a short, painful silence, he turned and headed for the door.

Beth didn't go after him, but watched him leave. And once more, the tears streamed down her cheeks.

"ARE YOU REALLY gonna leave?" Allison asked Beth for the umpteenth time that afternoon.

"Yes, I have to go back to work."

"But you can work here. At the clinic," Kayla said, looking just as unhappy as her sister with the prospect of losing their aunt.

"I wish there wasn't an Iowa," Allison pouted, her arms folded across her chest.

Just then the front doorbell rang. Kayla ran downstairs, while Allison stayed with Beth, watching her fold her clothes and put them in the suitcase.

A few minutes later Kayla said, "You've got company."

Beth's heart skipped a beat. She hoped it was Charlie, although after ten days without hearing from him, she doubted he'd suddenly show up on Ed's doorstep.

And she was right. Sitting in Grace's living room was Nathan, not Charlie. When he saw Beth, he said, "Can I talk to you in private?"

"Sure." She chased Allison and Kayla from the room, then sat down on the sofa next to the boy.

"I heard you were leaving," he said gently.

"Yes. Like you, I'm only here on a visit."

Nathan nodded and looked down at his hands, which Beth noticed were trembling slightly. "I have to ask you something."

The question was obviously causing him a great deal of anxiety. "I'm listening."

"You like Charlie, don't you?"

"Yes." She didn't hesitate to answer.

"And it's true you were once married, right?"

"Yes, that's true, too."

"And on the boat...were you just doing all that together stuff so I wouldn't feel bad?"

Beth wasn't sure what he was trying to ask her. "Nathan, I enjoyed our time together on the boat."

"Then why did you leave?"

"Because I had to come stay with my nieces. I told you that."

"Yes, but you didn't have to stop coming over and playing games and stuff."

Suddenly she felt like the most insensitive woman on the planet. Just because her and Charlie's relationship had soured, she shouldn't have forgotten Nathan. "I'm sorry. It's just that I didn't think Charlie wanted me at the houseboat," she said honestly.

"Why would you say that? He loves you."

She smiled then, wishing she knew how to explain to a fourteen year old that kissing didn't mean love.

When she didn't say anything, he blurted, "Can't you get married?"

"No, Nathan, we can't. It just doesn't happen that way."

His eyes narrowed. "So you don't want to marry him." Accusation laced his words.

"I didn't say that. And what makes you think Charlie wants to marry me?"

"He told Lucy he did. They had this big fight..."

He stopped in midsentence. "I wasn't supposed to tell you," he said in a low voice.

"It's all right, Nathan. I won't mention it to anyone."

He stood. "I better go. Are you coming to Lily's art show tonight?"

Beth had received the invitation, but had decided against attending because of Charlie. She knew he'd be there.

"I don't think I can make it," she answered.

His face fell. "Then you won't get to see it."

"See what?"

"My comic book. Lucy put some of my drawings together into a book, and she's going to have it on display at her art show."

Beth knew she had no choice. "Then I'll be there."

SHE HAD A PLAN. To go early to the art show, sneak a peek at Nathan's art, say hello to Lily and leave.

Only, she discovered that several other people had the same idea including Lucy Garvey. She was not the person Beth wanted to see on her last night in Riverbend, but short of being rude, she couldn't avoid her.

Beth wished she could ignore her—just walk away and pretend she wasn't in the same room, but she knew she couldn't. If there was one thing her mother had taught her, it was to be polite—even to her enemies. How sad, she thought, that she now regarded Lucy as her enemy.

"Hello, Beth."

"Lucy." She smiled politely.

"I was hoping you'd be here tonight. I...I owe

you an apology for what I said at the fair." Lucy's normally calm features looked as tense as they had the day she'd had to get up in front of the entire high school and give a speech. "I'm sorry."

An apology was not what Beth had expected to hear coming out of those quivering lips. She'd thought she'd leave Riverbend with her relationship with Lucy finished, just as her relationship with Charlie was. It was little consolation, but she accepted it graciously. "Apology accepted."

Lucy bit her upper lip, then added, "I'd like to put the past behind us if we could and maybe make a fresh start."

"Because you know I'm leaving to go back to Iowa," Beth couldn't help saying.

Lucy blushed. "I know I deserve that."

Beth immediately felt very small. "No, you don't." She sighed. "I'd like to start over, too, Lucy."

Charlie's sister smiled, then said, "Good, but first I need to tell you about that summer you left." Beth wanted to say she wasn't up to revisiting the past, but she could tell by the look on Lucy's face that she was determined to right a wrong.

"I wanted to be your best friend back then, but I had my own hurt to deal with and I guess I didn't know how to see beyond that," Lucy said on a wistful note.

Beth knew the other woman was talking about her basketball-ending injury. "Maybe we both were hurting so badly, neither one of us could see each other's pain."

She nodded, still chewing on her lip. "I didn't

know how to handle your success. You had what I wanted—the opportunity to go away to school.''

Beth felt a lump in her throat. She knew how difficult it was for Lucy to admit such a thing. ''I was lonely at school, Lucy. And there are those things in life that once they're lost…well, life can never be the same.''

Lucy nodded in understanding.

''When we were kids we promised that we'd never let anything come between us,'' Beth reminded her.

''Do you think we're too old to try to mend that broken promise?'' Lucy asked, her eyes hopeful.

Beth shook her head. ''I don't think so. Do you?''

''No.''

There was an awkward little silence, then Lucy said, ''I've missed you, Beth.''

''Do I dare ask for a hug?''

Lucy opened her arms and embraced her friend. ''It's been a long time. Too long.''

Beth agreed. They both dabbed at their eyes with tissues, glancing around the room to see if anyone had noticed their emotional display.

''Guess we should view the art show.''

Lucy smiled. ''Sure. Lily tells me Nathan has you to thank for getting him into art lessons,'' she said as she admired his comic book.

''He has a lot of talent, doesn't he?'' Beth remarked, finally feeling as if the tension between her and her childhood friend was gone.

They made their way through the exhibit, not like two best friends, but like two adult women discovering that the bonds of friendship could stand the test of time.

"Grace said you're leaving tomorrow," Lucy finally mentioned as they neared the end.

"Yes."

"Then you didn't find anything to keep you here?" she looked at her expectantly.

She raised both eyebrows. "Such as?"

"My brother?" She took a deep breath and looked around the room. "I can't believe I'm asking this, but what is wrong with you two?"

"I can't believe you're asking that, either," Beth admitted.

"I spent so much energy trying to protect Charlie from being hurt again that I refused to see the truth."

"And the truth is…" Beth prompted.

"He's crazy about you and you've always been crazy about him, so why are you apart?"

"You can't just erase a bad marriage, Lucy," Beth said with a sigh.

"Was it that bad?" she asked softly.

Beth shrugged, not wanting to experience the pain the subject of her marriage always produced. "It doesn't matter. We can't change the past."

"No, but you can learn from past mistakes."

"Unfortunately, the mistake was our marriage," Beth said sadly.

"You really believe that?"

"What else can I think? Charlie didn't want a baby."

"He might not have been ready to be a father, but he wanted that baby, Beth."

Beth didn't believe her, but simply said, "It's probably better if we don't discuss this." When she turned away, Lucy reached for her shoulder.

"You don't think Charlie wanted that baby?" she asked, forcing Beth to face her. "That night you spent in the hospital...he came home and cried. I heard him tell my mom that he felt as if a part of him had died, too."

Tears misted in Beth's eyes. "I didn't know. He never said anything."

"That's because he's like my dad. Callahan men aren't supposed to cry, you know."

"He never talked to me about his feelings."

"Did you try talking to him?"

She hadn't. She'd been so overwhelmed with her own grief, she hadn't been able to think of anything else. "I didn't know," she said in a painful whisper.

"I'm sorry," Lucy said softly. "I didn't mean to upset you."

Beth sniffled and shook her head. "I'm okay."

"Good, because Charlie just came in," she said, nodding toward the door. "Actually he's coming this way."

Beth turned and found Charlie standing right behind her. "I'd like to talk to Beth alone, Lucy."

She looked at Beth as if seeking permission to leave. Beth said, "It's okay, Lucy. I'll be fine."

"She's usually protective of me, not you," Charlie remarked as his sister left them. He stood before Beth looking incredibly handsome. It was only the third time she'd seen him in a suit and a tie. The first had been the spring formal dance, the second at the courthouse when they were married by the justice of the peace.

"We're trying to put our friendship back together," Beth told him.

"Then everything is okay between the two of you?"

She smiled. "Yeah. It is."

"Good." He didn't return her smile, but continued to look at her with an expression that made her long for the intimacy they'd once shared. "So why are you here?"

"I wanted to see Nathan's art," she said, gesturing at the comic book.

"He told me he visited you yesterday."

"Yes. He did."

"He misses you."

"I know. And I'm sorry about not visiting him these past couple of weeks."

"I miss you."

She had deliberately avoided his eyes, but upon hearing those three words, she met his gaze. The look on his face made her tremble.

It also gave her the courage to say, "I'm sorry I slapped you that night at Ed's."

He shrugged. "I shouldn't have said what I did."

"Lucy said some interesting things tonight," she commented.

"Such as?"

She didn't answer his question but asked, "Why did we get divorced, Charlie?"

He pulled her into the empty hallway. "I divorced you because all you'd ever talk about was going away to college. That had been your goal ever since I can remember. When you found out you were pregnant, your first words to me were, 'You think you're upset? I'm going to have to turn down my scholarship to Kansas.'"

"I was upset. So were you. Any two teenagers would have been in our situation."

"You blamed me, Beth."

"No, I didn't," she said, although she knew it wasn't true. She'd thrown all sorts of accusations his way—most of them out of frustration and fear. "All right. Maybe I did blame you. I was just a kid, Charlie."

"You're not a kid now, Beth."

"No, I'm not."

"So are you still blaming me?"

"For getting me pregnant?"

"No, for not being there for you when you lost the baby."

"Oh, Charlie, I wasn't there for you, either! You were hurting, too, yet I couldn't see that," she said, smoothing her fingers across his cheek. "We were so young and so unprepared for the emotions we had."

"You cried for days, Beth, and you wouldn't talk to me," he said.

"I didn't know what to say…to anybody. It hurt so badly." A tear trickled down her cheek at the memory.

He wiped it away with the pad of his thumb. "I wanted to help, but didn't know how."

"No one could help me at the time." She pulled his hand to her lips and kissed the palm. "I wished I hadn't lost your baby." Now the tears fell more swiftly.

He simply pulled her into his arms and held her. "The doctors said it wasn't your fault, Beth."

"I know that," she managed. "But if I hadn't lost the baby, we might still be married."

"Is that what you would have wanted?"

She nodded. "I love you, Charlie. I have since I was thirteen."

"We can still be married," he said, lifting her chin with his finger. "But only if you can forgive me." His eyes pinned hers. "Do you forgive me, Beth?"

"I've forgiven both of us," she answered softly, her eyes confirming what she said as they stared into his.

He hugged her tightly, then let her go so that he could reach into his pocket and pull out a small blue box with a silver ribbon. "This is for you. It's your birthday present."

She opened it and saw two gold bands intertwined and suspended on a matching gold chain. "Are these...?" She looked up into his eyes.

"Our wedding bands."

"You kept them all these years!" She pulled the chain from the box and slipped it around her neck. "How does it look?"

"Perfect. Does this mean you still want to be married?"

For an answer she gave him a kiss and said, "But this time it's for the right reasons."

"There's only one reason. I love you, Beth." Then he reached for her hand and led her back into the art exhibit. When they were in the middle of the room, he took her in his arm and kissed her, long and hard.

When he lifted his mouth from hers, they were both breathing heavily. "Guess everyone in River-bend will know about us now, won't they?" he whispered in her ear.

"Good. It's time people realize that what we have is no summer thing. It's the real thing," she said, enjoying the stir they'd caused among the small crowd.

"You're right as usual. Oh, and one more thing," he said as they left the exhibit. "There is one more birthday present waiting for you."

"And what might that be?" she asked with a seductive grin.

"Nathan's spending the night at Lucy's."

She tucked her arm in his and gazed at him with love in her eyes. "I think it's time we visit our houseboat, don't you?"

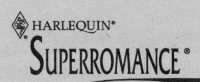

HARLEQUIN®
SUPERROMANCE®

You are now entering

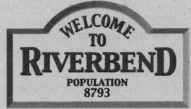

WELCOME TO RIVERBEND

POPULATION
8793

Riverbend...the kind of place where everyone knows
your name—and your business. Riverbend...home of
the River Rats—a group of small-town sons and
daughters who've been friends since high school.

The Rats are all grown up now. Living their lives and
learning that some days are good and some days
aren't—and that you can get through anything
as long as you have your friends.

Starting in July 2000, Harlequin Superromance brings
you Riverbend—six books about the River Rats and
the Midwest town they live in.

BIRTHRIGHT by **Judith Arnold** (July 2000)
THAT SUMMER THING by **Pamela Bauer** (August 2000)
HOMECOMING by **Laura Abbot** (September 2000)
LAST-MINUTE MARRIAGE by **Marisa Carroll** (October 2000)
A CHRISTMAS LEGACY by **Kathryn Shay** (November 2000)

Available wherever Harlequin books are sold.

HARLEQUIN®
Makes any time special ™

Visit us at www.eHarlequin.com

HSRIVER

Your Romantic Books—find them at

www.eHarlequin.com

Visit the *Author's Alcove*

➤ Find the most complete information anywhere on your favorite author.

➤ Try your hand in the Writing Round Robin— contribute a chapter to an online book in the making.

Enter the *Reading Room*

➤ Experience an interactive novel—help determine the fate of a story being created now by one of your favorite authors.

➤ Join one of our reading groups and discuss your favorite book.

Drop into *Shop eHarlequin*

➤ Find the latest releases—read an excerpt or write a review for this month's Harlequin top sellers.

➤ Try out our amazing search feature—tell us your favorite theme, setting or time period and we'll find a book that's perfect for you.

All this and more available at

www.eHarlequin.com
on Women.com Networks

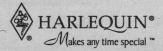

**Don't miss
an exciting opportunity
to save on the purchase of
Harlequin and Silhouette books!**

Buy any two Harlequin or
Silhouette books and save
$10.00 off future Harlequin
and Silhouette purchases

OR

buy any three
Harlequin or Silhouette books
and save **$20.00 off** future
Harlequin and Silhouette purchases.

**Watch for details
coming in October 2000!**

PHQ400

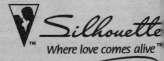

HARLEQUIN® SUPERROMANCE

COMING NEXT MONTH

#936 BORN IN A SMALL TOWN • Debbie Macomber, Judith Bowen and Janice Kay Johnson

Here's what small-town dreams are made of! This is a special 3-in-1 collection featuring *New York Times* bestselling author **Debbie Macomber**'s latest Midnight Sons title, *Midnight Sons and Daughters*. There's also a new Men of Glory title from Judith Bowen—*The Glory Girl*—and *Promise Me Picket Fences*—a return to Elk Springs, Oregon, by Janice Kay Johnson.

#937 HOMECOMING • Laura Abbot

Tom Baines, one of Riverbend's favorite sons, has come home to recuperate. After the year he's had, he needs the peace and quiet. More important, he wants to reestablish a relationship with his estranged children. But he never expects to meet Lynn Kendall, a woman unlike any he's ever met. Living in Riverbend might just have its advantages!

Riverbend, Indiana: Home of the River Rats—a group of men and women who've been friends since high school. These are their stories.

#938 MATT'S FAMILY • Lynnette Kent
The Brennan Brothers

Kristen had known the Brennan boys forever. She'd loved Luke as a friend,but she'd been *in* love with soldier Matt Brennan for as long as she could remember. Then Matt was reported missing, presumed dead. Luke persuaded the young, scared and pregnant Kristen to marry him. Slowly they turned their marriage of convenience into a real one. A second baby was born. Then five years later Matt Brennan—the man she'd never stopped loving—came home.... By the author of *Luke's Daughters*.

#939 SNOW BABY • Brenda Novak
9 Months Later

Two strangers spend a snowy night together. Chantel Miller falls for Dillon Broderick, the man who helped and comforted her during the blizzard—and then she discovers that her estranged sister, Stacy, is in love with him. The sister whose affection she's trying to regain... It's a painful coincidence that becomes devastating when Chantel discovers she's pregnant.

#940 THE NEWCOMER • Margot Dalton
Crystal Creek

Is the town of Crystal Creek for sale? Read *The Newcomer* to find out what happens when an eccentric movie star sends Maggie Embree to put in an offer on her behalf. Maggie runs into stiff opposition from the mayor of the town. Now she has to choose between her loyalty to her boss—the woman who helped raise her—and the man she's beginning to fall in love with.

#941 THE CATTLEMAN'S BRIDE • Joan Kilby

If Sarah Templestowe finds the wide-open spaces of central Australia unsettling when she arrives from Seattle, wait until she meets Luke Sampson! He's part owner of the isolated cattle station her father recently willed to her. Laconic and self-reliant, the quintessential outback hero, he's been managing the station for ten years, and he's about to turn Sarah's world even more upside down than her trip Down Under already has.

CNM0800